FIGHTING STOCK

TOMMY CONLON
BOOK 2

DAVID MICHAEL NOLAN

ROUGH
EDGES
PRESS

Rough Edges Press
An Imprint of Wolfpack Publishing
9850 S. Maryland Parkway, Suite A-5 #323
Las Vegas, Nevada 89183

roughedgespress.com

Paperback ISBN 978-1-68549-253-3
eBook ISBN 978-1-68549-252-6

FIGHTING STOCK

1

THE MAN WAS IN HIS LATE FORTIES, PERHAPS, HAIR GONE gray in all but a black streak back across his crown, his eyes still sparkling light blue electricity. Which was probably what the girl liked about him, Conlon thought, observing them from across the hotel dining room. That was if she actually did like anything about him besides the money he was worth to her.

The man—his name was Austin Davitt—had a face already lined with deep wrinkles. But with her, he smiled perpetually and the wrinkles melted away, replaced by dimples like sinkholes in each cheek, his beige teeth on full display, face a torch of light and amusement. He was obviously a man in love. He was wearing an expensive suit; light blue, the sort of thing a wealthy man might wear on holiday. A cravat; brown, shiny shoes, a hat in what looked like cream from this distance. His wedding ring was not on his finger.

The girl—one Molly Fagan of Irishtown—was less than half his age. She was a pretty girl, the kind that would be noticed in any room anywhere in the world.

Even now, in this dining room of an expensive hotel on the South Wales coast, Conlon was aware of the various currents in the room centered on her. It was a big room with high ceilings, glittering chandeliers, tablecloths of undeniably expensive lushness and the sort of heavy cutlery that suggested it cost more than most of the meals eaten with it ever had, and yet the men in her immediate vicinity were all aware of her, and either trying not to show it or openly stare. Even beyond those men, there was a general awareness of her presence. Wives felt irritated that their companions seemed distracted. Men peered at her, as if she were some exotic animal, with a mix of fear and wonder.

At nineteen years of age, she still had the warm, supple beauty of youth. It glowed from her. She wore her dark hair in long rolling waves under a tiny hat and a summer dress with a simple pattern to match her lover's suit. She was smoking a cigarette and laughing as Davitt spoke to her, and her laugh, voluptuous and excessive, drew even more attention her way. She was the kind of woman other women hated but all men loved. She understood this and embraced it—and laughs like that one were all part of that.

Tommy Conlon had been watching them since they had arrived for breakfast. In that time, he had eaten some bacon and a fried egg and two slices of toast, washed down by a pot of strong tea. She had seen him as she entered the room—their eyes had fleetingly met —but he was willing to bet that her eyes had fleetingly met those of a half dozen other men also dining here this morning. For the moment, her eyes were on Davitt. Occasionally they would reach out and touch hands, briefly.

Conlon finished his last slice of toast and took a final mouthful of tea. Unlike many in the room, he did not smoke. His lungs had been weak as a child, and cigarettes had a wicked effect upon his ability to breathe. Standing, he adjusted his jacket and walked across the room to their table. He was light on his feet, and even if you knew nothing of his life or history, you would look at him and assume that he had once been an athlete.

He did not ask for permission, just pulled out a chair and sat down, close to the girl, facing the man. He made sure he kept his face pleasant, not unfriendly. They both stopped speaking and stared at him for a moment, as if waiting for an explanation.

"Good morning," he said.

"What—who are you?" Davitt said, recovering some poise.

"My name is Thomas Conlon. You would be Austen Davitt, and Miss Molly Fagan. Pleased to meet you." He smiled at the girl, and she could not prevent herself from smiling back at him.

"Why...what—how did you find us?" Davitt had a wheedling, annoying tone in his voice, disdain mixed with a whine. Conlon disliked him instantly.

"Is that really the question you want to be asking now, Mr. Davitt? Sure, shouldn't you be more worried about why I found you? And what I intend to do now that I have found you?"

As Davitt stared at him, Conlon could virtually see the whirl of questions and possibilities in his eyes.

"Helen sent you," he finally said with a defeated kind of certainty.

"Well...not quite. But I have spoken to Mrs. Davitt,

and she's not too happy with you at the moment, Mr. Davitt."

Miss Fagan said, "Austin?"

Conlon looked at her. "Miss Fagan. You should get out of this unharmed, as long as you go along from now on. You'll have to come back to Dublin with me, though."

"What about me?" Davitt said.

"Have you figured out who wants you badly enough to hire me?"

"What are you? What kind of job do you do?"

"I find people. People disappear all the time, Mr. Davitt. Sometimes because they want to, sometimes because somebody else wants them to. I find them, either way."

"That's no sort of employment I've ever heard of." He sounded personally affronted by it.

Conlon chuckled. "Well let's see. You are the head of your firm's Dublin office, are you not? But you ran off with quite a few hundred pounds of their money and a young girl from the office. I'm not sure you're any sort of reasonable authority on employment, Mr. Davitt."

"They sent you."

Conlon nodded. He watched as Davitt bristled, anger evident in the bulge of his cheek and slight reddening of his face.

Davitt said, "What now, then?"

"I'm goin' to let you decide, Mr. Davitt. There are two options I can see. One, you come with me, right now, to the police station in town. The police are looking for you over here, too, they're just not looking too hard. If you were to just fall into their laps, that'd suit them just fine. Peelers are lazy all over the world."

"And Molly?" Davitt said.

Conlon could see his eyes going as if he was looking out the window of a train, calculating odds and potential.

"Miss Fagan would join me on a train and then a ship back to Ireland."

Davitt nodded, a smug, knowing look in his eye at that.

"What's option number two?"

He was growing more confident by the minute, Conlon saw. He thought he had Conlon figured out, believed he had some sort of leverage somewhere.

"I let yourself and Miss Fagan go upstairs to pack your bags, and then we get the 11:35 London train."

"London?"

Conlon nodded. "Once we're there, I'm to deliver you to their offices. And bring Miss Fagan back to Dublin with me."

"Oh you are, are you? And what do you suppose they intend to do with me at their offices?"

"I don't suppose anything."

"Well what do you think?"

"I don't care what they do to you. I imagine that they'll soften you up a bit, and then charges will be pressed."

Davitt nodded and took a drink of his coffee. He then lit a cigarette. His eyes had changed, there was a set calm in them now, and he stared levelly at Conlon. "I have another option, Mr. Conlon."

"Do tell, Mr. Davitt."

"Well, it seems to me that we started off on the wrong foot. There is no need at all for us to be in opposition here. Just the contrary in fact. We can assist one another."

Conlon nodded. This always came. They always tried it.

"The sum you mentioned. I am still in possession of the majority, which is a considerable amount. I would be willing, given the circumstances, to perhaps pass yourself some of that amount. A fair sum, I think can be agreed between us, as reasonable men?"

"And in exchange?"

"Look the other way this morning. Allow us to escape. Nobody need know about this."

Conlon fixed him with a look. "But I'll know."

"You'll know that you are a far richer man than you had been."

A note of expectation was there in his voice. It had not occurred to him that Conlon might refuse the offer, and that was reflected in the open, confident expression on his face as he looked to the younger man, awaiting the expected agreement.

For his part, Conlon just stared at him, silent, for half a minute until Davitt blinked, reddened and looked away.

Conlon looked at the girl now. "Miss. Are you willing to come with me? Back to Dublin?"

She was staring at him with those huge wet blue eyes, her mouth slightly open. He instantly understood the effect she might have upon a man.

"Sure I won't have a job," she said.

He had to stop the laugh that came at that, and said, "The firm is willing to take you back. They don't see you as culpable."

At this, Davitt scoffed. Conlon looked at him again.

Davitt said, "So that's the lamentable way they see it, is it? As if she just fluttered her pretty little eyelashes at me and I devised this scheme for us to run away together? Well, come now Mr. Conlon, you seem a man who can read people and understand what drives them. Look at the girl. She knew exactly what she was doing. 'Not culpable'. Such a nonsense."

"Austin!" she said, her anger obvious in each clipped syllable.

Conlon ignored that and kept his tone even. "Have you made your decision, Mr. Davitt?"

Davitt's eyes narrowed. "And what, Mr. Conlon, is to stop me simply taking my sweetheart by the hand and walking out of that door in the next moment or two?"

"Well, I would've thought that was obvious. I am."

Davitt steeled himself. "And what exactly are you going to do, Mr. Conlon? You have absolutely no authority here. You are just another Irishman. Barely a gentleman, from what I have observed of your manners and breeding. You would be best served carrying bricks somewhere, I would imagine. What exactly could you do to stop me?"

"You do not want to find out, Mr. Davitt."

"Oh but I do, you oafish blackguard. I surely do."

Conlon nodded and lowered his voice to a flat, low, emotionless growl. "Very well. If you take a step in a direction I don't like, I'll break your nose. I'll probably knock out a few of your teeth at the same time. If that doesn't stop you, if you have more guts than you look to have, then I'll have to break a few of your ribs. Maybe I'd snap a few fingers, too."

Davitt, to his credit, rode over his own fear and blustered, "And then? Then, Mr. Conlon, you are in trouble."

"No. Then, the police arrive, and find a wanted man unconscious on the floor. When you wake up, me and your 'sweetheart' are already on a ferry back to dear ol' Dublin, and you're in a cell. So, how does that sound?"

Davitt's eyes roamed over the table, desperate for a way out, a weapon, a solution. Conlon watched him calmly.

Finally, he said, "Very well, Mr. Conlon. You present a convincing case, it seems. I think I would like to spend as many hours as I possibly can with this lovely young lady, so if you don't mind, we'll travel to London with you, to the company offices. I can at least enjoy the rest of this day, before my life as I have known it ends completely."

Conlon nodded. "That sounds fine, Mr. Davitt. You'll need to pack your things."

"Shall we meet you in the lobby in, say, fifteen minutes?" Davitt asked.

Conlon looked at his watch and agreed. Davitt stood and helped Miss Fagan to her feet. As they moved off through the restaurant, she looked back over her shoulder at Conlon, her expression unreadable.

He gave them two minutes, and then he got up and walked out into the lobby, then turned and moved up the stairs. He had checked their room number as soon as he arrived, and now he went to the third floor and along the corridor to room thirty-six. The corridors here were light, with plenty of ornaments and plants on small tables between rooms, and large windows at the end of each stretch, light falling through white curtain.

Conlon leaned against the door and pressed his ear against it. He could hear Davitt's voice, high with anxiety, through the wood, and the girl's occasional, musical replies. After perhaps a minute the door burst open, and Davitt came out, a case in one hand, the girl's wrist in the other. He did not even look toward Conlon but allowed the girl to slam the door as she stumbled after him, and instantly headed away from the stairs towards the far end of the corridor and the fire escape Conlon knew was waiting there.

He was walking as quickly as somebody could walk without quite running. Conlon had to clear his throat loudly to attract his attention.

Turning his head, he did not stop walking until he saw that it was Conlon. Then his shoulders drooped a little, and Miss Fagan ripped her hand from his grasp and took a few steps away from him.

Conlon shrugged. "I suppose this makes the local police station a better option for us, doesn't it?"

Davitt began to nod and then suddenly launched his bag at Conlon. Conlon batted it away, covered the distance between them in a flash, and hit Davitt twice— a body shot with his left and a straight right. Davitt went down hard and lay on the carpet whimpering, blood already escaping from his face between his fingers. Conlon flexed his stinging knuckles. The girl looked at him, smiling.

2

THE LOCATION OF THE MEET MADE GRANT NERVOUS, FOR a start. If it was routine, they could've met in Dublin somewhere. The docks or Sandymount or the Phoenix Park, if they wanted some privacy. Any pub, if they didn't. But all the way out here? That told him that something was off. And that made him nervous. So he had brought some of the lads out, to back him up, just in case.

He was smoking at the back of the ruined old building, looking down at the city. It looked small from up here, and Grant could see right across to the rump of Howth Head, sitting squat in the Irish Sea through the clear summer air. All the people he knew down there, getting through their days. He watched a couple of birds twisting in the blue of the sky and then turned to look at the building. The Hellfire Club is what everybody called it. Even though it was a wreck, it was still impressive. It dominated the hill it sat on, its big empty black windows like eyes over the city, the slanting shoulders to its smaller wings giving it a continued grandeur even though it had been uninhabited for decades. It was a fine warm summer afternoon, but still there was something dark and doleful about the place. He understood all the tales of ghosts and haunting, even if he couldn't quite believe any of them. Life was frightening enough for the living without needing to invent stories about the undead to make it worse.

Cal and Gearoid were upstairs smoking and drawling at one another in a window. Like a married couple, the two of them; always together, always arguing, always laughing. But they were handy in a scrap. Gearoid was a giant, six foot three and built like a cart horse. Grant had seen him lift a man clean off his feet with one hand in a warehouse in Inchicore. He had a placid demeanor and an easygoing nature to match. But get him going, and he would take some stopping. Cal was fundamentally different. He carried a knife, and he was lightning fast with it, and his temper could be triggered by the most trifling of things.

Sharpie and Joey Brannan were somewhere around the other side of the building. Brannan had fought in the Great War, and he carried a revolver inside his coat, just in case. He was quiet and had a coldness to him that Grant disliked, but which he was grateful for on days like this one. He acted as if he had killed before, whereas most of them tried to act like that and failed. His service and the way his mouth always seemed to be turned down at the end gave him a weight and gravity that impressed the other lads, even if none of them would ever admit it. Sharpie was just along for the laugh, as he always was. Right now, Grant supposed, they would be smoking in silence, stood together without speaking. Sharpie would be in agony, wanting nothing more in the world than to have a simple, polite little chat, and Brannan wouldn't even notice.

Grant finished his cigarette and lit another with the dying butt before he flicked it away. He should bring Maureen up here, he decided. She liked strange things; she would enjoy this. Her dark imagination, she said with that lovely light little laugh of hers. He felt a sudden bolt of despair at the thought of her, a near certainty that he would not be seeing her again. For comfort, he touched the pistol in his coat pocket. He was prepared. Nothing here could threaten him, not today. He had this gun and the lads, and they were ready for any foul play or double cross.

He thought about Maureen again. He remembered how she had looked walking away from him the other night, her hips swaying in that dress. Smiling back over her shoulder at him. But she didn't even know what he did, not really. That had bothered him of late. Since they had gotten involved with these boys, anyway, and everything had seemed more serious and more dangerous. She thought he was some kind of messenger, he suspected, based on an assumption he had allowed her to make. How she squared that with the money he obviously had to take them out for dinners and cake and to the pictures, he could not figure out. She must have known, deep down, that he was involved in something. She probably thought he was a Fenian, one of the Rebels, out to kill Englishmen, and that was why he couldn't speak of it, and why she didn't press him. She was a good girl in that way. She was a good girl in most ways.

He had met her at a wedding, over a year before. His old friend Bobby Foster had married a country lassie, which meant that the whole place was packed out with culchies, which meant that there were a few brawls late on, but by then he was already at home in bed, in love and dreaming of the pretty brunette he had shared perhaps a whole minute of conversation with.

He nagged at Bobby for a solid month before he arranged for them to meet again. Back then she had worked as a secretary in some company in the docks, so she was always being courted by young dockers, and she was very picky, said Bobby. But Grant knew that he was charming, and all he needed was a chance to show it. They had met—

An engine rumbled. It was the kind of violent sound that tore at the fabric of a day, and it made him wince now. He also knew it was them. It had to be. Not many people would be up here, not in an automobile, anyway. He looked around at Cal and Gearoid and nodded. Cal copied the gesture and stubbed out his cigarette. Stomach crawling, flopping inside him like a gasping fish, he felt a bolt of nausea, acid in his throat, and turned grimly towards the sound of the vehicle approaching up from the valley.

What could he tell her, though? Not what he had actually been doing for these people. She would never understand. He barely understood. A year before, he had been doing smalltime stuff; criminal yes, but nobody was being hurt. Now though, he knew this wasn't true. He knew it in his heart. He himself hurt nobody—not directly, anyhow—but he was fairly sure that they were hurt afterwards. He had avoided details of what happened to the girls for exactly this reason; he had a conscience. He didn't want to know. All he really did, if he had to explain it and keep it vague and not incriminating, was charm some young ladies, and arrange some transport. Innocent enough. But then it wasn't. Some of the girls got scared, and he and his lads had to be rough with them. And he knew what would happen to them, didn't he? If he allowed himself to think about it? He knew.

The engine noise raked to a stop. The silence left in its wake was shockingly clear; he could hear the faint breeze moving through the trees perhaps eighty yards away, a spray of whispered foliage. Cal and Gearoid had moved from their position, and he could no longer see them, but he knew they were nearby. A bird burst from the branches and arced low over the ground. Three men came walking out of that same tree line a moment later.

He knew none of them. The one in the middle was tall and broad-shouldered, and had a swagger about him, his chin high and wide like a boxer's. He wore tweed and a waistcoat as if he were going on a hunt. His hat was wider than most, almost like a cowboy hat from a picture show. He had a dark mustache, extravagantly oiled. The other two were older, more familiar types— soldiers, enforcers. Grant had been surrounded by their like for years.

Movement in the corner of his eye as Sharpie and Brannan came around the building to watch the men approach. The man in tweed spoke to him from thirty yards away.

"This is a spooky place to meet, ain't it?"

Grant almost started. The man was American.

"I didn't choose it."

"Ah, my people? I'm not from these parts, so I let a

local pick for me. He chose well. I like it." This man was supremely relaxed and confident.

Grant nodded. "I'm not sure why we're here."

"Well sir, I like to meet the people who work for me."

"I work *with* you."

The American stopped now, perhaps ten meters away, and a soft smile flicked across his mouth. "You take my money to provide a service. Where I'm from, we'd call that employment."

They watched one another for a moment before Grant acceded with a curt nod.

"So, what can I do for you, Mister...?"

"My name is Gunnar. And you don't need to do anything for me. My boss has been checking out your operation for the last few weeks, and he's decided we don't need you anymore. So I guess you could look at it as me being here to fire you, Mr. Grant."

"You're fucking joking, wha?"

"Now, I didn't come all this way to make jokes with my Irish underlings and my boss doesn't really have much of a sense of humor, so you need to start taking this seriously."

"You can't just come to Dublin and think you can start doing our kind of business here, for fuck sake. That's not how it works."

Grant felt a sense of panic he couldn't really understand. Something else was happening here, just beyond his realization. And that scared him.

"You should have done some research into who you were working for, Mr. Grant. My boss hasn't just come here. He's *from* here. He has strong links with the community. He has friends. And they know exactly what we're doing."

He had to mean the Fenians, Xavier, Fitzy. Grant couldn't comprehend this. He needed to talk to the lads who made decisions above him—Doyle or Waters—and see what they knew.

"Ok. So why are we here? All this could've been said somewhere else. You could've made a telephone call." He shrugged. "I don't understand why you had to drag us all out here."

Gunnar grinned, but his eyes were untouched by any amusement. They were cold, empty. He said, "You were the one we thought might make some trouble."

He cocked his head, raised his right arm, then dropped it sharply.

Gunfire from the tree line. A tattoo of blasts. Sharpie and Brennan fell, shot.

Snipers.

Sharpie was dead, but Brennan kicked and bucked in a circle on the grass, blood bubbling from his neck. Grant looked around for Cal and Gearoid. Gearoid was running for it, headed for the trees, downhill, legs windmilling madly, looking as if he might fall at any second. A shot from the tree line missed him.

More gunfire from nearby. Cal was fighting back, perhaps on the other side of the building. Grant's eyes met Gunnar's as they listened to the shots intensify, and then they stopped entirely.

One more bark from a rifle, but Gearoid disappeared into the trees down the hill, running flat-out, like he was about to take off.

Grant slowly moved his hand for the pistol and

Gunnar met his eye and slowly shook his head. The two men flanking him were watching, expressionless.

Grant felt baffled. Why was this happening? He saw no reason for it.

"But why?" he asked. "What's the point of—"

"We like to keep things neat. No loose ends. It's good business." A slight shrug at that.

Grant nodded, absently. He was thinking of Maureen, and how he wished he could tell her sorry and kiss her again, one more time. He pictured her face and smile as his hand moved for the gun he carried. Gunnar was already crossing the ground between them, covering the space with shocking speed, and as he struggled to release the gun from his clothing, Grant had time to take in the big man's posture and realize that he was a boxer, and that he was about to punch Grant in the face.

The first punch made the world explode into light and threw Grant onto the grass, on his back. It felt as if everything had been turned upside down. Distantly, he felt Gunnar's great weight as it pressed upon his chest. He felt the second punch, and the third, but he was beyond such sensations by the fifth, and by the tenth, the big American was just pounding what had been the face of a now-lifeless corpse.

When Gunnar was done, he stood, drew a handkerchief from his breast pocket, and wiped off his knuckles. He had expected more of a fight, somehow. But then this country had been pitifully easy, so far. No fight, no balls from anybody they had encountered. They seemed soft and fat on their assumptions of power to Gunnar. If all the Irish were this accommodating it was no wonder the English had controlled this little country for so long. He almost longed for a challenge, someone to step up and make him work for it.

He nodded at the trees down the hill. "Make sure they get that one." Then he headed back to the car. Swaney was arriving in a few weeks. There was still much to be done.

3

TOMMY CONLON WAS IN A HURRY. HE LIKED TO EXERCISE in the mornings when he could. It was a habit he had picked up from the Major, and a habit he liked, and had continued since he had returned from the war. It kept him feeling sharp, alert, physically ready for whatever might come his way. Some mornings he ran in the Phoenix Park. Others, he shadow-boxed in his own living room, did sit-ups, press-ups, skipped rope, lifted the dumbbells he had ordered a few months before. And at least once a week he came to Clontarf Baths and swam.

He had chanced that today, even though he was due to meet Theresa in Bewleys on Westmoreland Street at Ten. He had swum for almost forty-five minutes and now he was dressing after hastily drying off, then combing his still-damp hair, one eye in a gray, misted mirror, listening inattentively to the two sons of Clontarf loudly discussing London politics at the other end of the changing room. Finally, he was done, his things packed into his bag with a precision and efficiency learned in the army, and he walked quickly out of the baths then headed towards the tram station.

It was a fine May morning, he thought, Dublin finally risking displaying its summer color to the world after months of drab gray, rain and snow, bitter winds and creeping fogs off the Irish sea. Now the trees lining the road vibrated with green, the sun bounced off windows and automobiles, horses glowed with health and people's faces reflected the weather, too; they looked a little livelier, a little more cheerful, their smiles upturned to the sun and the blue above.

He had to wait ten minutes or so for a tram and had neglected to either buy a newspaper or pack a book into his bag, which would have been his usual practice. So now he watched the crowd develop, waiting for the tram. Businessmen in smart suits, shiny shoes and fashionable hats, each with his head in a newspaper, smoking cigarettes, were scattered around. There were ladies, too, of varying ages and classes, based on their dress. A man stood in front of him, squinting at a paper which he held up high, and Conlon read over his shoulder about the Dockers Strike that had begun a day or two before and the "black flu" that had first afflicted some in the city the previous summer but seemed to have returned in the first months of fine weather. His mother had visibly shivered when they discussed both issues, reminded as she was of the horrors of the lockout a few years previous and of epidemics from her childhood. With its teeming slums, awful sanitation and miserable winters, Dublin was not a healthy city, and the tales of dozens of seemingly healthy people suddenly falling ill and dying were disturbingly easy to believe.

That all felt distant here, in this well-to-do suburb on a sunny morning, when he felt strong and energized by his swim. Here the streets felt wide, and the sky was open and huge and blue above, and it felt like possibility. But he had grown up in a slum, where the sky felt gray and glimpsed between buildings or through a greasy, cracked window, and he knew the way the smell and the lice and the dirt seemed to drag people down into the earth itself, until their bodies gave out from the strain. He had escaped that life, but he understood it, and he had to hold onto that understanding and draw strength from it, because it separated him from so many others, from the people stood around him here and now on this platform, waiting.

The tram arrived, already quite crowded, and after waiting while people levered themselves on and found space, he stood by a door and watched the light flickering on the sea and then the familiar streets roll by.

At Sackville Street he helped a young lady climb down and then he was hurrying off, already late, anticipating Theresa's cutting jibe with intense pleasure.

Bewley's was the smell of coffee. The Major had loved coffee, and in France, whenever he had sat in his study and listened to him talk, the smell had cast his memory back to Dublin and this place. This place where he and Orla—the girl he had loved and watched die and who would haunt him, he believed, until he, too, died—had once come and sat at tables on other sides of the room, casting glances at one another, fearful of discovery by Xavier, the gang lord who owned them both, to some extent, but unable to resist their need to see one another.

When he walked in, the noise was what struck him:

a dozen conversations, laughter, the efficient rattle of china from the kitchens, music playing from somewhere he could not see like the sun behind a cloud. It was crowded. Breakfast smells beneath the coffee, the strong cologne or hair wax of the maître d, already approaching him with dark, arched eyebrows high up on his lined forehead.

Theresa was in the back, near the staircase. She wore a dress of dark green he had not seen before, and she saw him coming and a small grin flicked across her face.

"It is nice of you to decide to show up, I suppose. I should be grateful."

"I'm sorry, Theresa. You look lovely."

She blinked in confusion at this. Their unspoken rules did not allow for compliments. They sparred and parried, insulted and teased, but there was never any acknowledgement of attraction. They were both waiting for something, although what it might be neither would be able to identify.

"T—thank you, Tommy. This is a new dress."

He nodded, satisfied to have distracted her from the anticipated fusillade. "For me?"

She laughed at this. "No. I am having dinner with a gentleman."

He didn't know what to say or how to react to this, but he felt his guts churn. To cover any physical sign of that, he waved for a waiter.

She said, "I've already ordered a pot of tea, and a bacon sandwich for you."

"And maybe I'm not in the humor for a bacon sandwich?"

"Sure when are you not in the humor for a bacon

sandwich? I'll make sure one goes in the coffin with your corpse and you'll eat that, too."

He laughed. She always made him laugh.

"So who is this gentleman?"

She didn't look at him as she answered. "Nobody you know, I hope."

"Are you courting?"

Now she looked him in the eye. "Tommy. You're not my daddy."

"I know that. But George—"

"George would like him. George wouldn't want me to be the mourning widow forever."

"Alright."

"I don't ask questions about your girls."

"What girls?"

"I'm not stupid. I run your business for you, I deal with these women. Miss Fagan. Mrs. O'Kane. That Englishwoman from the theatre in February."

He felt blood in his face, but he just nodded.

"Trust me," she said. "He's a gentleman. And I'm tired of waiting around with my mother-in-law."

He read the implied criticism in that and knew it was deserved.

A waitress arrived with their tea, his sandwich and a slice of sponge for her. He poured the tea for both of them, and he was momentarily transported again by the wonderful burble of the liquid into the bottom of each cup. They ate silently for a moment.

"Just—" he said. "If you need me..."

"Of course, Tommy," she said with kindness.

He nodded and chewed furiously. After a while she moved on to business.

"Mr. Davitt's company have paid. I put most of it in

the company account. The Watsons are paying in installments, you'll remember. They have three install-ments left."

"I feel bad about that. Can we not let them off the rest?"

"Do you want to?"

He shrugged.

"We're not a charity, Tommy. You work hard. It can be dangerous."

"I know. One more installment, then write off the rest."

"You're too soft."

"Only when I need to be," he replied.

She nodded and made a note.

"Anything coming in?"

"Two this week. One I chased up already. Husband run off to America without telling a soul."

Theresa had become adept at quickly determining which cases were nonsense and which required actual investigation. She had a little office in her flat which was a miracle of organization and tidiness and from there she ran this part of his life, making it easy for him to focus on the actual legwork—chasing people down, asking questions, piecing things together. Meanwhile she fielded clients, dealt with all of the money, and had already amassed a sea of contacts across the city which meant he was rarely without work.

"The other I think you should meet."

"Who is it?"

"It's a nun."

"Jaysus."

She giggled at this, and her girlish laugh made him laugh, too.

"Has God gone missing again?" he said and she laughed louder.

"She works with charities, helping paupers and people on the streets. She says some of the young girls have been going missing."

"Street girls?"

"Beggars, urchins. Not boys though, only girls."

"How did she seem?"

"Sharp the way some nuns and priests are. Like she missed nothing. She was absolutely convinced and very persuasive."

"Ah, but you were educated by nuns, weren't you? You were always going to be trembling before her."

"They were all old wagons. She seemed nice."

"Surely the Church could investigate."

"We both know the church doesn't care about a few street kids."

He rubbed at his face. "What do you think?"

"You might as well meet with her and see how you feel about it then..."

"Right so. Tell her I'll meet her—when?"

"I told her you'd be there this afternoon."

"Of course you did. Where am I going?"

"She says the convent in the Coombe. Do you know it?"

"I do. Am I looking clean and tidy enough to be visiting a convent?"

"What do you mean?"

"I have to look like a respectable, god-fearing young gentleman, or they won't even let me into the place. So should I be changing my cap for a smarter hat, maybe?" He said this with a twinkle, teasing her.

She caught this and threw it back at him. "Ah I'm

sure the sisters will be wanting to adopt you. You're only the sweetest young man in Dublin."

He laughed again.

"Do you have a smarter hat? You're always in that cap."

"I have other hats. I like the cap. It helps me blend in more. A top hat tends to get noticed more easily."

"I'm sure. Maybe I'll go and buy myself a hat after this."

"You could ask your gentleman to buy you one."

"I could. He has plenty of money, he could afford it."

That stung him somehow, and he swallowed the last of his tea, and sat up straight. "Right so, I'll be off. I'll drop by later this week and we'll chat."

She nodded, watching him. "Be careful with those nuns."

He was standing, his cap still in his hands. There was always this feeling between them. Like leaving was wrong. Like there was more to say.

"You know I'm never careful, Theresa," he said, turning away with a wave.

"Tommy," she called.

He looked back. "Her name. Her name is Sister Diana."

———

CONLON DROPPED his bag off at home before heading for the Coombe. His flat was just off the Quays, in Smithfield, and though he had moved in over two months before, he felt as if he had barely spent any time there. He was still sleeping on a cot, like the one he had had in the army. The whole place needed a coat of paint, and though he'd planned to do that since his first night there, it somehow still hadn't happened.

His books were piled up in tired and pitiful-looking towers, tottering against the wall where he was intending to build a bookcase. The spines were all brown and maroon. He had at least a closet and a few presses, where he kept his clothes. There was also a table and a few chairs, and now he spread his wet towel and swimming suit out on the backs of those, hoping that the sun into the kitchen would warm them through. That was the best thing about the place—it was bright, with big windows and sunlight filling the living room for much of the day.

In his bedroom, he pocketed his father's old miraculous medal, its shine dulled by age and wear, just in case he needed to play the old altar boy in order to win somebody over. Nuns, like priests and monks and Christian Brothers, could be awkward if they believed they were dealing with a non-believer. And though he had stopped attending Mass in his teens, and had what last vestiges of faith remained slammed out of him by the things he had seen and experienced in the War, he was diplomatic enough to stay silent about this when he dealt with the Church. In fact, he believed that his lack of faith made him better at his job. He was not superstitious and utterly without sentiment. He treated the clergy like human beings, and was not cowed or intimidated by them, but saw them the same way he saw somebody else. A few months before, a search for the vanished son of a Dun Laoghaire doctor had led him to the door of the parish priest. If he had been a believer, if he had bowed before the might of the Church, then he might have hesitated, but he had done what he had been hired to do. And so now the Church in Ireland knew of him. Which might prove a good thing in the future, or a bad thing. When he knocked on the Convent door, he was thinking that it was a good thing.

A young nun answered the door. She blinked at him for an instant with utter incomprehension. Finally, she said, "Hello? Can I help you, sir?"

"Hello. I'm here to see Sister Diana."

The nun nodded slowly at this. She was still holding the door over so that only one side of her face was revealed into the street. She looked just like all of the girls he had passed on his way here—her nose upturned, lips pursed in either irritation or confusion, eyes dark and brown. She was pretty, he saw, something pleasing in the set of her features, a spark in her eyes. Only she wore a habit, concealing her hair, framing her face and making her age impossible to guess. She looked at him in silence as the seconds dripped past.

He said, "Is she here?"

"Yes. You have a meeting with her, you said?"

She opened the door a little wider to speak this to him.

"Not quite. She is expecting me though."

"Would you mind waiting?"

She closed the door on him with a loud bang before he could answer. He chuckled at the exchange, then turned to watch the street as he waited. Perhaps a minute later she returned and asked him in. Briskly she walked him through a hallway marked only by a long line of coat-hooks and some religious icons of varying size and color along the right wall. He had—ridiculously—expected it to smell of incense, but there was instead the faintest wet odor of boiled vegetables.

She did not speak or look at him. He watched her black-wrapped head bob and sway as she turned up a staircase and he followed her.

On the first floor, lighter and fresher than the one below, he was taken to an office at the back of the building, and there, behind a large desk in a room with one wall lined with books and another filled with wooden filing cabinets, sat an older woman with kind eyes and laugh lines creasing the corners of her face.

"Sister Diana," he said.

"Mister Conlon. Thank you for coming so soon."

"Not at all. And it's Tommy, please, sister."

The nun nodded, and gestured to the younger woman, who moved around the table and sat on a chair near the filing cabinets.

Sister Diana saw Conlon's eyes on her and said, "You must forgive Sister Maude, Tommy. We're a bit nervous here today. We had a break-in the night before last, and she is still recovering from the fright. She got an awful shock."

Conlon nodded. "I'm very sorry to hear that. Why would somebody break in here?"

"Well, I have a feeling it might be to do with what you're here to talk about."

"Girls disappearing."

"Yes. I think they were here trying to scare us."

"Who might they be?"

The nun shrugged. "That I cannot say. I suppose that is where you come in."

"Well, let's hope so, Sister."

He reached into his inside pocket and drew out his notebook and pencil. They were mainly for show, and had been Theresa's suggestion. As so often, she had been correct. People seemed to be comforted by them, by the suggestion that he was paying attention, making notes of the salient facts. For his part, the whole thing felt too theatrical, but he respected the fact that it worked. So he persisted.

Now, he wrote the date and the word NUNS. And tried to stifle a laugh at this.

"So, how did this all start?" he asked.

"A young girl I've grown quite fond of and knew well just vanished."

"And that would be unusual? For a street girl?"

"More unusual than you might expect. This isn't Calcutta, Tommy. Dublin is still quite small; everybody knows everybody—on the streets at least. The others would know where she was sleeping, where she was begging, and so on. But there is no sign of her at all."

He nodded. "What's her name?"

"Saoirse. I never knew her surname. Those details aren't as important on the street. Some of the children we know only by nickname."

"And when did she disappear?" He was scribbling in his notebook now. Though he would remember all these details, he played his part.

"A month ago. She used to come to us at least twice a week, every week. A conflicted girl."

"What does she look like?"

"Extremely pretty. So pretty you'd be surprised she could be living on the street."

"Hair color? Eyes?"

"Black hair, long. Blue eyes. Tall for a girl her age."

"How tall?"

"Around Sister Maude's height, I'd say." She gestured to the younger woman, who blushed at the mention of her name. "Her skin is quite pale, and she has a scar over one of her eyes—the right one, I think. Quite a strong Dublin accent, I'd say. A bit like yourself."

"Do you know where she was staying? Any friends I should talk to? Family?"

"We can introduce you to some others she was friendly with, and they might be able to help you."

"That would be helpful, Sister."

"Would you want to do that now?"

"When we're finished here. She was the first one to disappear, was she? Have there been others?"

The two nuns shared a look. "We don't know for certain, now. She was the first one I noticed, and then... when we thought about it, we realized a few regular faces weren't regular anymore. They just weren't around."

"But there's no evidence, no witnesses to something odd?"

"No. They...they aren't keen on opening up about anything like that. Not a soul would talk if we asked."

"Could she have gotten sick?"

"The Spanish Flu? No, no. The children are all very aware of that. They would have known."

"Right. This break-in."

"Yes."

"Tell me about it. What did they take?"

"Not a solitary thing."

"Did they hurt anybody? Was it even a "they"? Did you see them, or him?"

"Sister Maude did. Tell him, Sister."

He looked at the younger nun. She had tears in her eyes before she had even begun speaking, but she fixed her eyes upon his and spoke with an edge in her voice. After a moment, he recognized that it was anger.

"I heard a noise late. It woke me."

"What time?"

"Half past one. I checked my clock so I know. I went out of my room and could hear someone moving downstairs, but it didn't sound like one of the sisters was in the kitchen..."

"Why not?"

"It was too loud, and it sounded violent. There was a lot of smashing, and the sounds of things breaking, like glass or delph."

"What did you do?"

She let a little laugh escape her. "I didn't want to awaken anyone in case it was nothing."

"Of course."

"So I went downstairs, on my own."

"That must have been awful scary."

"It was. There were two of them, just outside the kitchen. And they'd been all over the house, from the look of things. It was an awful mess."

"Did they see you?"

"Yes, they stopped what they were doing when I came into the doorway and stood just gaping at me. Then they ran."

"What did they look like?"

"They had handkerchiefs over their faces, and hats."

"What sort of hats?"

"Flat caps. One of them was tall and the other one was average. And they both wore black or dark gray jackets and trousers."

She could be describing a few thousand men in the

city on any given day, and from her apologetic expression, he saw that she was aware of this.

"What were they doing? Just breaking things?"

Sister Diana said, "It would seem so. Cutlery, some delph, some jars of various foodstuffs. They were just trying to scare us, I think. They broke a window to get in as well."

"If they've done that once, they won't be afraid to do it again."

"Well. Now we won't be confronting them, if so. Now, do you want us to bring you to meet these children?"

Conlon liked the way she took charge—no-nonsense, no tolerance for any wasted time.

"That could certainly be helpful, Sister, yes."

He waited in the kitchen where Sister Maude had seen the two men. They had entered by breaking a pane of glass in a door and opening the lock from inside. The pane had already been repaired and replaced, the mess the men had made cleaned away as if it had never happened. He was already wondering who they might be and how they could be wound up in all of this. Hired thugs? Or something else, something stranger.

Or this was entirely unrelated.

He had a sense he could barely articulate to himself that this job would be unusual. Something felt off, and though he couldn't put his finger right on it, he was strongly aware of it. The nuns and their oddly truculent impatience only added to this feeling.

He leaned against one of the worktops. This kitchen, like the rest of the building, from all he had seen, felt cold and impersonal, bereft of individuality or personality. Not quite what he had expected.

The sisters eventually came and fetched him, then led him through the streets without speaking. They had a habit of acting without speaking; spending so much time together had given them an oiled, wordless efficiency, and it was as if they expected him to slip right into their system, to do as they did without questions or need for explanation. Because he watched and listened and paid close attention, they weren't wrong.

They made their way out across the city, bustling and busy by then, the sun high in the sky and baking the buildings and cobbles they crossed. Men wore shirt-sleeves rolled to their elbows, women fanned at themselves and lurked beneath awnings and in shady doorways. He walked behind the two women, memories of his brief early education making him grin as he went. It was odd to watch the ways they glided along, crowds parting before them, their heads rarely wobbling like a pair of dark swans, elegant and untouched.

People looked at him strangely as they passed; he was an incongruous sight accompanying these young women. Every so often Sister Maude would look back to make sure he was still following, and once, when their eyes met, he gave her a warm smile and she smiled back, the most open expression he had seen on her face to that point. When they crossed the Liffey and headed North up the wide, sunbaked valley of Sackville Street, he began to have some idea of their likely destination.

They turned up Sackville Place and then into Earl Place, the twinned bulk of Clearys and the Pro-Cathedral looming from different sides, and here they were, little groups of children; boys and girls coagulating on steps and stoops, dirty faces and fingernails blackened with the grime of Dublin, their clothing tatty, and, on some children, torn and worn away in large patches.

Sister Diana was speaking to him as they approached. "One of the problems we find with the poor in Dublin is that there isn't any one group overseeing all the charities trying to help them. There are instead various churches and groups involved, giving them things and asking them questions and trying to come up with ways to make their lives easier. But sometimes they're working at cross purposes. So imagine a young boy, whose mother has died, and whose father likes a drink a bit too much. His daddy can't guarantee regular money coming into the room they share, if they're lucky, on Clanbrassil Street. So the boy is out, trying to earn money, or at least earn food. And he'll steal if he needs to. Sure if a charity comes along, offering him bread or potatoes, he'll bite their hands off, won't he? But then the same day, another charity gives him more bread or maybe some carrots. While the young boy who lives around the corner from him and whose daddy has been killed in the Great War gets nothing."

He nodded at this.

"They're like feuding neighbors sometimes. They won't work together. They won't swallow their pride, any of them. Some of them men of the cloth. So we have to work around the edges of what they have wrought. Try to keep an eye on the details, because somebody has to."

"If you hadn't been doing that, nobody would've noticed that this girl is missing," he said. A cluster of children had already broken away from their own groups, drawn like birds to the prospect of the two nuns and whatever treats they might provide.

They had no treats today. Instead they talked to the children, asked them questions, made them laugh. Conlon hung back, watching. The children lost interest and began to drift away. Sister Diana was involved in a conversation with two young girls, but Sister Maude moved over to stand by Conlon's side.

"Usually we'd bring food for them."

He nodded. "So they...beg?"

"Some of them do. Some of them steal. Some of them are already starting to burgle. The gangs recruit them around ten or eleven, especially the boys. The girls will try to sell flowers on Sackville street or at Stephens Green. Some of them end up in the Monto."

"Some of them end up as nuns," he said.

She laughed at that and he saw that warmth again flash through her face. "Maybe they do, Mr. Conlon."

"Tommy, please. Is that how you came to be a nun, Sister?"

"Oh no. I'm not—"

"From this part of Dublin, I know. Bray? Graystones? Somewhere out in Wicklow, I think."

"Very good. You are a detective, after all. I'm from Rathnew. You're a city boy. From not too far away from here?"

He nodded. "Stoneybatter."

They were silent then, watching Sister Diana's intense conversation.

"Is she asking about Saoirse?"

"Maybe. You have to wait until you can feel that they're ready to talk about something like that, or else they'll just close the door on you."

She went on talking, but his attention had wandered. There was a man watching them from the street corner. He had a newspaper out, and was leaning against a lamppost to read it, but Conlon knew he was watching them. Something in the body language and one head movement had given him away. Conlon stared at him for a moment, then stopped. Had they been followed? He supposed that they must have been. He should have noticed, but he had been distracted. By what? He had to admit that it had been by the young nun who was even now still talking to him. Sloppy and unprofessional, he told himself, annoyed.

This man didn't know Conlon, didn't know who he was. If he did he would never have been so careless as to let himself get made as easily as he just had been.

And now he was intrigued. The two things seemed unconnected, although they obviously were, somehow. Street children disappearing was one thing, and it was a thing he felt he could approach a certain way. But men intimidating and observing nuns felt like something utterly different, and his response to it felt different, too.

He needed to be clever, and not confront the man, as much as he might want to. He glanced in that direction again, taking in as many details as he could capture in an instant. He was a big man, six feet three or four, and with a build like a stag, but young, with the broad face of a farmer. Not experienced at this sort of thing. So why was he here? Conlon wondered as he directed his attention back to the nuns and the children. Something did not make sense. You would not send such a giant to follow people. He was too conspicuous. But he was not trying to intimidate them, either. So what was the point of this clumsy surveillance?

One of the children interrupted his thinking. "Mister, have you got any change for us? Any change, mister?"

"Where are you from?"

"King Street. Have you any change?"

Conlon dug in his pocket and tossed the only coins he had to the boy. Looking up, he saw Sister Maude regarding him with an expression he could not read.

He said, "Without being too obvious, tell me if there's still a big man watching us from the corner?"

Sister Maude's eyes narrowed a little but aside from that, she managed it with no little subtlety. "The one reading a paper?"

"That's him."

"Did he follow us?"

"I don't know. Is he one of them from the other night?"

She looked again, and he winced, because this time, the involuntary glance had been obvious, unmissable to anyone who might be watching her.

"No. He's too big. He's leaving now. Oh no, did he see me look at him?"

Already turned, he made after the giant, telling her, "Don't worry," over his shoulder. Her face shrunk in displeasure.

When he reached the corner, the giant was already turning onto Sackville Street, moving into the crowds, and heading south. Conlon swore and almost tripped, trying to increase his pace without actually running.

On Sackville Street he picked out the head easily as it was gliding above the mass of people, one of many similar hats, but a good foot higher than all of the others, crossing towards what had been the General

Post Office. As Conlon turned the corner, the man looked around and Conlon knew he had been seen. The giant was too far away for him to make out his face to be certain of that, but he could feel it.

Sure enough, as he approached the corner with Abbey Street, the giant began to run. He disappeared around the corner and Conlon broke into a run of his own in order to keep up. He had to let a tram pass and jump over a steaming pile of horse shit, but when he got to Abbey Street, the giant had vanished. He could have gone down Williams Row and through the Lotts or into one of the many shops on either side of the street. Either way, he was gone.

Conlon stood there for a moment, unaccustomed to this feeling of utter powerlessness. Then he returned to the nuns and the children.

4

ACCEPTING AN INVITATION TO DINNER OUT OF CURIOSITY, Conlon returned to the convent with the sisters that evening. He was becoming frustrated with how little there was to go on here. They knew little to nothing about the missing girl. After circulating through a few more regular gathering points for urchins through town, Sister Diana estimated that perhaps as many as ten other children they were used to seeing were no longer around. She also conceded that some of these may have found employment or returned to families or simply moved on. But she said she just had a feeling that there was something wrong here. Conlon agreed with her, but was confounded as to how he could approach whatever that wrong was. Confounded even as to how he could determine its exact nature.

A possible course of action was to stay close to the nuns. If these men who had broken in were somehow related to the disappearances—and he was assuming that they were, even though this was a huge and very possibly incorrect assumption—then it was likely that they would return.

But that could also be a fruitless waste of time. And Conlon had always been aggressive in his approach to investigations; he made things happen, he was active, he provoked a reaction. But right now he had nothing and nobody to provoke. And he hated the feeling of power-lessness this brought. Hated it.

They ate in a large dining room with a high vaulted ceiling, shelves of books forming one entire wall, and three large tables running the length of the room. This conformed more readily to the mental image of convents he had been carting around, and he found that almost comforting.

There were perhaps a dozen other nuns, mostly sat in two groups at the other tables, as Sister Maude led him in and ushered him to a place at the only empty table.

A hush had taken hold of the room at his entrance, and she raised her eyebrows at him. "They're not used to men eating here, except for the odd priest."

"Priests do love a free meal, don't they," he said.

"And the company of nuns..." she said with another eyebrow raise, which made him laugh out loud.

She beamed at this, then spent a minute or so describing the drunken lechery of one of their regular collared visitors. Sister Diana interrupted them when she arrived, trailed by another nun. Both carried trays, with three large bowls of steaming stew, cups and a jug of water.

When the bowls had been placed in front of them and the other nun retreated to the kitchen, Sister Diana said, "Were you just telling Mr. Conlon about Father Brailsford?"

Sister Maude reddened. "I was. I'm sorry, Sister, it—"

"Sure he is a source of regular amusement." She looked at Conlon. "He has taken a liking to Sister Maude, to be sure."

Maude said, "He wanders into my room and pretends he's lost."

"Hoping...?"

"Hoping I'll be dressing, I expect."

Conlon laughed again.

"Aside from that unfortunate side of his character, he's a fine priest," said Diana, with a mocking tone. "No, really. A wonderful speaker, a kind man, no politics in him, cares about his parishioners. He's just an oul' divil. He's awful into the horses. A gambling man."

"Aren't we all, sister, in one way or another?"

"If you say so, Tommy. But he loses all his money to the bookies. Which isn't one of the ten commandments. But it should be, if you ask me."

They laughed, and when she began to work on her stew, Conlon and Maude followed.

"This is lovely," Conlon said after a moment.

Sister Maude said, "Sister Eilish is a wonderful cook. She used to work in a kitchen."

"Do either of you have old careers I should know about?"

"Sister Maude came to us straight from school. I was a teacher, briefly. That feels like another life altogether. What about yourself, Tommy? You didn't always find people for a living."

"No, I didn't. I was a boxer, for a while."

"I have heard that, when I asked around about you. Some of the priests spoke very highly about you in the boxing ring."

He shrugged. "I wasn't bad."

"You don't seem the type," Sister Maude said.

"What would the type be?"

"I'm not sure. Stupid, I would've thought."

"Maybe a few are. But then there are stupid people in every walk of life, aren't there?"

"Sure we have our share of sisters who aren't the best for thinking," Sister Diana said, deadpan.

Conlon chuckled and went on, "But it's a surprisingly complex sport. I don't think I encountered many stupid boxers. I probably met a few who couldn't read, but they were far from stupid."

"So why aren't you still boxing? Why isn't Tommy Conlon a champion?" Diana asked gently.

"I gave it up."

"Why did you do that?"

"A girl. That ended badly, and then...the War." They were both silent at that. "And then when I came back, I just fell into this."

"How do you fall into such a peculiar station?"

He shrugged. "I was looking for somebody, for a friend who went missing. It was complicated, but I found them. Somebody heard about it and gave my name to somebody else. And so on..."

"Do you like it?"

"It's never dull. There's something new every day."

"You must see some awful things," Sister Maude said.

He looked at her for a moment and then they both had to look away. "Yeah, it can be a bit grim, but it's not the trenches. And I always get to walk away and sleep in my own bed every night. That can't be so bad."

"That War..." Diana began, then stopped. "It's a terrible thing."

"We can agree on that, Sister."

They talked for a while longer, about Dublin, the Spanish Flu and how they were considering opening up the convent to take in victims, about music, about the rebels. He was given a dessert of strawberries and cream, and they drank tea after that. Then he excused himself and, prompted by Sister Diana, Sister Maude walked him to the door, her head down as they exchanged a few sentences about what time she had to rise in the morning.

She walked as if being marched to a firing squad, as if he had a gun to her back. Her need to do that drove him to look at her, to make sure she was ok, to see if she would return his look. But she did not, replying to him with her eyes on the floor as they walked. When they reached the front door, she unlocked it, pulled it slowly open, and stood there beside it, her hand on the handle, all of it accomplished with her face down. Yellow light filled the doorway from the lamps in the street, which were just beginning their nocturnal efforts against the dark.

She looked up for an instant, as if to check that he did intend to leave, and their eyes met, and then she looked away, furtively and anxiously. He wondered if it was the absence of Sister Diana now that made her so nervous. He wanted to tell her that it was fine, that she could trust him, that he was a good man and would not hurt her or even talk to her if she did not wish it. Instead, he said he would be back the next day, she nodded, thanked him politely and closed the door.

He stood there a moment alone, feeling confused and stupid. He had never really spoken to nuns before. And of course they were just people, women, human beings.

But he had been expecting something else. Nothing so complex and interesting. He stood and thought and dismissed it. He had a job to do, now. He turned and made off. He knew where he was going.

———

IT WAS a nameless pub upstairs from a butchers, on a side street in the ragged, wild land between the docks and the Monto. You had to know it existed and go hunting if you hoped to get in. Even then, you might not pass the inspection of the two burly men perched on stools in the shadows hanging over the landing.

But they knew Conlon well, and there were quiet "Evening's and nods at his arrival. The door opened with a neat click, and in he went. Everything stopped for a moment, as it always did. The music continued to play, but it always seemed as if the entire room turned to look at him. The air was as smoky as ever, men masked their faces with splayed cards and drank at every table. Heads were without hats, and there was a sweaty musk, combined with the sweetness of brandy and cheap perfume. Prostitutes circled the room slowly.

Conlon brazened it out. He could kill all expression in his face, as he had done before fights, and he did it now. The mass looked at him a moment, then returned to their distractions.

Conlon moved in. The manager—who he had every suspicion was one of Xavier's underlings—had knocked down all the walls, leaving the entirety of the building except for the landing outside as one big saloon. The bar ran along the wall and was manned by a grumpy, middle-aged Scotsman by the name of Watt. The clientele obviously named him Watt the Scot, which he hated while always answering to it.

Conlon wound his way to the bar between tables crowded with sweaty dockers and flirting working girls.

He nodded to Watt, who warily said, "What'll it be for the gentleman?"

"Give us a pint, good man."

While he pulled and waited, Watt said, "You're only ever in when you're looking for something. So ask away. I probably won't be able to help."

Conlon laughed at his miserable outlook. "It's always a pleasure to share a cheery word or two with yourself, Watt."

"Ah, fuck off wit tha shite. Wha'd ya want?"

"There are children disappearing off the streets. You heard anything about that?"

"No, no. But there are a lotta strange things happenin' now."

"Like what?"

Watt shrugged. "Ask around. You'll hear stories."

"Because of the rebels?"

"No. Nothin' to do with em. Somebody new."

"Somebody new?"

His pint was slid before him.

"Aye, it seems so. Nobody knows who, is the problem."

A skinny man in a waistcoat at least one size too big had approached the bar and stood there expectantly.

Watt said, "Tell him, Brendan."

Brendan looked at Conlon, and Conlon saw the recognition do something to his eyes.

"Tell him wha'?"

Watt rolled his eyes so hard it looked as if they might fall out of his skull and only his irritation kept them there. "Tell him wha people are saying, ye fuckin' eejit."

"Ah. They say there's a new outfit come in, from abroad, from England, they say," said Brendan.

"Who's they?" asked Conlon.

"Everybody, sure."

"And what are this outfit up to?"

"Nobody knows. But there's talk."

Conlon looked at him.

"Talk of what?"

"A few lads murdered. A few more disappeared."

"By Englishmen? Not the army or special branch?"

"No, but nobody really knows. Lot of the lads around town are spooked about it."

"So you're saying there's a gang of English gangsters moving into the city, and they've killed a few lads, but nobody really knows if they're even real? Is that what you're saying...?"

Brendan looked desperately to Watt for support.

"Well, yeah. But...no—"

Conlon stared at him. "Have you heard of anyone abducting children? Street urchins, like."

Brendan and the barman snatched a glance and Conlon caught it on the way back.

"Tell me," he said.

Brendan frowned, then looked at Conlon and spoke quickly. "Some of the lads were involved in something that sounded like that. Last month, I think."

"Give me a name, Brendan."

"Andrew Grant. He was boring the arse off us about the job a few weeks back."

"Where'll I find this Andrew Grant? Is he one of Xavier's lads?"

"I don't know that much. He used to hang around at the Gravediggers."

"Kavanaghs? That'll do, I suppose. Thank you, Brendan."

Brendan nodded, nerves still plain on his face.

"Something else you need to tell me?"

"There's been a bit of talk that Grant's gone missing. Nobody's seen him for a week or so."

Conlon nodded. "So you think there might be some relationship between these two things?"

One of the prostitutes had noticed Conlon. She put her arm around his shoulder, the better to pull him close and whisper into his ear. He smiled at her and was delighted when the smile she revealed was a dazzling split in her face, unmasking the scared little girl inside this bored, hopeless creature. She moved on, away from him, trying to keep that smile at bay, but it returned when she looked back at him.

Conlon returned his attention to the two men. "This Grant—does he have a gang? People around him?"

"Yeah, he pals around with a few lads," Watt said.

"Muscle, would you say?"

Watt and Brendan looked at one another.

Brendan said, "Couple of shooters, I'd say. They

wouldn't be welcome in polite company, let's leave it at
that, wha?"

Conlon nodded. "You seen them around? Or is it
just him that's missing?"

"I haven't seen any of them, no."

Watt was shaking his head, too.

Conlon said, "Is that strange? Are they regulars here,
on the scene?"

Watt looked thoughtful, in that his craggy, crinkled
eyes became even more craggy and crinkled. "They're
around. You'd see one of them every day or so, I'd say."

"And you haven't?"

"No. Not for days."

"Alright. Well if I turn up dead, lads—you were
right."

Watt chuckled. "If you turn up dead, we're all
fucked."

———

THE GRAVEDIGGERS SAT beside Glasnevin cemetery, and
it was what Conlon considered a decent pub. Nice pint,
normal crowd, fine grub. He had been many times with
the lads before everything with Xavier and the War. But
he hadn't been back since his return. This had become a
common experience for him. Places remained the same,
but Conlon was changed. And that made them feel
different, and that often felt frustrating, or even sad.
And then, sometimes, occasionally, it was fine.

He was recognized by the barman as soon as he
walked in.

"Tommy Conlon, isn't it? Jaysus you should still be
fightin', son, you were a pugilist of magnificent skills."

Conlon laughed at that, but felt the compliment warm him nonetheless. "Thanks very much. I think I missed me chance, though."

"Ah never. You're only young still. Life has a way of providing us with second chances when we least expect them, so it does."

A couple of old men turned to regard him. The barman said, "Frank, Dave, did yis ever see this lad fight? He was like a bleedin' tiger. Who was that lad you battered in—was it 1914? From Belfast, like most of them fighters. Red haired lad, big hands like a bleedin' ape. What was his name? He was the favorite, right, and then Tommy here bet the head off him for two rounds and knocked him out cold with the best right hook I ever saw in me life. The whole place groaned at the sight of it. You could feel it in your innards. You were better than any of them Belfast lads."

Conlon nodded and laughed. "Ah stop."

"Why aren't you fightin'? The War, was it?"

"Something like that, yeah."

"Ah well. What're ye having then, son?"

"Pint please."

When he had been served and had paid, the barman said, "I heard you're some sort of detective now."

"Did you? I didn't know it was common knowledge."

"Dublin is a small town."

"True."

"So're ye here for information? Tracking down a suspect of some description? Or just the fine pint that I pull?"

"I'm looking for someone."

"Go on then."

"Andrew Grant."

"Yeah, he's a regular alright. Haven't seen him in a few days now, though."

"That's what I've heard. You have an address for him?"

"No. But I know where his lassie lives."

"That'll be more than enough, then, I think."

"He's a bit of a gangster then?"

Conlon shrugged. "I don't know the man. I'm looking for somebody else and he might be able to help find them."

"He is alright. Nice lad though. No malice in him, ye know? He's just a bit lazy about how he earns his money."

"Sure, aren't we all?" one of the old men at the bar growled and they all shook with laughter.

The barman slid a piece of paper across the bar at Conlon. He glanced at it, then nodded his gratitude. But then the barman crouched down, palms apart, and Conlon knew he just had to explain the writing on the piece of paper. Conlon slumped.

———

THE BARMAN HAD GIVEN him a set of complicated directions complete with a backstory about his sister-in-law being a neighbor of the girl, but he found her tenement easily enough in one of the shabbier bits of Ballybough.

The streets were quiet at this time of day, and he knocked, entered and had one foot on the bottom step when somebody called out, "Hello?" from the darkness upstairs.

He said, "Hello? I'm looking for Maureen. Does she live here?"

"Who's asking?" A head appeared over the banister, peering down into the gloom for him—a woman, middle-aged and weatherworn.

"She's not in any trouble. I'm trying to find her fella."

"Isn't everyone? Sure we haven't seen him for days."

She was clumping down the stairs now, and came into view at the bend. She stopped to look at him, a frank, appraising air to her steely gaze, a scarf concealing all but a cow lick of her dark hair.

He said, "My name's Conlon. I'm trying to find a girl who's gone missing, and I was told Mr. Grant might be able to help..."

"Only now you're tryin' to find him? Ha!"

"Is she here? Can I talk to her?"

"She's out. Some of us work for a living, Mr. Conlon."

"But not you?"

"Oh you're a cheeky get. I like a cheeky get. Is this your job, or does he owe you money?"

"I've never met him. I find people."

"And get paid?"

"Not much but yeah, if somebody wants them found."

"Could you find me a husband? I misplaced mine twenty years ago." At this she cackled, and her laughter made him laugh, too. When she stopped chuckling, she blinked at him as if she had forgotten he was there.

"She sells cigarettes and sweets at the Dorset Picture Hall. You'll know her. Pretty girl. She'll talk to you. She's been pining for him something fierce. She's awful scared he's got himself the black flu and collapsed in a canal somewhere, but then she does have an imagination."

He nodded. "Thanks very much."

"You're welcome, darling. If you think of any solutions to my husband problem, you come back and let me know, won't you?"

He was backing out already, unsure how to respond.

"I can think of one solution already..." she said with that dirty chuckle, as he shut the door.

————————

THE DORSET PICTURE Hall was a big cinema off Dorset Street. There was a small queue for tickets when he arrived, people hurrying to get out of the summer drizzle and shelter beneath the canopy. Another queue for smokes and chocolate at the second counter. Inside the plush, deep red lobby, a few people sat smoking on the purple sofas, reading newspapers.

The program on the wall suggested that there were a lot of Harold Lloyd comedies playing, together with Douglas Fairbanks in *The Americano* and *20,000 Leagues Under the Sea*. He had seen them all at a variety of the many picture houses scattered around the city, but still he felt tempted. He loved the feeling of escape from reality a daytime trip to a cinema offered; the enveloping darkness, the warmth, the vividness of other lives and souls on a big screen. But when he reached the ticket desk, instead he asked if he could speak to Maureen.

The man behind the counter rolled his eyes. "Buy

yourself a ticket and you can find her and chat as long as you want."

So he did just that. He had to stand at the back of the cinema for a good minute or so, allowing his eyes to adjust to the darkness. It was a large auditorium, perhaps one third full. On screen, Harold Lloyd was alternating between joy and panic in shining gray American rooms and streets. The audience, scattered in clumps around the auditorium, rumbled and barked with laughter. Smoke hung over their heads in a form-less sag of gray.

He saw her perhaps a minute later, leaning by the wall to his right, her eyes on the screen but expression suggesting she was somewhere else entirely. She was pretty as the woman had said; neat and with a perpetual half smile on her lips. The tray at her waist was filled with an array of cartons and wrappers, and she was standing so that her jutting hip propped it up so that she could bite a thumbnail and worry her own hair.

She jumped when he spoke to her.

"Maureen? Can we have a quick chat? I'm looking for Andrew Grant."

Her eyes went teary at the mention of the name and, nodding, she led him along the wall and out of an emer-gency exit. She made sure that her fingers were on the wall at all times, as if for support. There they stood together in an empty corridor, and she seemed to be struggling to breathe.

"Is he alright?" she gasped.

"You're misunderstanding. I'm trying to find him. Why wouldn't he be alright?"

"Who are you?"

"My name is Conlon. I find missing people."

"Somebody hired you to find Andrew? Who would do that?"

"No, I'm looking for somebody else altogether. But his name came up. Why would he be missing?"

"Ah, he's involved with gangsters somehow. He thinks I don't know, but I'm not stupid. I don't care. He's a good man."

"So why would he be missing? How long since you've seen him?"

"Five days. I haven't heard from him. Nobody has seen him at all. But that's not the thing—the thing is that he was scared beforehand. The last few weeks I'd say, he's been different. Whatever he's been doing, he was scared by it. It made him quiet."

"And that's not like him?"

"Not at all. He'd talk the hind legs off a horse, Andrew. Could talk you into anything, believe me."

"His pals. The lads he hung around with, do you know their names?"

"Only nicknames. He keeps them away from me. Trying to be clever. Why? Who are you looking for?"

"A girl. A street-girl."

Her eyes narrowed. "How does he know her?"

"I'm not sure he does. I think whatever he might've been doing could be connected to her, though. But it's just a theory at the moment."

"A young girl?"

"I'd say so. A child."

She looked thoughtful, twisting on one heel.

"What is it?" he asked gently.

"We had a few chats about children, street children, the last few weeks. I didn't think anything of it at the time, but now that you've said that..."

"What did he say?"

"He was—talking about where they slept and how they made money...the way they all knew each other. Like he'd been studying them, almost."

He nodded, but he could feel frustration rising slowly inside him. This was interesting, but it was getting him nowhere. He reached into his pocket and gave her one of the little cards Theresa had had made up.

"Can you do me a favor? If he shows up, or even if you hear anything, let me know?"

"I will," she said, her eyes brimming with tears.

He was about to leave, but he stopped himself, and took her hand. "It'll be alright, Maureen." He squeezed her hand and she managed a brave little nod.

———

SLEEP WAS hard to come by that evening.

Conlon stopped off for a few pints at his local, and sat there drinking in isolation, nodding hellos and pantomiming reactions to other regulars. Once he'd finished his beer, he had a whiskey, too. Then he made his slow way home and washed and undressed, studying his own frown in the shaving mirror, the lines pinched above his nose by joy and terror.

And then he lay in bed in the dark. He would close his eyes but nothing was coming. Something about this case and his inability to get anywhere was under his skin. He thought his way around it, lying there, conscious of the fragility of the cot bed under his frame on this night, when he felt the need to toss and turn.

He could not see a break. Nothing that he could do,

at any rate. It was far too reliant on luck for his liking. Either somebody would decide to walk in and confess something, or somebody would get sloppy and let something slip... He just needed to make sure that he was around when they did. That was how to win a case like this; patience.

Was this girl alive? That was the question. Did he have the time to wait?

He realized also that he was distracted by the nun, Sister Maude. Her face had been in his head all day, since he had left the Convent, in fact, and he was anticipating returning there tomorrow, partly because he wanted to see her again, and see if he could draw one of those heart-stopping smiles from her, or get her to laugh.

He would have guffawed at himself if this realization hadn't made him so thoroughly miserable. All of the women he had been interested in since Orla were women who were unavailable in one way or another. Married, in the main. Promised to a gang lord. And now a nun.

But he could not take the glow of her eyes from his mind, the strange light there, the pain he could see, the suspicion that she just needed somebody to hold her, and that he could easily be that somebody.

Was this ridiculous; this sentimentalizing of a nun? Was that what he was doing? Projecting onto her because he was in fact the lonely one, in need of somebody?

He thought about Theresa and whatever their relationship was. She was available, and he knew that she wanted him, that she was waiting for him. That even this courting with this man was her letting him know this, giving him a signal, because she thought he was otherwise too stupid to do anything.

He thought about the women he had been involved with lately. He did not know what he was doing, with his life.

Sister Maude. Her face came to him, again.

5

GEAROID WAS SLEEPING THAT NIGHT IN A GARDEN SHED IN Kingstown. He knew the area well enough, having once courted a lassie from nearby, and he had remembered where the really big houses were situated.

When he arrived at the road he had in mind, he did a bit of peeking and estimating, and once it was dark, he scaled a wall, dropped stealthily down into a vast back garden, and approached the shed, sat green and solid beneath the shade of a creaking, massive chestnut tree. There was no lock on the door, and inside there were some folded lawn chairs leaning in a row by the wall, their clean quality evident in the manner moonlight gleamed upon the wood of their arrayed legs. Pristine gardening tools dangled from hooks, shovels and hoes and rakes nearby.

He cleared some space for himself and finally settled down in the corner, in the darkest area, using his own forearm as a pillow, keeping his shoes on for warmth; already knowing he would probably regret this when he woke the next morning, stale and aching.

He knew he would be safe all night here. No gardener worked in the dark, and no one who actually lived in a house like that one would ever stoop so low as to actually enter a shed. He was at least fifty meters from the house's backdoor here. That should give him at least ten hours to rest and recover before he had to move again.

But still he felt skittish and uneasy. The problem was that he didn't really know what he was doing. He didn't know who these men who were after him were, he didn't really know if they even really knew who he was, meaning that he was unaware of where he could go and what he could get away with. Did they know what he looked like? Could he be spotted on Grafton Street and knifed?

A problem here was his height—he always stood out, no matter where he was, because of it. All of the ways to attempt to combat that just drew more attention toward it. If he stooped, he looked like he was a cripple. It would be ridiculous if he wasn't so scared.

Scared of what? All he really knew was that they were serious, dangerous people. The ambush at the Hellfire Club still shook him to think about, and it had already acquired the odd cast of a dream in his memory —sensations twisted and distorted by unreality, his own remembered emotions now the numbed, futile sensations of one who can only witness.

At the time it had been terrifying—to see his friends shot and killed so brutally, the lack of hesitation from their attackers. The violence had begun and went on until he was running, his breath shuddering from him, all of the others dead high above in the hills. Then of course he had had no idea what to do, or how to do whatever it may be that needed doing; no idea how to get back to Dublin, or stay ahead of them and alive, or how to tell anybody that the others were dead, or how to stay in Wicklow and survive somehow. He just felt petri-fied and very alone.

It had taken him a day to get back to Dublin. He kept off the roads but kept an eye upon them, in case the men's cars came looking for him, but this just meant that he took longer to get anywhere, trudging across fields and through forest, throwing himself to the ground in a breathless panic whenever he heard an engine noise—even if it might be miles off—until he found himself wandering off a hill and into one of the villages on the Southern edge of the city.

That was the morning after his friends had been killed, and he had passed a fitful, cold night lying under some bushes on a bed of dry leaves, slapping insects off his head and listening to every crack and stir in the wood at night, every inch the city boy lost in nature.

When he had slept—in awful, tortured snatches—he had dreamt that he and Grant had been playing cards in a field, Grant's face hidden behind his hand, and when Grant lowered the cards, he revealed a face where one eye socket was a blown-out blossom of blood and gore. Gearoid awoke panting and shuddering against the earth.

But he had risen some hours later and made his way through the gloom towards Dublin, not really knowing what else he could do. Eventually he had seen smoke curling into the sky—from a chimney, he assumed. He headed towards it, crested a hill and halfway down he could see rooftops before him, roads beginning to emerge, more smoke rising from other chimneys. A village, and beyond it, the murk of Dublin.

He had barely known where he was, but he kept on walking.

Ten minutes later, he was sitting in a café, eating butter on toast and drinking very milky tea, wondering if it was obvious to everybody that he had slept under a tree, and more conscious than ever before in his life about his height.

When he was full and warm he began to think—where could he go, what could he do? He had no answer. He had to assume that they knew who he was, and so he could not return to any of his friends. But he was aware that this could be utterly misguided. He had to assume that all of the boys were dead. If they had hit Grant, then nobody was safe. And they had hit Grant so hard that there was no doubting that their intention had been to kill him. But they were supposed to be meeting employers or senior partners or players from somewhere else, he thought, so how did that work?

This was the problem. He had never listened when they talked business. Grant was always going on about something or other, but he talked so much that you often just had to stop listening and let it fade to background noise. So Gearoid knew little; certainly not enough to be able to help himself now. He overheard the odd detail, but really he hadn't cared. They didn't tell him because he didn't ask. He didn't know why they did the things they did, he just went along with the lads and enjoyed it.

But he knew he needed help. He couldn't go to the

peelers; he'd end up in jail. The only friends who could help him were dead.

He thought about what they'd been doing these last few weeks. The chislers. That had made him feel queasy, for all Grant's chat about helping them. People would be interested in the chislers. The right people. Who would care but not have him arrested? Who could protect him?

It took him most of that day to arrive at an answer. When it did he was on his way into the Phoenix Park where he passed a nun in the street. As usual, his head went down out of some vestigial respect and shame. She was an older woman, she was wearing eyeglasses, and she gave him an expression that was half-wince, half-smile. And suddenly he thought, *the nuns.*

There were nuns around the children, giving them food, trying to find beds for them. They were there at random, unpredictable times. He and the boys were wary of them. They tried not to even be seen by them. They would scout the kids out before approaching them, purely to see if there were any of the sisters around.

The women always seemed to be there in a small group, but he knew their Mother Superior by sight. A bit older, stern and intimidating. They would help him. They were god-fearing, they would protect him. They would want to find the children that Gearoid and the others had taken.

It was warm that night and he slept better—even though he was sleeping under a tree with his jacket rolled up for a pillow, and he was terrified, and even though he had spent the day cowering around the fringes of his home town, and he was traumatized by what had happened to him—because he felt he had some hope.

Then he had gone to see if he could contact the nuns. He had no idea where they were based. What did he know about nuns or the church? So instead he looked for the children. He knew just where to find them. They had their usual spots. His method for observing them had not changed; he walked past the streets and alleys where they congregated. He never ever walked down those streets.

That day he had found them in the morning, then kept on walking. They were near Sackville Street, in their favorite haunt. It was close to the clamor and crowds of the busiest part of Dublin, yet private and relatively quiet. They were spread over a small area, noisy, dirty and energetic. There were no nuns. He'd paused long enough to establish this.

So he'd continued walking, and over the course of the next few hours, he turned in wide loops to bring him back down by the urchins. He stopped for a pint in the afternoon; the last of his money gone now. Unless he was happy to become one of the city's many tramps, he would have to do something very soon.

And then, on his fourth pass, there they were. Only two of them, but one of them, he was quite sure, was the one he was looking for.

This time he only went as far as Sackville Street, purchased a newspaper, and wandered slowly back to the corner. He leaned on a lamppost, reading the paper, watching them, trying to keep calm. There were the two nuns, perhaps fifteen of the street children, and a man he did not know. He squinted, trying to make out the man's face. Was he one of them?

The man turned, talking to the younger nun. There was something familiar about him, but his head was down as he spoke to the smaller woman, and the details of his face were frustratingly elusive, no matter how hard Gearoid stared. Even without that, he was familiar. Something about him. Gearoid felt certain he had in fact seen this man before, somewhere. He must be one of them. He must be.

Just at that instant, they made eye contact. It lasted only the briefest time. Gearoid was quick enough to look back at his paper, and when he risked a rapid glance back, the man was chatting again, smiling at something and seemingly oblivious.

But Gearoid's heart was thumping in his chest. He waited, back to his paper, risked another glance. Then the same again. He could feel that something was up; his stomach felt off now.

Sure enough the man was making his way towards him, his hard face and cold blue eyes all purpose, some-thing about the way he moved scaring Gearoid as much as anything he had seen in the last forty-eight hours.

Gearoid was already shifting, his long legs breaking him through the crowds like a Viking ship cutting fast upon the ocean; upright, chin up, quick and smooth in his movement. He crossed Sackville Street and kept moving, upping his pace as he turned the corner. He didn't look back.

GEAROID THOUGHT about trying to find a bed in a shelter that night, maybe even in one of the halls that had been opened up across town for people with the Spanish Flu.

But, afraid he might actually catch it, he risked the same shed again, squeezing his long frame in against the wall yet again. Sleep didn't come so quickly. He was starving; running out of money meant that he hadn't eaten since that morning. His stomach felt raw and almost hollow, hunger scraping at his insides with bony fingers. But worse than that, he had placed a lot of hope with those nuns and that man's presence and pursuit had rattled him, robbed him of his last scrap of hope.

Though once he had considered it and justified it to himself, he reasoned that the man did not—of course not—live with the nuns. It was just about timing. And if he tried to contact them again, he might be luckier. He would be luckier, he told himself. He had to be. He was owed that much. He had to be luckier.

He fell asleep telling himself this.

The next day, he took some more assertive action. In the morning, on Westmoreland Street, he approached one of the older boys he recognized from the group, gave him his last few coppers, and asked, "Those nuns who help yis out sometimes. Where do they come from?"

"Sure God sends them personally," the boy said, deadpan.

Gearoid just looked at him, stumped by that answer, for at least ten seconds.

Then the boy laughed. "Ah no mister, they come because they want to help us."

"Yeah, but where are they from?"

The boy frowned. "The young one is from Dublin, but well-off. I don't know where the ol' one is from."

"No, I mean, are they from a church? One in particular?"

"Do you know nothing? Nuns don't live in churches. They have a convent."

"Well, where is it?"

HE HAD HIS HAT GRASPED, twisted in his hands when he knocked on the door. His heart was thundering and he felt unsteady on his feet. The sister who answered was not one of the two he had seen with the children, and he was prepared to have entirely the wrong address. There could be five convents in the Coombe for all he knew. This nun was middle-aged and tiny, wizened and with piercing green eyes, and her expression was one of curiosity to see this extremely tall man standing at her door.

When he explained that he was looking for the ladies who helped the children in town, she smiled and nodded, and asked him to wait. He felt a wave of relief sweep him. He closed his eyes for a moment. He needed a wash, he thought, suddenly very aware that he would soon be in the company of nuns. He had a healthy fear of nuns, having been raised by them in an orphanage after his ma had died when he was five. They had always been nice to him. Strict of course, but never unfair.

Which perhaps explained why he assumed that they would help him in this situation, even though he knew that they were not like this with everyone, that they were capable of horrendous cruelty. But these ones, surely, they were helping the children. They must be nice, he thought, they must be kind.

He looked up at the convent before him, stretched

and yawned. There was a voice from behind him, a man's voice, and he whirled so fast that he almost slipped off the porch and down the steps where he would have found himself colliding with the man who stood there looking up at him.

"Howya," the man said.

Gearoid tried to speak, but only a dull, spit-addled noise emerged.

The man put his hands up, an image of non-violence and reasonableness, and Gearoid, his fear and panic mixing when he realized that this was the man from the day before, put his hands up, too.

"I just want a little chat with you," the man said.

Gearoid nodded, and then he launched himself off the steps at the man, desperate to put him down so he could get away. But his fist moved through only air; the man not where he had been an instant before.

There was a flash in Gearoid's vision and a heavy, loud noise. He could not see or hear or process anything for a moment. His head was suddenly ringing and he realized he was sitting on the path beside the steps. It felt as if his nose was running, and when he reached to stem the flow with his hand, it came away red. That man—the man had hit him. Hard, and it had put him onto his arse.

He looked up. The two nuns he was looking for—they were on the steps now, peering at him with concern. Like that, his hearing suddenly slid back into place.

"He went for me," the man was explaining. "I only hit him once."

"Is he alright?"

"He'll be fine."

The man bent down and helped him to his feet. "Why don't you come inside with the sisters and myself and we'll all have a little chat."

Gearoid nodded and, like a child, allowed himself to be led up the steps and into the convent.

6

THEY GAVE HIM A CUP OF TEA, AND WHEN HE SAID HE WAS hungry, he was given some soup and bread and butter. He ate it all ravenously, as if he had not eaten in days, and Conlon could feel the tone in the room shift, as they all began to feel sorry for him. Despite his size, he had an air of innocence, of childishness, clinging to him, and sitting there in the airy kitchen he looked lost and scared, and Conlon could see that both of the women wanted to look after him.

"What's your name?" Sister Diana asked him.

"Gearoid," he said.

"Gearoid. I'm Sister Diana, and this is Sister Maude."

He nodded respectfully at both of them, and then he looked towards Conlon, but his head would only allow him to look directly up to a point; his eyes refusing to meet Conlon's, he was like a beaten dog.

Sister Diana went on, "This is Mr. Conlon. He's a friend of ours, he won't hurt you."

Conlon spoke, "I only hit you because you tried to hit me."

Gearoid nodded. "I'm sorry, Mr. Conlon. I got scared. I thought you were one of them."

"One of who?"

"Are you Tommy Conlon? The Tommy Conlon?"

"That's me."

Gearoid laughed in disbelief.

"Who were you afraid of? Who did you think I was?"

Gearoid sat there, shaking his head, plainly conflicted and confused.

Conlon watched him, then his eyes met Sister Diana's. He avoided looking at Sister Maude, though he was all too aware at every moment of where she was in the room, and where her eyes were pointing.

"Listen, Gearoid," Conlon said gently. "We're looking for some children that have disappeared. Street children, urchins, like the ones you saw us with yesterday. Do you know anything about that?"

Gearoid's features wobbled, trembled, and Conlon thought that he looked as if he might cry. Then he did cry, dissolving on the chair into a sobbing ball, hands over his face, huge gulping moans shaking from his body. Conlon and the nuns looked at one another, and then Sister Maude was at the young man's side, hugging him, Sister Diana hovering nearby. They were both making soft sounds.

Conlon had not seen a man cry since France, and he stood back and let him collect himself. It was perhaps better to let the sisters handle this. He watched, his eyes were drawn to Sister Maude again and again and, again and again, he dragged them away. She looked at him once, and gave him a genuine, lovely grin, as if to acknowledge the silliness of the scene, and he grinned back, unable to help himself.

Finally, Gearoid felt sufficiently recovered to speak.

Sister Diana said, "So, Mr. Conlon's question about children. That upset you. Can you tell us why?"

"That's—that's what we've been doing. Getting children. Street children."

"Getting them? For who? For what?"

He shrugged. "I don't really know. Grant dealt with all that side."

"Where is Grant?" Conlon asked. "I've been looking for him, but he's disappeared."

"I think he's dead. We were meeting them—the people who were taking the girls—"

"Girls?" Sister Diana said.

"Yeah, they're all girls. No boys at all."

They all looked at each other then, thinking the same thing.

Gearoid continued, "We were meeting them, and Grant was worried. I think he thought it was a bad sign that they wanted to see him face to face."

"Why? How had they communicated before that?"

He shrugged. "I don't know. Not in person. But they demanded this, he said."

"He must have had a messenger or something. It can't all have been telegrams and letters, can it? Telephone calls?" Conlon pressed.

Gearoid said, "I'm sorry. I didn't pay attention to any of that. It wasn't my concern, like, I was just there to hang around with the lads. Like, I grew up with them. Grant handled all the business, all the money, and that was fine with me."

Conlon nodded. Gearoid made a hacking, shuddering noise, the last vestige of tears leaving him, and Conlon thought of how odd it was, watching this giant weeping like a baby.

"So what happened?" he asked.

Gearoid shook his head and his eyes became distant, focused on something they could not see. "They wanted to meet at the Hellfire Club. Do ye know it?" He looked around at them all, and when they nodded that they did, he continued.

"Grant wasn't happy about that, he complained about it all the way up there. He thought it meant something bad, so he brought his gun. He never brought his gun. And he made us bring ours as well." He stopped for a moment, breathing. Then he looked at Conlon, "That story about you in the Warehouse, is that true?"

He felt the eyes of both nuns shift his way.

Conlon said, "Most stories you hear about most people in this town aren't true."

"But is that one?"

Gearoid looked at the nuns and explained. "The story goes that Mr. Conlon was cornered in a warehouse —unarmed—by twenty men with guns, and got out alive. But none of them did."

He looked at Conlon again. "So is it?"

"Not entirely. Some of it is."

"So how did you feel? When you heard the first shot? Were you scared?"

"I was in the War, Gearoid. I'm probably a bit more used to being shot at than you are. But yeah, of course I was scared."

Gearoid nodded. "I soiled myself. This car pulled up and three men came out of it to talk to Grant and the next minute there was firing from the trees. They had men in the trees shooting at us, like snipers. Cal started firing back, but I just ran. Just legged it, like me arse was on fire—sorry, sisters." A sob escaped him. "They got Cal, and Sharpie and Brannon. And Grant was on the ground the last I saw of him. But I just ran."

"Snipers," Conlon said.

"What would you have done, Mr. Conlon? Fought them?"

"I'd be dead if I had. You did the right thing. You survived. Don't feel bad. This way you can help us and the people who killed your friends—we can get them."

He nodded and pawed at his eyes.

Conlon said, "So you're afraid that they're after you now? Because you survived?"

"Yeah, the must be mustn't they?"

"They probably don't even know who you are. If you keep your head down, you'll be grand."

"Sure he can stay here, for a while," Sister Diana said. "But you'll have to earn your keep. Do us some jobs."

He was nodding, nodding, eyes dumb with gratitude and bafflement.

Conlon said, "It's important though—anything you can remember. Anything Grant might have said, any name, a place, anything. I need something to go on to find these people."

Gearoid shook his head and looked thoughtful.

"What was your impression of these people, from what he said? Start with that."

"He—he...didn't like what we were doing. He was the one who always talked to the girls. And then we just delivered them. They were picked up at night by a car."

"Who was the driver?"

"Nobody I knew, and it was dark, so you could barely see a thing. Then we didn't see them anymore."

"Where were these pick-ups?"

"They were always somewhere different. Around town." He shook his head.

Conlon kept looking at him. He squirmed under the eyes upon him.

"They paid well. We had more money than any of us had ever seen before. After the other lads got their cut."

"Who are the other lads?"

"Ah, like Grant's bosses, so they are. They actually meet Fitzy."

"You worked for Fitzy?" Conlon said, and felt both the women look at him again because of a new sharpness in his tone.

"Not really. But the lads who sometimes gave us jobs were his boys. We paid them off, too."

Conlon looked at Sister Diana. "There are basically two big gangs who run the city. One is controlled by a man called Xavier, mainly operating on the northside. The southside is controlled by Fitzy. Sean Fitzgerald."

"Do you know him?"

"We've met, Sister."

"What's he like?"

"He's a businessman. Who also has a liking for nailing the hands of people who displease him to floors."

He looked at Gearoid. "These other lads, what are their names?"

"Doyle. Doyle and Waters."

"Do you know them?" Sister Diana asked again. Conlon could sense her excitement at all this, a sort of professional interest, from somebody fascinated by people and the way they made the world work.

He shook his head. "No. But I will."

———

BEFORE HE LEFT, they had settled Gearoid in a little room in the cellar, where he had a bed and his own sink. He was told he would be working as a caretaker, and would have certain tasks to fulfill. His gratitude was heartbreaking, but as soon as he saw the bed he began yawning and explained it had been a few days since he had enjoyed a decent night's sleep. Conlon said goodbye to him, but promised that he would keep him informed about what was happening.

At that, Gearoid looked him in the eye and said, "What are you going to do, if you find them?"

"I'll get those girls back."

"Yeah, but what are you going to do to them? The men who killed my friends?"

Conlon looked at him. The nuns were out of the room at that moment, and he nodded. "I have friends in the police. But yeah, if I have to, I won't involve them at all."

Gearoid nodded, too, his eyes already drooping.

Outside, Sister Diana said, "Would I be right in assuming that this just became an awful lot more dangerous for you?"

Conlon chuckled. "I wouldn't argue with you, Sister."

"But that's also the first real lead you've had in a few days."

"It is. And one I have to follow up."

"Well. Be careful, then Mr. Conlon. We've become quite fond of you here."

"I'll do my best, Sister."

"I know you will. Good luck. May God bless you and save you."

He nodded and turned. On his way out, Sister Maude was lingering near the front door.

"Will you be ok? It sounds awfully dangerous."

"I'll be fine, don't worry."

She nodded, but her eyes were tight. "But I do worry, now."

"Don't," he said. "This is my world."

"What he said about the warehouse..."

"Yes."

She shook her head, unable to articulate whatever it was she was feeling. He so desperately wanted to put his hand to her cheek it was like an ache in his gut, burning away inside him.

They stood there, two feet apart, staring at one another.

He said, "I know. I'm not thick, Maude. I won't do anything stupid."

She nodded. "Right. Well, find those girls, then, Tommy." She laughed, a nervous laugh.

"I'll do my best."

"Be careful."

"I always am."

"Well. Good."

"Right."

"Right."

He stepped beyond her and had opened the front door when she said, "Tommy."

He turned to her again, and she smiled. "Nothing."

He smiled, too, gave her a little half-wave, and went out the door, thinking about the way he got goosebumps when she said his name.

———

HE NEEDED information before he actually approached anyone. Fitzy's gang would know him, and that meant that any direct approach could have serious, violent consequences. So he needed to try a different way.

He stopped in a smoky, crowded pub near Christchurch and used their telephone to make a single call. Then, after a quick pint, he made his way out to the Quays and leaned against the wall, watching the Liffey float past, a sluggish gray under the sunlight, diffuse and flat through the cloud ceiling.

Barry spoke from behind him, then leaned against the wall, back to the river, eyes on Conlon's face. "So, Tommy. Have you got something for me, or do you want something from me?"

Conlon smiled at him. "Good to see you, too, Barry."

"Ah sorry, did I forget me manners again? Police work brutalizes men, I'm told. Hello Tommy. How are ye?"

"Surviving."

"If anybody else of my acquaintance said that, I'd know it was a joke, but with you, that's liable to be the honest truth."

"How are you?"

"Ah, this city." It was all Barry needed to say. He turned around so that he and Conlon were side by side, watching the waters movement.

"So, what are you working on, Tommy?"

"Some street children have disappeared."

"That's not unusual."

"I know. But the details here make a difference, Barry. They were all girls. All of a certain age, all within a few weeks of each other. Somebody's come in from outside and hired some of the local small-timers to deliver them."

"Who's 'somebody?'"

"I haven't got to that yet."

"But you have an idea, I'd say."

"People are scared. They know what they're doing."

"We haven't heard anything about any of this."

"Like I said, they know what they're doing."

"Have you any proof?"

"I have a witness, but he got a terrible fright."

"And what exactly did he witness?"

"Four murders, by the sounds of it."

"Where was this?"

"The Hellfire Club, a few days ago."

"Four? Nothing to do with the rebels?"

"Nothing. This doesn't seem to be political at all. Maybe ex-army."

"For Jaysus sake, Tommy, what is it with you and fecking gangs of armed killers..."

"I'm finding it hard to break the habit."

Barry sparked up a cigarette and stood smoking quietly for a moment.

"I'll send somebody up to check out the Hellfire Club. What are you going to do? Do I have to worry about cleaning up another gunfight in some warehouse?"

"Not if I can avoid it. Tell me, do you know a couple of Fitzy's boys by the names of Doyle and Waters?"

"Aye, I do. Like Siamese twins, the two of them. They involved in this, are they?"

"They might have some information I could use."

"Pair of scumbags. Doyle is a gambler, bookie, loan shark, the money man. My favorite story about him is that he sometimes lets husbands pay debts by lending him their wives. Or daughters if he likes them. And they come back the worse for wear."

Conlon was looking at him.

Barry shrugged. "Nasty piece of work. Waters is the muscle. Dapper, the two of them. Waters has a thing for young girls, too, so their involvement isn't a surprise."

"Are they close to Fitzy?"

"I doubt it. He's clever that way."

"Where would be the best place to look for them?"

"Today? They'll be at the races in the Phoenix Park along with half the crooks in the city...and a fair few of my colleagues."

Conlon nodded.

Barry said, "You'll need to get your shoes shined if you're going to pay them a visit there. They won't be in the cheap seats."

"Ah, now, you know I can fit in anywhere, Barry."

"I'll look for news of the place getting burned to the ground, then."

Conlon laughed at that and Barry took a long drag.

"How's your mother?" he asked.

"She's good, thanks for asking. The family?"

"Grand, grand. Surviving."

"That's a good answer."

"I thought so. Should I be worried about this case you've got, Tommy?"

Conlon shrugged. "Maybe. I've got a funny feeling about it."

"That makes me nervous, sure enough."

"And if they're abducting young girls..."

"It can't be good. I'll ask around, put the word around the lads."

"I'd appreciate that."

"But we're fierce busy at the moment."

"Sure aren't you always?"

"'Tis true. Well, is there anything else?"

"Not at the moment, Barry. You're fierce busy, apparently."

"Right so. You know how to reach me if you need me."

"I do. The problem may be that if I do need you, I won't have time to reach you."

"Well do what you always do, then, Tommy."

"What do I always do?"

"Break everything and everyone in sight. Good luck!" And with that he strolled away in a plume of his own smoke.

———

CONLON HADN'T BEEN to the racing at Ashtown since his time as a fighter, when Xavier liked him to be seen, and he and his promoter, Fergus Fallon, had drunk champagne and eaten strawberries until Fergus was loudly sick in the upstairs restaurant. He hadn't placed any bets or even seen any horses. It was just another of Xavier's parties, in a different, novelty location, with many of the same odious people, and he had been there because of his minor celebrity.

Now he had to pay for a ticket, and he would have to sneak into the upstairs bar.

It was busy, but not as busy as he remembered. The Spanish Flu had been affecting crowds for days by this point, but all that still felt surreal and at a remove from his life. The day had brightened and the sun set off the violent colors of the many ladies hats moving through the crowds. There were men in tops and tails, and more canes than he had seen since a military parade near Guildford during the War.

The grandstand was filled with patches of people, and below it others milled around. The sound of such a mass of humanity was like waves near shore; a constant undertone, always there, in the air. Bookies yelled odds and gesticulated in a sign language he did not understand. Horses were paraded around a circle. Waiters hurried past him, trays laden with drinks. Several hundred conversations overlapped, and somewhere beyond the stand, horses and men created a galloping storm of cacophony and energy, tearing around the track. The noise reminded him of a crowd before the game started at Dalymount.

There was the strong smell of food on the wind, the trees shaking behind the course, ladies holding their hats in place.

He moved around the back of the grandstand and the crowds thinned out instantly. Here it had a more threadbare, backstage air. There were kitchen porters and waiters smoking by doorways, trolleys used for transporting kitchen equipment, large bins circled lazily by wasps, patches of weed squeezing through broken brickwork.

The doors all led into rooms where people seemed

frantically active—movement and noise briefly
glimpsed. He ducked into one, walked through a busy,
clamorous kitchen, his chin up, without any hesitation,
making eye contact with no one. Then, through a corridor, he followed the noise up a flight of stairs, then two
more, to emerge through the service doors into the bar.

He dimly remembered it from last time, but that
memory was mainly formed of the color purple, the
richness of the food and the swollen faces of the many
people shaking his hand.

Now the place was revealed in all its specificity—
thick carpets, deep colors, expensive fittings, lots of
polish. Paintings of horses in motion on the walls, a
portrait of a long-nosed gentlemen who at some time
over the last century had been a patron of some sort.

The odors of food from the kitchen were dampened
here, underhanging the fog of smoke—cigar and
cigarette—of port and wine, of perfume and hair oil and
wax. It was all suffocating.

Waiters were positioned around the large room, eyes
restless and ceaselessly scanning. One or two had
marked his appearance through the wrong door, but
none would speak up.

Most of the people had finished eating and were
grouped around the windows and balconies at the far
end of the room. They were overlooking the race course
itself, and the light the floor to ceiling windows gave
meant that this end felt gloomy and slightly sad.

He plucked a mostly empty glass off a table and
moved along the wall, eyes picking through the faces
he could spot. Rich people, for the most part, and
then there at the center, a knot of purest Dublin
crime. Gangsters in sharp suits with oiled hair,

women scattered in their midst, smoke curling from their group the way it would from a shelled battlefield.

He recognized a few faces—no Fitzy, which was a relief. No sign of Xavier or Finch either, though he assumed they would be here somewhere, perhaps in one of the smaller private rooms. But he did not know who was Doyle and who was Waters, and walking over to the group like this would be unwise.

He took a seat and watched the race as the crowd roared and sulked and flung betting slips to the carpet in devastation.

One of the girls in their group celebrated extravagantly when the race finished. She clutched a slip tightly in one hand, her bag in another. Her red hair was contained under a green hat to match her jacket and skirt, and she seemed to be hovering near the arm of one of the men, a young man with a moustache, who was spitting words at her as she virtually danced her joy at victory. She spat something back and stalked off, throwing a comment about "winnings" back over her shoulder.

Conlon followed her.

Down at the counter, she joined a long, snaking queue, and he stood in the one next to it, right beside her. When she glanced at him, he gave her his brightest smile, and she smiled back instantly.

"Hiya," he said.

"Hello." She looked around as she said it.

"Did you win much?"

She laughed. "Not much. A few shillings."

"But that's not the point, is it? It's fun to win."

"It is! I was just saying that. Did you win much?"

"I never win much. That's the whole point. Keeps me coming back."

"And the fun...?"

"And the fun, of course."

She looked around again.

"Are you alright?" he said.

"Yeah, I am. Just—I'm here with somebody. He wouldn't like it if he saw me talking to you."

"Sure we're just talking. No harm in it."

"I know, I know. He wouldn't see it that way."

"Ah, I see. He's the jealous type, is he?"

"I suppose so."

She looked glum. The queue had barely moved.

"What's your name?" Conlon asked.

"Virginia."

"That's a beautiful name."

"Thank you. My mother is from there."

"America?"

"No, no—Cavan."

They both laughed.

"What's your name?"

"Tommy. So is it serious with this fella you're here with?"

She made a face. "I hardly know him! He has a lot of girls, I think. We met the other night and he invited me and I'd never be able to afford this on my own and I'm not working today so why not?"

"But you don't seem happy."

"I might as well not be here. He doesn't want me talking to any of his pals but he hardly talks to me. Sorry. I don't mean to moan."

"I asked. I can't imagine why any man in his right mind wouldn't want to talk to a girl who looks like you."

He watched her stop her reaction to that reach her face. "You say things nobody else has ever said to me."

"Most men are stupid. They don't know how to talk to a woman like you."

"What does that mean? 'A woman like me?'"

"A beautiful woman. A woman who should be adored."

"You're some kind of chancer."

"Maybe I am. But I'm telling the truth. You are beautiful."

It was easy for him to say these things, because she was. Seeing that it made her feel good only made that easier still.

"Go away out of that."

"I'm not trying to get anything out of it, I'm just saying it. You deserve better than whatever gobshite you're with who's not even talking to you."

"Sure you've talked to me more in two minutes than he has in three hours."

He shrugged at that, as if to say, see?

She screwed up her face. "What do you do, Tommy?"

"For a job? I find people."

"How do you mean."

"People sometimes go missing. I track them down."

"That sounds interesting. Like a detective?"

"Exactly like a detective, yeah. What do you do, Virginia?"

"I work in the Laundry at the Mater."

"Do you like it?"

"I like the girls, but it's boring. It's certainly not being a detective, so it's not, washing sheets and drying towels."

"Listen, why don't I take you home."

She looked horrified.

He put up his hands. "I don't mean anything inappropriate. I was just about to go anyway. I could take you, too."

"That is very kind of you, Tommy, but... but—"

"Just go and get your things."

"He'll kill you."

"Will he?"

"He's a gangster, I think. All of his pals are, too. Some of the things they've been talking about." She shuddered.

"All the more reason."

"No. It's a lovely offer, and you seem very nice, but I think they'd hurt you."

"What's his name?"

"Liam. Liam Doyle."

"Right. Have you left anything with him?"

"My scarf."

"Once you've collected your winnings, we'll go back, and you can get it. I'll talk to him. It'll be fine."

She wavered, looking unsure.

"I know those kinds of men, will you believe me. It'll be alright."

"Alright," she said. "Alright."

When she busied herself at the counter, he slipped out of the queue and waited for her, thinking of what was the best way to get Doyle away from the others.

She joined him, and he said, "Does he know where you live? Or where you work?"

"No, he picked me up in his automobile at Clearys. And he hasn't asked me a thing about myself."

"Well that's good."

They were going up the grand staircase to the restaurant now.

"When you get there, tell him somebody called Fitzy said he was to come to the door—just him. Then you go. Wait for me at the main gate."

Something dawned on her. "Who are you?"

He gave her his smile again. "I'm getting you out of a situation you don't want to be in, trust me."

"You know him?"

"Sort of."

He found her hand with his and squeezed it and she nodded. At the top of the staircase, he took in the landing.

"The main gate?" she said.

"The main gate. I won't be long."

She went inside, and reappeared, wringing her scarf around her fists, perhaps thirty seconds later. Doyle was at her heels, talking as he came through the door.

Conlon nodded to him, said, "This way," and led him across the landing and into a service door. He looked and nodded to her as she descended the big staircase. Through the service door lay another, narrow, claustrophobic stairwell, and as soon as Doyle came through the door, Conlon swung and delivered a right hook to his gut. He made a noise and doubled up, falling as he did so. Conlon let him fall. His shoulder and head struck the wooden banister as he went down.

Doyle was sucking for air, his hands clawing the floor. Conlon grasped him by the lapel of his fancy suit and yanked him roughly to his feet.

"Do you know who I fucking am—"

Conlon hit him again, another hook to the stomach. Not hard enough to do any damage, but hard enough to hurt. Doyle bent and vomited over the banister, sobbing as he did so.

"*Aurgh*...we're gonna fuckin kill you!"

Conlon pushed him back against the wall and punched him once in the face—a right cross that took out a few teeth and cut his lip in a couple of places. His head slapped the wall behind him.

He began to cry.

Conlon slapped him hard. "Stop crying."

Doyle made a huffing noise, trying to breathe, and Conlon slapped him again. "Stop crying. Calm down. You're still alive. Don't make me hurt you more."

"What do you want? What the fuck do you want?"

"You're going to answer some questions for me."

"About what? About what? I don't know anything..." He whimpered the last words through a stream of blood and spittle.

"You've had some of your boys taking girls off the street."

Doyle's eyes changed at this. "Are you one of them? Oh Jesus don't kill me, please, don't kill me."

"One of who? Who are you working for?"

"We don't know who they are. We never met them. We think they're American."

His legs wobbled and Conlon held him up.

"American? Why would you think they'd want to kill you?"

"Some of the boys went to a meeting with them and we haven't seen them since. They have to be dead...we don't know, we don't know..."

"How do you communicate with them?"

"Who are you? Why do you want to know?"

Conlon slapped him, hard. He began to cry again.

"Stop crying. How do you contact them?"

"We leave a note with Annie on Moore Street. They do the same. We haven't heard anything since they asked for the meeting. We don't know what they're doing..."

"Fitzy thinks they're trying to move in."

"Everybody's scared of them. We don't know who they are."

"Why do you think they're American, then?"

"We had to drop off the girls to them."

"Where? When?"

"Last week, last week— The middle of nowhere in Wicklow, I swear..."

"And?"

"One of our boys heard two of them talking. He said they were yanks."

"Where did they take the girls?"

"I don't know..."

Conlon raised his hand.

"I don't! I swear to God, I don't know!"

"So what's the plan? If Fitzy thinks they're a threat, what are you doing about it?"

"I don't know, he wouldn't tell me, I'm nobody! I swear!"

Conlon let him go and he sagged against the wall, his head hanging, blood and mucus pouring from his face in a steady drizzle.

"Who the fuck are you..." he moaned.

Conlon said, "My name is Tommy Conlon. Have you heard of me?"

His eyes widened a little at that. Everybody in their circles knew who Conlon was.

"Yeah, I have... I'm sorry, I didn't know it was—"

"If I ever see you again, I'll kill you. If you see me in the street, if I was you, I'd turn and run."

He took a fistful of Doyle's hair and wrenched his head up until his face was exposed again.

"Do you understand?"

"Yeah—yeah..."

"Do you believe me, Liam?"

"Yeah...yeah...I believe you..."

Conlon nodded. Then he punched Doyle one more time, a short uppercut, throwing his head back and spinning him off his feet onto the floor. He lay there, breathing but unmoving. Conlon made his way slowly down the stairs, thinking of Virginia waiting for him by the gate, and Annie, on Moore Street, and how she could help him.

7

ANNIE HAD A FISH STALL. CONLON KNEW HER WELL
enough; had known her for years. Everyone knew her.
The area around Moore Street and that cobbled lane
were filled with tables and piles of crates from behind
which traders sold fruit and vegetables, flowers, meat,
material, milk, butter, cutlery, plates, clothing, buttons,
antiques. Annie was one of the most memorable.

Her stall was on Cole's Lane, just off Moore Street.
You could hear her voice carrying over the cries of the
other traders and stallholders as you approached, and
not long after that you would smell her product: a wash
of fetid, pungent seawater transplanted miles up the
Liffey to this small corner of the Northside and stinking
as it dried and rotted.

She smoked behind her stall, wrapping fish in paper
and chopping off heads with a knife that looked as dull
as a rolling pin, her cries of prices and wares issued
casually out of a corner of her mouth at a deafening
volume. Her accent was thick, old Dublin, stretching
single syllable words to two or even three, dropping t

sounds at every opportunity, a harsh yet somehow warm sound that was as close to the spirit of this city as he could begin to imagine. She said she was the fourth generation to run this stall and that her daughter would take it over once she was gone, while her daughter slopped down cobbles and skinned fish behind her.

As he approached today, Conlon could not hear her voice bouncing off the cobbles. And indeed, her daughter was there alone. She recognized him, too, and they shared a warm greeting.

"Is your Ma around?" he asked, after a few moments of pleasantries.

"She went home. She had terrible stomach cramps and felt all weak. I've worked on here twenty odd years with her and she's never done that before. She looked awful. Her skin was a funny shade."

Seeing the expression on his face, she said, "Is it urgent?"

"It might be, yeah. Can you help me?"

"Sure we'll see. What is it concerning?"

"She's been passing messages between some of Fitzy's lads and another gang."

She was shaking her head. "I'm sorry, Tommy, she keeps me out of that part of the business. That's only for her, she says."

"You must have seen people?"

"Do you know how many people she holds messages for? I don't even look up half the time."

"Alright. So can I find her at home?"

"You should, yeah. You know where you're going?"

"Have youse moved into a fancy Townhouse out in Sutton yet?"

She laughed. "Not yet, sure."

"Then I know where I'm going."

Where he was going was a tenement on Lisburn Street, not that far from where he had grown up and where his mother now lived. The street was like so many that were host to teeming, infested tenements—shabby but obviously lovely beneath recent hardship, dirty and crumbling but still somehow proud and even stylish—if you ignored the dirty-faced urchins on the front step, the rubbish on the path and cobbled roadway and the smell of waste, both food and human.

Two women were hanging washing from upstairs windows and chatting across a twenty-foot gap. Conlon watched them, took everything in. He had run these streets as a boy, barefoot half the time and dressed in something close to rags. And though there were children playing on the street in front of the various tenements at this end, something felt off to him. It seemed quiet, or muted at least.

He knocked and waited, then knocked again. A young woman, perhaps his age, answered after another wait. She looked tired, sweat plastering some strands of hair to her forehead, squinting out at the daylight. She looked at him quizzically.

"I'm looking for Annie," he said.

"Are you a friend?"

"Yeah, I've known her since I was a baby. Are you her daughter?" She looked like the woman he had spoken to on the stall – they had to be sisters.

"Aye. She's sick."

"Your sister said."

She shook her head. "I'm worried it's this Black Flu. She's gone a funny color."

"Black?"

"No, no, come in, come in..."

She led him into the gloom of the tenement hall. He knew these buildings so well; the patches of damp on the walls, the feeling that all was crumbling around these people, the stench of humanity, unwashed; food and sweat and sex and dirt, too close, always in your nostrils. It made him nostalgic, was the thing.

She was beckoning silently, summoning him up some stairs. He pulled himself out of his reverie.

Annie was in bed in a similarly darkened room, moaning to herself, and when he peered at her, he could see that her skin appeared thoroughly purple. She was bleeding from the nose and laboring for breath, and the room already had the sweet, rotten smell of disease.

"She's been getting worse since she got home. She had a flu about two months ago and I've heard that's what happens. You get it, and it's not too bad, then you get it again and it's terrible."

Annie spoke, "Spanish Flu they called it in the paper. It came from Spain. Is that Tommy Conlon, Grace?"

"It is," he answered. "How are you, Annie?"

"Sure how do I look, ye gobshite?"

He laughed and looked at her daughter. "Have you called the doctor?"

"He's coming. But there are a lot of people have had it."

Annie spoke again, "Why...are you here, Tommy?"

"I was hoping for some information, Annie."

"Are you looking for...somebody missing?"

"I am."

"Ask away." She coughed and coughed, then

wheezed. "I've got...nothing else...to do while me girls do...all the work."

"You've been holding messages for some of Fitzy's boys and another gang."

She looked at him, her chest rising and falling rapidly, eyes a little too wide and desperate as she sucked for breath, then managed to get out, "The Americans...?"

He nodded. "That sounds about right. What's going on?"

Even with the illness that was gripping her, he saw something else carry across her face, a tremor of feeling: fear.

"I—I only put things...together."

He nodded.

"They—they...don't...tell me... anything"

"I know. Nobody's blaming you here, Annie."

She nodded faintly, then indicated to her daughter that she wanted water. The mug beside the bed was held to her lips and she drank, then lay back, eyes closed, her bosom heaving with the effort.

"They—they want girls—young girls"

Her eyes opened and found his.

"Are you—are you...looking for a girl?"

"More than one."

"Good...good"

"Who are they, Annie?"

"I've worked...some things out. They...don't tell me... anything. From Boston. Irish—Irish links. Irish names. Fitzy's men are...afraid of them."

She waited, eyes closed, breathing, pain in the set of her jaw.

"I think...they—they seem like...soldiers. Remind me of soldiers."

"In what way?"

She shook her head absently, eyes elsewhere. "Organized. Focused. The way they—the way they dress."

He nodded.

She coughed again and he waited for her to collect herself.

"Do you have any idea where they are? Who they are? Any names, anything?"

She shook her head. "No. No. I'm...sorry, Tommy. They're far—far too careful...for that."

"Alright. Annie, thank you. I appreciate it."

"Be—be careful, Tommy."

"I will. I hope you feel better soon. I'll tell me Ma to say a prayer for you."

"A—rosary, please..." And she smiled, and he was ushered out by her daughter.

Outside, he took in the fresh air in great gulps as his eyes adjusted to the sunlight. A woman with a face creased like an accordion came from the house next door, having obviously been waiting his exit in the doorway, and looked him over. "How's Annie feelin'?"

"She doesn't look well."

"Half the street has it. Johnny O'Shea died two days ago and Brida Lawlor died this morning. It's like the feckin' plague, so it is."

"You feeling alright, Missus?"

"Ah I never get sick. Me mother gave me Guinness instead of milk," she cackled. "But it's spreadin' through the whole city. You get it and you die the next day. And these are young healthy people. Just dead, like tha'."

She was loving this, he thought, watching her fascinated enthusiasm for this disease.

She nodded, to him, to herself, and retreated back through her front door, leaving him standing on the step, realizing why the street had felt so quiet when he arrived. The flu had taken it a kind of prisoner. He had one last look around, and then he set off.

———

CONLON HADN'T SEEN THEM. He didn't until it was almost too late. They were good, and that was proof. They had some sort of training.

On Capel Street, one stepped in front of him, and as Conlon made to sidestep around him, there was the other one, and a revolver was pressed against his ribs so that he could not mistake it for anything else.

He didn't panic. He looked them both full in the face, and said, "What's this about?"

They wore flat caps, jackets and shirts. One was extremely dark; swarthy, even. The other had ginger hair and blue eyes. Both of them were thin, hungry-looking. They trained and worked and kept fit physically. They had that hungry, strained look he recalled men have when they drill and march and run day after day. Annie had been right—some sort of military training.

"We need to ask you some questions, pal," the swarthy one who held the gun to him said.

Conlon looked him in the eye. Pal? "You could've just asked..."

The ginger one faked a smile. "Well we're asking."

Both of them had American accents. The swarthy

one nudged him and they headed up the street, the gun still pressed to his side.

He knew he had little time. Based on what he had heard about these men, they would kill him in the next minute or two without pause or remorse. They were trained soldiers, so he had to assume a certain level of combat acumen and give them some respect. But he needed to do something quickly and not give them an opportunity to put him in a situation where he had no options. In the alley, with two guns on him, back against the wall, he had no options.

There were a few people on the street. One motorcar passing, a horse and cart moving by towards the Liffey. A man approaching, two women across the road. He would have to go all out, he knew. Each strike to do maximum damage.

He felt the calmness that had always fallen over him in battle, in fights. Life became a series of decisions and rapid-fire calculations. Cause and effect, action and reaction. If I hit that, this will break.

He knew what to do, in what order, where to move; he knew how it would go in an ideal world. But this was not an ideal world, and his own peculiar gift had always been an ability to respond instantly and decisively when plans went awry.

As they neared the approaching man, the swarthy one had to withdraw his gun to some extent, to make his walk seem more natural. Conlon felt the pressure of its muzzle relieved. The swarthy one turned and walked beside him, the gun tucked under one arm.

As soon as the man was behind them, but before the gun was back at his ribs, Conlon grasped the wrist of the swarthy one tightly. He whirled in a sharp semicircle, dragging the gun-hand behind him so that it was pointed roughly towards the ginger one.

The swarthy one was off balance, and began to shout something to his colleague, but Conlon was already using the momentum from his turn to transfer a big right hook up from his hip. It was as true a punch as he had ever thrown and it landed on the Adam's apple of the swarthy one with devastating force, collapsing his larynx like a rotten fruit. The shout turned into a sickening cracked noise and the swarthy one fell to his knees, the gun skittering off over the cobbles. His hands clawed at his throat.

Conlon had already turned onto the ginger one. He was groping for the gun he had inside his coat, but Conlon didn't allow him the time he needed to retrieve it. He threw a sharp overhand right to the man's nose, which bent and cracked, then followed it with a left hook aimed at his liver. With each shot the man cried out—little surprised cries of pain—as Conlon ducked and pivoted and knocked him off his feet with a right hook to his jaw. He scrambled away from that, falling back to his feet.

The man who had walked by had turned and was gaping at the carnage, and the ginger one grabbed him as he ran, then was away, sprinting down Capel Street.

Conlon let him go, and looked at the swarthy one, lying, writhing on his back, his face turned a bruised purple, eyes bulging as he smothered, unable to breathe. He was dead perhaps twenty seconds later.

Conlon strode into the road and pointed at the pistol, then looked at the witness.

"When the bobbies get here, make sure they see that."

Then he turned and headed for home, increasing his pace until he was running.

On his way he stopped in a pub and called Barry, who finally came to the phone after an interminable wait, all shouts and clatters and mumbled chatting.

"Tommy. I know this is bad. You never use the telephone."

"Two men just jumped me. With guns. You'll find one of them dead on Capel Street."

"Oh Jesus Mary and Joseph. Who are they?"

"Americans. I think they must have been watching Annie's stall on Moore Street and followed me from there."

"Where's the other one?"

"He got away. They were good. Trained, dangerous. I'm alive because they didn't know who I was and underestimated me. Be careful. Make sure your men are careful."

"Is this linked to the street girls?"

"It must be, no? They must be the outsiders who've come in. Doyle said they were American."

"You talked to Doyle?"

"Yeah. Don't worry, he's alive. He didn't know much beyond that. You should probably warn Annie's family. They might be in danger."

"I'll see to it. Jaysus, Tommy, it's never boring with you, is it? Anyhow, this conversation never happened. Let me know if you need anything. Goodbye."

At his place Conlon packed a bag. This was an eventuality he was prepared for, but still bridled at. The feeling hanging over his shoulders—that of a fugitive—he hated. But after the last time his life had been exploded by the enmity of a criminal gang, he had made plans on the off-chance that it might happen again. He had somewhere to go, systems in place, money put aside.

He packed some clothes, retrieved his gun from under a floorboard in the kitchen. Then he headed for Theresa's.

He took quiet back streets, kept his head up and his eyes constantly moving. He was assuming that the Americans had not learned his identity yet but that it was only a matter of time. And when they did, they would fall on his life like a hammer. He had to warn everybody around him about the possible threat. And then he could begin to plan to destroy the Americans instead.

He had a constricted feeling; his throat and chest felt tight at the thought of what might happen to Theresa, to his mother. Dublin criminals generally had a sense of honor about such matters. Xavier, for instance, would never think of going after his mother. That just wasn't the way things were done. But something about these Americans felt different. They were taking street children, and they had killed some of their own people, for some reason he still didn't understand. The training, the aims—they seemed like a different sort of dangerous.

Theresa knew from his face that there was a problem.

"What's wrong? Why are you here, Tommy?"

"Remember we spoke about you having to go down to the country for a while?"

"Yes, but why? What's happened?"

"You need to pack a bag now, Theresa. You need to

go and get my Ma, and the two of you need to be on a train today."

"Tommy, tell me what's happening."

"We don't have time. We need to be moving."

"Tommy!"

She took his hand, and he could see the fright on her face now. He stopped and pulled her to him and embraced her. Then he held her away from him.

"Is it that case? The nuns? It can't be," she said.

He made a face even he could not have described. "It is. There're people involved." He shook his head. "Bad people."

"Who are they?"

"I'm not sure, but they're dangerous. And it's only a matter of time...I need you gone so I can fight them without having one eye on whether you two are safe."

He shuddered. A stab of pain lanced through his gut.

"How dangerous?"

"They've killed a few. They tried to kill me today, on Capel Street. They're serious in a way I've rarely seen before." He stopped. "You should be packing, come on. We can talk while you do it."

In her room, while she folded and pressed items of clothing into her bag, he gave her the key events of the past few days, and at the end of it there were tears in her eyes, though she was trying not to give into them.

"It'll be alright," he said. "They've already underestimated me. If they do that again, that'll be all the advantage I need."

"What if they don't do that again, Tommy? What if they're ready for you?"

"Well I'll just have to be ready for them, too, won't I?"

She gave a sharp little laugh, a laugh without any discernible humor.

"They're taking little girls, Theresa. Jesus Christ, I can't just let that happen, can I?"

"No. You can't."

She came into his arms again and they held one another for a long time, tightly, until he could feel her heart thudding against his own chest.

———

HE TOOK her to his mother's, where they had to pass a few anxious minutes waiting for the woman to return to her house from the market. When she arrived, breezily carting some onions and potatoes in her bag, she seemed remarkably unsurprised and asked only a few questions, recognizing from her son and his friend that the situation was grave. She packed in a couple of minutes, and seemed excited by all of it, joking as she prepared herself, telling Theresa tales of their destination and its many characters.

He did not risk traveling to the station with them, and instead said goodbye outside his mother's house.

After he and his mother had hugged and said farewell, she sauntered away and busied herself lighting a cigarette, staring across the road, giving him time with Theresa.

She stood in front of him and shook her head faintly. "You don't—you just do what you do, Tommy. You're a survivor. You survive."

"I will," he said.

"I can't lose you. Not now. Not after everything."

It was so unlike her to speak to him so directly of her feelings that he was shocked. And that feeling made him nervous, too, as if this altering of the dynamic between them might in some way be bad luck.

"I know. You won't lose me, Theresa."

"You're all I have."

"That's not true."

He held her again, his gut twisting with pain.

She said, "We—we never..."

"I know. Don't worry. I'll be fine."

She nodded, her eyes large and filled with pain.

He said, "When it's done, I'll come for you myself. Nobody else. If it's not me, it's not safe. Only me. Alright? It might be two days, or it might be two weeks."

She nodded again.

"Right. Goodbye, Theresa."

"Goodbye, Tommy."

He watched them walk away from him then, his mother, and the girl who more or less ran his life and meant more to him than anyone else did. He didn't know when or if he would see them again, and for a moment he wished he had said more, had told her how he felt about her.

She knew, he thought. She knew.

———

THE PAIN in his gut worsened. It had started as some minor ripples of discomfort, the awareness that perhaps he needed to use a toilet. As he crossed the city, the cramps became so bad he had to stop and wince and prevent himself from grunting aloud. His teeth ground together, his jaws tight with the effort of containing the pain.

He was heading for the tram, then out to Tallaght village where he had arranged the use of a room. Somewhere to lay low for a few days, rest and plan his next move. That was the plan, at least.

But after five minutes walking, he realized he might not get there. He was hot—sweating, but also his skin was almost painful to the touch. Aches had opened like clawed hands under the skin within his arms, his legs—even his fingers—and seemed to be worsening with every step he took.

He tried to think. He was having difficulty focusing. The Spanish flu. It had to be. Most people who caught it were said to have suffered a flu for a few days, weeks before. And so had he. Three days of cold symptoms, pain and a stuffy head. He had shaken it off, but now it's significance was frightening. As was the way it was affecting him now; he was limping along, head down, the aches in his limbs and joints making him feel old and fragile. Shaky.

He would not make the tram at this rate. He felt weak now, and his breathing was starting to tighten. Within a few moments of this thought he was sputtering and racked with wheezes. It felt as if somebody had jammed his windpipe shut and he barely knew what to do as his lungs felt like they might rot and fall out his mouth in a fine spray. He stopped walking and leaned against an iron fence, head hanging. He recognized that what he needed was to be in bed, sleeping. That was all he needed. He could feel his strength ghosting out of his body with each passing second.

Just then he was racked by another sudden twisting

stomach cramp. He barely stayed on his feet. Where was he? He looked around. Where was nearby? Who did he know around here? He had to push through. Find somewhere he could rest and recover.

The pain was subsiding now, but his lungs were still gripped by a vice and every breath felt as if it put unendurable pressure on his chest and shoulders. He wanted to sleep, for this pain to be over. Where had it come from, so suddenly?

He moved again. He thought about who he knew nearby and suddenly it came to him. It was five minutes from here, he told himself.

He started to walk again, extremely conscious that he might look like an old man, stooped and slow and moving gingerly, his joints stiff and aching. But then another wash of pain came over him and he ceased caring about how he looked, put his head down and waited for it to be over.

That five minute walk took a lot longer, but finally he found himself climbing the steps—one step, slowly, at a time, one foot and then the other—and somehow summoning the strength to knock upon the door. When Sister Maude answered, he nodded, began to speak, found he had no breath, then collapsed face first into the doorway.

8

GUNNAR TOOK FOUR GUARDS OUT TO KINGSTOWN TO meet Swaney's ferry. He didn't trust the local muscle much yet, and didn't respect it either, so he ensured that there were two of their boys alongside the two hired Dublin boys.

The Dublin boys were quick studies—already they had adopted the stone-faced stoicism of the Americans. They were four men with no expressions, eyes constantly on the move, revolvers under their coats.

They drove out in two automobiles. Distrustful of European cars, Gunnar had found himself delighted to discover that Ford had a factory in Manchester, England, and that consequently the streets were full of them. But then he had driven a Rolls Royce a few days after his arrival here, and he forgot all about Fords. So now he was behind the wheel of a Silver Ghost, while two of the men drove behind in a Ford.

He was already bored of Ireland. The food, the weather, the people. He missed Boston, the bars there, the girls he knew. He missed the little Italian place where he took his dinner three nights a week. This filthy, squalid little city with its pale little people and its lowering skies and its flu burning its way through tenements made him feel claustrophobic, made him want to hurt somebody.

Which, knowing Swaney, the boss had expected, and was exactly why he had sent Gunnar.

Gunnar had always been good for a clean-up job. Swaney had sent him in before with instructions to wipe out the opposition. Give Gunnar that brief and four or five good men, and he would level a small town in a few hours. He had done that to Kemmelmann's people. Then he had done it to Rosso's people, with a body count above thirty, and lots of garish headlines after gun battles spilled into city streets. Gunnar was a hammer, not a scalpel.

But here it had been different. He had needed to get the lay of the land first. Swaney had asked that he learn the main players, identify weaknesses, strengths, allies, opportunities. Be a little closer about his team, keep things close to his chest, and, meanwhile, ensure that the pipeline of young girls went uninterrupted.

Everything had been going absolutely smoothly and as he had predicted until the last few days.

He was worried about how Swaney would take this news. Swaney liked solutions, not problems, and wasn't shy about saying so. So Gunnar mentally rehearsed what he was intending to say, considering nuances, different tones, dropping phrases and changing them around. It was only Swaney who had this effect on him. Only Swaney who forced him to think so hard about how he came across, how he might sound. Only Swaney who made him so nervous.

They were parked now near the dock. The ship was approaching, carving across the harbor towards its berth. He took his pipe from an inside jacket pocket, then tortuously began to clean and fill it, his eyes never leaving the prow of the approaching ferry.

The other men knew better than to talk to him. They had also witnessed his mood change over the last few days, and if they were good at reading people or had observed him well enough, they would have realized that this change in his temper had more to do with the anticipated arrival of Swaney than with the new problems they were encountering in Dublin. There was precious little in the world that scared Gunnar. But Swaney did.

He had heard Swaney's name around Boston for a long time before he had ever run into him. Back then Gunnar was an enforcer for the Hurleys. He broke down doors, he broke fingers, he broke noses. He even enjoyed a lot of it. But the cops were a problem. He was smalltime; he had no protection, nobody who even cared if he turned up stabbed to death in some gutter.

Swaney was known as a man with a plan. A facilitator. He planned jobs but never executed them. Hits, robberies, prison breakouts. If it worked like a Swiss clock, Swaney had planned it.

And then somebody crossed him. There were different stories about who and about how. The one Gunnar heard had it that three men robbed a rich man's house using a Swaney plan, and refused to give Swaney his share. Within two days all of the men were found dead and all missing a hand—Swaney's warning to those who would steal from him.

Steadily he had acquired a reputation after that. People began to fear him. The jobs he planned were not contracted, he started to arrange crews for his own jobs, and he kept the proceeds. When another crew—Feeney's—tried to lean on one of Swaney's men, Swaney responded with one of his plans. A plan for war. Within two weeks the Feeney family was shattered. Assassinations and intimidation were timed and weighed and delivered with devastating precision. When Old Man Feeney was shot and killed on the steps of his church on a Sunday morning in front of most of his community, Swaney's reputation was sealed. Boston was his.

Gunnar had been recruited through other men and shown his talent for bloodshed quickly, but it was perhaps six months before he actually met Swaney. Few of his men ever did. And now here he was, about to disembark from a ferry in Dublin, and Gunnar, the man he trusted to deliver the city to him.

Swaney was accompanied by three other men when he eventually appeared on the dock. One of them was Krakowski, his enormous Polish bodyguard. A smaller man, with glasses and a ratty beard, flitted around; this was Williams, who dealt with the banalities of the world on Swaney's behalf. The third man was unknown to Gunnar, but he was more or less a pack animal, carrying Swaney's chest upon his back.

And then Swaney himself, as surprisingly unimpressive as ever. In his early 60s, he was entirely gray, clean-shaven, and starting to bald. He wore eyeglasses and a cravat. He was slight and of average height. His eyes were the feature few people were likely to forget;

purest black and empty of all feeling, they nevertheless shone with an intelligence and cunning that was instantly chilling. His mouth was thin, teeth brown and jagged inside its smear.

He, alongside Williams and Krakowski, climbed into a car which Gunnar would drive, who dutifully climbed into the driver's seat and started the car, aware as he was of Swaney's impatience.

Everything had to be done at his pace. And his pace was unflagging, exhausting, ferocious.

Nor did he believe in pleasantries. "You have news for me, Gunnar."

"Yes, sir, I do."

"Have you encountered resistance?"

Gunnar was negotiating a busy Kingstown street as he weighed this question.

"We have, yes, sir."

"Some of the local criminal fraternity? The Royal Irish Constabulary?"

"Neither, sir. We're not exactly sure, sir."

"Tell me."

"A local man appears to be investigating the girls, sir. I'm still not certain of the identity of the individual who hired him, but he is formidable."

"What do you know about this man?"

"He works as a detective. He mainly seems to find missing persons."

"Why is he not dead, Gunnar? That is your usual solution to a man like this one, isn't it?"

"He—I wasn't sure who he was. I sent two men to question him and dispose of him. He killed one, and the other returned hurt and scared."

"He shot our man?"

"No sir. He was unarmed and appeared to crush the larynx of our man."

"A private dick who can kill an armed man with his bare hands? The motherland is filled with unpleasant surprises, Gunnar. Who is he?"

"Thomas Conlon, sir. A known former associate of Mr. Xavier. He fought for the British Army in the War, sir. A boxer of some note prior to that."

"That doesn't explain the fact that he is still alive, Gunnar."

"My men have asked around, sir."

"Your men?"

"Your men, sir. Apologies."

A curt nod. "And what have they learned."

"He was in some unit in the war. Special training. When he returned there was trouble with Xavier's people. Lot of men died. Conlon did not. He appears to be quite the accomplished killer."

"And still I await your explanation..."

"Yes, sir. He has gone underground. As soon as he knew that we were onto him, he dropped out of sight. His mother has also disappeared. No sign of him for three days now sir."

"That is troubling. Have we increased security?"

"Yes, sir."

"The Police? The 'Royal Irish Constabulary?' The 'Dublin Metropolitan Police?'" This said with an unmistakable sneer.

"The correct payments have been paid sir. We haven't seen any police since we've been here. They're doing what we asked them to do."

"Good."

They drove in silence for a minute or so, the noise of

the engine filling the cab as it bounced and rocked over Dublin's streets.

"When are we moving the girls, sir?"

"Either three days or five. A telegram tomorrow will tell me which. Is all ready here?"

"Yes, sir."

"My hotel?"

"We've paid for the best suite, sir."

"Some company for after dinner?"

"Arranged, sir."

"You seem to have done well here, Gunnar, for all your reluctance to come."

"I don't like the place, sir. But I've done my job."

"Yes, you have. Yes, you have."

Gunnar waited for more but it did not come. So he asked.

"How long are we planning to be here, sir?"

Swaney chuckled mirthlessly. "Not long Gunnar. Mr. Fitzgerald falls. Then, in time, Mr. Xavier. Then, once the city is pacified, and the underworld is controlled by parties with our best interests at heart, we can leave. I estimate five or six weeks, depending on Mr. Xavier's capabilities and manpower."

"I have a few men on that, sir."

"Good. But this meddler, this Conlon—find him, first. Then, we move for the city. Once we have the city, well, then, you are a key cog in an International machine, Gunnar. And the potential is limitless."

They had arrived at the hotel. Swaney let Krakowski and Williams climb out of the car first, and then he followed. Gunnar remained behind the wheel. He had work elsewhere. Swaney leaned in through the window. Gunnar could smell his sour breath.

"Gunnar—the Private Dick. His head. Make an example of him. A statement, so that the city knows what happens to those who oppose me. Be creative."

Gunnar smiled at this. "Yes, sir."

Swaney turned and was gone.

9

His first solid thought was a memory—Orla. A dark room, in bed. The warmth and welcome pressure of her head on his chest. The thin line of light from the edge of a curtain widening just enough to find the gold in her hair, there in the corner of his eye.

As always, her memory brought Conlon a surge of purest pain. And that was what woke him, brought him back to himself. The unendurable pain of losing her had become his anchor, had been with him through the war and everything since. It was part of who he was. And now it had dragged him up out of what felt like an ocean and into the light.

He blinked his eyes. A dark room, but the dim light was still too much. He could remember recent dreams —dreams that felt like reality. He had been awake but not fully conscious? Hallucinating? He could not remember.

He narrowed his eyes and tried to move. His limbs felt hollow—weakness he could barely comprehend. He lifted his head and it lolled back onto the pillow.

He had been sick. He remembered now. Staggering along the streets as the flu took control of his body.

He was alive.

He tried to raise his head again. There was someone in the room. A shape over by the light. A window? He tried to speak. A rasp tore from his tongue. Dry.

A voice.

"Tommy?"

A woman. A young woman. His eyes searched the gloom for her. She moved away again and light filled the room; she had opened curtains. He blinked and squeezed his eyes shut for a moment. He felt the weight in the bed shift, and then she was holding his hand, and he knew it was Sister Maude.

"Maude," he whispered. He could not quite see her yet, his eyes still adjusting to the light.

"Do you want some water?"

He nodded faintly.

The gentle lapping of water into a cup, then her small, strong hand holding the back of his head, and he drank, enjoying the cold of the mug against his mouth, feeling the water rolling through him like life itself. He lay back, exhausted from the exertion.

"Sleep now, Tommy. Rest. Your fever only broke this morning. Sleep. I'll be here when you wake up."

He began to say something but—

———

IT WAS MORNING. He could tell from the sounds, the smells of the house, even the light. He raised his head slowly. Maude was asleep, sitting up in an armchair beside the bed, a blanket over her legs and most of her body. She wasn't wearing her habit. It was folded in her lap, and her hair fell across her forehead. She was strawberry blonde, her hair in thick waves down to her shoulders. She looked younger, somehow, with her hair on display. He watched her for a moment, and then he tried to sit up. The room reeled around him, and he lay back, eyes closed. How long had he been here?

He could hear voices downstairs somewhere, smell bacon, the charcoal scent of toast, hear cutlery's tinkle.

"Maude," he said. His voice sounded odd, more musical than he was used to.

Her eyes opened in a flurry of shy blinks and she rubbed at them, yawning, and then focused on him.

"Morning," he croaked.

She smiled, the open smile of a young girl, and he felt that deep inside. "Good morning," she said.

"Could I have some water, please?"

She poured some from a jug, and helped him drink, and then he lay back, regarding her while she drank some, too. Just then she realized that her head was uncovered and, without panicking, she put her habit on, with a shy smile for his benefit.

"What happened?" he said.

"What do you remember?"

"I was sick. Trying to get to Tallaght." He shook his head at the gaps in his memory. "I could barely walk."

She nodded. "You came to us. You collapsed in the door."

"Spanish Flu?"

"Oh yes."

"But I survived."

"You did. We weren't sure you would for a while there."

"My lungs..."

"Yes?"

"I have weak lungs. Pneumonia when I was a baby. That's why I don't smoke."

She nodded. "That does explain it. You were breathing like an old boiler. The noise outta ye!"

The door opened and there was Sister Diana, smiling at the sight of him. "I thought I heard voices. Tommy, it is wonderful to see you looking so much better."

"Thank you, Sister. Where are we?"

"We're at Father Brailsford's Parish House, in Graystones. He's been very kind."

"We couldn't risk keeping you at the Convent, in case they came looking for you," Sister Maude continued. "So Gearoid helped us get you in a carriage and we took you here."

"We weren't sure you'd last that first night, but Sister Maude hasn't left your side," Sister Diana said.

His eyes met Maude's and she didn't look away for once.

"How long have I been sick for?"

"Three days," Maude said.

"Three days!"

The women laughed. "You were in a bad way," Sister Diana said.

Three days. And the world had spun on without him.

"I'll get you some food. Toast to start," Sister Diana said, with that laugh in her voice.

"Thank you, sister."

When she was gone, Maude said, "Why were you going out to Tallaght?"

"They know who I am. I was going to lay low for a few days."

"How do you know that?"

"Two of them came for me in town."

"On Capel Street?"

"Yeah."

She nodded. "It was in the paper. You killed one of them."

"I did."

"Did you mean to?"

He shrugged. "They were going to kill me. I had to do something."

"Who were they?"

"I assume they're them. They tagged me because I followed a lead. And I was right. So I was going to keep my head down for a while, plan my next move..."

"You don't seem the type to hide."

"No. But they have all the advantages. I don't know who they are, really. I don't know where they are, how many of them there are, what weapons they have, what they know about me, what their plans are...they could kill me from half a mile away with a rifle, and I'd know nothing about it. So my only option is to hide. Fight when I can. Then hide again."

"Do you know anything at all?"

"They're American. Some of them have military training."

"How do you know that?"

"Something about these two. They were definitely soldiers."

"American soldiers? Maybe they're invading."

"They weren't very good soldiers. We should be alright, in that case."

"Not good enough to kill the famous Tommy Conlon, you mean?"

"Do you want to talk about that? It seems to bother you."

Now she looked uncomfortable. "Sure doesn't it bother you?"

"I've never killed anyone who wasn't trying to kill me or somebody I cared about."

"How—how many people have you killed?"

He shrugged and instantly regretted the gesture. "I don't know. I didn't count, during the war."

She nodded and looked at her hands, unable to meet his gaze. "Our Lord says—"

"You know I'm not religious."

"I know. But you're a good man, Tommy. A moral man. I know you are. But—I can't work out all this violence. Killing! How do you deal with it, in your head?"

"I don't think about it, much. I try not to dwell on the men I've killed, even though I know most of them deserved it and were trying to kill me. They were still people. They had mas and das, and sometimes wives and children, too...I can't think about any of that. I just put my head down and get on with it. I've known men who are haunted by it. Every man they've ever killed— they remember their faces, they can't let it go. That's never been the way with me. I don't think about them. I let them go."

She shook her head, baffled.

He said, "It was the first thing I was good at. Not killing, but fighting. It just came so easy to me. So easy. It still does. And—and part of what I do, and why I do this now, is because I can use that, sometimes, to help people. To do the right thing. Sometimes you have to do something nasty for the right thing to happen. That's one thing I've learned, and it's not a nice thing. You can't always turn the other cheek. And sometimes it even feels good not to turn the other cheek."

"It feels good to kill somebody?"

"Of course not. I didn't say that. Not many people can do the things I can. The War taught me that. And afterwards I didn't know what to do about that. I was going to try to forget all about it and try to be a normal person and get a job and all that. But if I can do these things—and help people, and if sometimes that means I have to hurt people—well shouldn't I do it? Wouldn't it be wrong not to do it?"

"I don't know," she said.

He lifted his hand towards her. She took it and held it, and he realized he didn't know which one of them needed that contact most.

He said, "These children. The ones I'm looking for, for you and Sister Diana...These men are taking them and they're selling them on. Or they're using them, like cattle, for sex. You know they are, we all know it. We just have to try to find them before they get put on a ship for America. Right?"

She nodded, eyes squeezed shut.

"So what lengths should I go to, to protect those children? Should I stop myself from killing these men? Because God might not like that? Or do I think that God gave me the ability to do the things I can do because he wanted me to use that ability, and use it to stop those men any way I can?"

She looked at him, her eyes large.

He lay there, suddenly exhausted, and laughed. "I

don't know either, Maude. When it comes down to it, I rarely have a choice, it's kill or be killed. So I kill, so I don't die."

She nodded. "I'd rather you didn't die."

"Thank you."

"You're welcome, sure."

They both chuckled. Then her face changed and she said, "But all of this—the world you live in...no, I know you live in the same world I do. It's normal. But you walk in this other world. With evil men. Evil, Tommy. You can't keep going into that world and hope not to take some of that evil back out with you. Evil is...it has an appeal, doesn't it? The devil comes as something attractive, something people want to be around."

"I don't believe in the devil."

"He's a metaphor, here. You keep on doing these things and dealing with these people, and you'll change. But you mightn't even notice, sure."

"You'll notice, Maude."

She looked at him for a moment, the silence between them loaded.

He chuckled. "The problem is, I'm not sure if I even can kill these men. They seem serious and motivated in a way I haven't really run into before."

"Are you scared?"

"Of course, I'd be stupid not to be."

She squeezed his hand and then looked down at it, as if surprised to find that she still held it.

He said, "Anyway...this all feels a bit stupid, all this talk of killing. I doubt I could stand up at the moment."

"You'll be fine in a day or two. Once you get your strength back."

"What about you. We've never talked about...why did you want to become a nun?"

Her face changed somehow at this question. Nothing obvious; no twitches or creases, no wrinkles of emotion. But a change was there nonetheless. She said, "I heard God's call."

"What was that like?"

"He spoke to me—not with words, not with any kind of voice. But I knew that was what he wanted from me."

"And how did you feel?"

"Scared. Scared I wouldn't be good enough or strong enough."

"I'm sure you have been."

"So far, please God."

"My da told me about the Call when I was a boy."

"You've never mentioned your da."

"He died when I was seven."

"I'm sorry."

"Thank you. Anyway, he told me that if God wanted you to become a priest he called you, and if you didn't obey the call, you would be unhappy all your life. And after that I was terrified that I'd be called. Because I knew I didn't want to be a priest, ever."

She smiled. "Would it be so bad?"

"For me, it would."

"Why?"

"The best moments of my life would never have happened if I'd been a priest."

"With a woman, do you mean?"

He nodded.

"Somebody you love?"

"Loved. She died."

"I'm sorry."

"You don't have to be."

The door opened and she released his hand instantly. He saw the blush rise to her cheeks then. Sister Diana was there, a tray carrying a plate with toast and a teapot, cup and saucer all spread out for him in her hands. She encouraged him to sit up more, then folded little legs down from its corners and placed it over his midriff, an instant little table.

He went slowly and his stomach made several wet, bubbling noises as he sipped at his tea. The nuns laughed.

Once he had eaten some toast, Sister Diana said, "So —and I know you'll be needing a day or two to get your strength—how are you going to proceed after that?"

"I'm thinking about it. All that really matters is the girls. All I need to do is find out where they are and go get them."

"Sure you say that as if it'll be easy."

"I know it won't be easy, Sister. I'll need some help. But I can get help."

"The right kind of help? Men like you?"

"At least one, yes. And maybe another kind of help, too."

Maude said, "If you get the girls they'll just take other children."

"I know. I'm working on it. I can't go to war with these men. But I might know somebody who can."

"I would've thought you'd seen enough of war," Sister Diana said.

"Oh I have. But some wars have to be fought, don't they?"

"I don't know. It's enough to make you despair, so it is."

"No. The strong prey on the weak. That's the way of the world, and it always has been. That's in the bible—that's everywhere in the bible."

"You know the bible?" Sister Maude said.

"I couldn't quote it, but I was taught by Christian Brothers. So the strong, the rich, the powerful...they do what they want, and the weak—the poor—they just have to take it. And not even complain. Well this war, when it comes, is the poor biting back."

The nuns looked at one another, trying to conceal amused smiles.

"He belongs in the pulpit, sister," Sister Maude said. "You should have heard him a minute ago. He sounded like one of them Russian fellas."

Conlon laughed at that, and they joined him.

10

HE RANG BARRY.

"I thought you were dead," were the policeman's first words. "It's been days, Tommy."

"I haven't been feeling well."

"Not the bleedin' flu?"

"That's it."

"Well you're doing well to be breathing, aren't you? Half the city's got it and half of those have died."

"It's not nice, trust me."

"Oh, I don't doubt it. Three of my squad are down with it."

"Well, I hope they're alright."

"Aye. I've heard your name a fair bit, too."

"Where?"

"On the street. Our friends are looking for you. The word is out. Every floozie and jewman and card player knows to keep an eye out, sure there might be money in it. Tommy Conlon—where is he? That's what we've heard."

"What about you lads?"

"The detective in charge of the investigation of the murder on Capel Street, if that is what you're referring to...?"

"It is."

"That'd be Detective Kavanagh. Good man, Kavanagh. He'd like to have a few words with you, so he would."

"So. Keep my head down?"

"Keep your head down."

"I might need some help, so."

"With keeping your head down?"

"No. I need to find these boys."

"I can't help you there, I'm afraid."

"Ah, of course you can, Barry, and we both know it."

A heavy sigh. "I'll see what I can do."

"Ah, and that's why you're my favorite peeler."

"Do you know any other peelers?"

"I do not."

They shared a laugh at this.

Then Barry said, with a note of unusual seriousness, "How bad a mess are you going to make here, Tommy?"

"No mess at all, if I can help it."

"That's not like you."

"These boys feel different. More serious and more dangerous. They had training, and they're here with a plan. I'm not sure I can take them on and survive."

"But if it comes to it?"

"I'll call the police, Barry."

"You only call me after the fact."

"Things happen and I react. It's not something I plan."

"Well then that's not calling the police."

"If it comes to it? I'll do what I always do. And hopefully be alive afterwards to call you."

"That'd be appreciated, Tommy."

"Well sure everyone likes to be appreciated."

"You keep your head down now."

"I'll try. See you, Barry."

"Tommy."

HE GAVE himself another four days to recuperate, reasoning that he if was to be a target on the streets of his own city, then he needed to be in the best condition he could be, ready for anything. During that time, he rested, he began to exercise, and he spent long hours talking with the two nuns.

Father Brailsford was rarely around—Conlon had never suspected how busy a parish priest might be—but the phone was always ringing for him to attend to Last Rites for a flu sufferer or counsel a parishioner or attend some community function on top of his usual duties of mass and confession. He was at evening meals; a warm, gently witty presence at the head of the table, generous with his wine, and seemingly comfortable with Conlon convalescing in his home. They chatted through the nuns but rarely without them; Conlon felt that the priest avoided him around the house, but he couldn't understand why. Perhaps he could sense Conlon's suspicion of the church in general? Perhaps he himself found Conlon's line of work distasteful?

Whenever they passed in the hall or Conlon found himself wandering into a room where the older man was reading a paper, say—he spent a lot more time reading a newspaper than a bible, to Conlon's gentle surprise—Brailsford would nod and avoid Conlon's eye, then leave within a minute or so. But it was not too pressing an issue, for the priest's home was big enough that they could pass hours without seeing one another.

And what a home it was. Parish priests lived in detached houses, generally within a short walk of their church, and this residence had four high walls surrounding its large house and extravagant garden. The church paid for Father Brailsford to have a house-keeper—Mrs. McCutcheon, a silent, constantly hovering middle-aged woman, who gave Conlon the same smile every single time he saw her—and a gardener.

In the sunny afternoons while he was there, Conlon would sit on a chair in the warm light in the garden while the elderly but bouncing sprightly Gardener pottered in the shade beneath the apple trees fringing the east wall. Sisters Diana and Maude moved back and forth between the garden and the house, picking fruit and herbs, bickering good-naturedly over one thing or another, teasing Conlon about his laziness.

He exercised in the garden early in the mornings, barefoot in the dew-damp grass, press-ups and shadow-boxing, chin-ups on the thickest branch of the chestnut tree in the corner nearest the gate until his vest was sticky and clung to the small of his back. After a break-fast of poached eggs and toast, he began to feel his strength returning.

One morning he spied movement in a window while he danced and flung hooks and uppercuts at the air before him and looking up he saw Sister Maude jerk her head back and behind a curtain.

While he sat in the garden in the sun, he was thinking—considering plans, means of attack, avenues of investigation. But it was difficult; there were too many things he did not know, too many areas where he would have to improvise solutions, act in the instant. It all necessitated guerilla tactics. He needed to be fast and decisive, moving and striking, moving and striking. He had been that way in the ring, when the opponent demanded it.

The first problem he had was that he did not know who to strike at, or where. And that was what he was thinking about, sitting there in the sun. For the first few days, he was frustrated. And then it came to him. He woke up with it, perfectly formed. Where to get information. How to approach it all. The beginnings of a plan.

————

FITZY WAS DOING his damnedest to lose himself in this moment. But that had become harder and harder for him as he had become more powerful, and older.

His mind these days was chock-full of problems, debts to be paid, credits to be collected, vendettas, slights, the way one of his lieutenants was getting a bigger head than was wise at his level, the rebels and the way their activities were making it harder to be an ordinary decent criminal in Dublin nowadays but also ways to exploit that—round and round his brain went.

So he came to see Patricia as a way to lose himself.

His wife was a lovely woman. Mother of his seven children, daughter of the same Liberties Streets that had produced him, they had known one another from childhood. She was where he left his heart, she was the one he would think of when the end came, as he knew it inevitably must, with a bullet in the head. But she was not the one he wanted to ride.

That was Patricia. He had a few other women around the city—it worked for him that way, not like Xavier, who he had heard was a virtual monk these days —some of them whores, some not. Patricia was the wife of one of his bookies. This bookie and Fitzy had an understanding. He looked the other way when Fitzy wanted to come around. He made himself scarce. He didn't ask her about it, or give her any hassle, or act jealous. He pretended it hadn't happened.

And Fitzy threw him more business than he could handle. Fitzy stopped his protection demands. He was a friend of Fitzy's, and all because Fitzy loved riding his wife.

She wasn't as beautiful as some of the other girls. Nor even as beautiful as his wife, who despite the strains of almost two decades of motherhood, still retained the bright eyes and full face and figure of her youth. But Patricia had something. The look in her eye had always bewitched him. Something sullen and unconquerable about her.

And she was pretty, with auburn hair and a tight little body, which was, at that moment, straddling his groin and grinding down into him as she moaned and sweated. His hands were on her midriff, and he was enjoying it, but...his mind kept wandering away from her.

Too many unanswered questions lately for Fitzy to sleep soundly.

These Americans he had made a deal with...what

exactly did they want? At first it had been a simple transaction. Not a pleasant one, not at all, but a lucrative one. He farmed it all out to the furthest reaches of his army and wanted no more to do with it, except for counting his money. But then it had gone wrong. His men went missing. And he knew that it was the Americans. That they were pulling something.

His gut told him that they wanted a piece of the city. The way they had moved men in, felt out his network, taken out a few key players on his side...it all suggested they were making a move.

So he increased his own security. What else could he do? He didn't even really know who he was fighting. It all made him furious with himself for letting them dictate the way they kept contact—the messages, the lack of a face to face...

He suspected that they didn't have all that many men, but that those they did have were well trained. He thought they had a plan, and they were confident enough to stick to it. That worried him.

He could feel himself wilting despite Patricia's best efforts, so he slapped her rump and thrust up at her a few times, willing these thoughts of Americans and assassination from his mind.

But stubbornly they remained. What he wanted was one location. Send a few men, kill them all and take one prisoner. Torture the gobshite until he told them everything they wanted to know. Then eliminate all of the American bastards.

Part of him was just offended at the way they had just come in and tried this. And that he had fallen for it. They hadn't targeted Xavier over on the Northside. He had initially been flattered that they had chosen him, and maybe that was why they had chosen him—his weakness to flattery.

So what he wanted to do, more than anything was kill them all.

And now there was this thing with Tommy Conlon. They had circulated his name. They wanted him dead, very badly. They were willing to pay to make sure that he got dead.

Fitzy remembered Conlon when he was a fighter. Something inhuman about him in the ring when he was on song—faster and stronger than his opponents, he was like a wolf fighting a sheep; he would tear boxers apart. It was impressive and chilling to watch. And then he had apparently ridden Xavier's girl. And Xavier had ordered them both killed.

There had been whispers that that job had been botched. That Conlon had put up a better fight than anyone imagined. But he was gone, she was gone, Xavier became a monk.

And then Conlon had returned. From the War, he had been told. And he made trouble, too. At the time, the rumors and informers told Fitzy about huge gunfights in warehouses and parks, about Conlon raiding safe houses and smashing up gun shipments. A few men wound up dead. But not Conlon. He was working as some sort of detective, finding people. Fitzy saw him once in a restaurant off Stephens Green. That danger he had carried into the ring he now wore over his shoulders like a cape, and it hung there in his eyes, too, and Fitzy saw why Xavier had backed off this man.

And now the Americans wanted him dead, and Fitzy was intrigued by this. His people said Conlon had disappeared, which meant either he was already dead or he was smart enough to know when to keep his head down and he'd be making a move soon. He might be worth finding and talking to. Fitzy needed allies against these Americans. Conlon had apparently killed one in the street a week before.

My enemy's enemy is my friend, he thought.

"What?" Patricia said, stopping suddenly.

"What?" he said.

"You said something to me."

He had said it aloud, he realized. She was now sat there, astride him, still, looking at him with confusion and perhaps a little accusation, too. His cock was shrinking inside her like a deflated balloon.

"Nothing," he said, shifting his weight and causing her to slide sideways off him.

"You mustn't be letting it all get to you," she said.

He looked at her, naked beside him, trying to comfort him in her clumsy way, and laughed in her face.

The door to the bedroom opened. He was up instantly, ready to hurl abuse at whichever one of his idiot guards was responsible.

There were four guards altogether. When he saw who had opened the door, he knew that all four were already dead.

It was a tall man, wearing a soft brown tweed suit, his moustache oiled and magnificent. A smaller man came in behind him, a pistol in one hand. He covered the room. Patricia had pulled the sheet to cover her nakedness but Fitzy stood naked in the center of the room and stared at the big American. For it must be one of them.

"What do you want?" he asked the big American.

The American grinned at that. "My employer wants

to speak with you. I'm just here to ensure that the room offers no threat to his person." He cast a glance down at Fitzy. "You offer no threat that I can see, Mr. Fitzgerald."

He nodded at the gunman, who disappeared down the stairs.

"Who are you, then?"

"The name's Gunnar."

"You're not in charge?"

"No, I am not. Although it has been me these last few weeks kneecapping your organization. Which has been surprisingly simple."

"Did you kill all my guards?"

"I think the one outside the door is still breathing. He's gonna have a bad headache when he wakes up though."

Fitzy nodded. He wasn't dead, which meant they wanted something from him. If he kept his head, he might still profit from all this.

"I'm going to put on some trousers, if you don't mind," he said.

Gunnar smiled. "Be my guest, Mr. Fitzgerald."

"While we're waiting for Mr. Swaney," Gunnar went on, as Fitzy fished for his trousers from a pile of clothes on the floor by the bed, "do you have any idea where I could find a man named Thomas Conlon?"

Fitzy repressed a smile as he pulled on the trousers.

"The boxer?" he said.

"He was a boxer, yes."

"He has a place in Smithfield."

"He hasn't returned to his residence for quite some time."

Fitzy said, "You made it too obvious you were after him. He's no fool, he's hiding out somewhere."

"Where would a man like Conlon hide out?"

Fastening the trousers, Fitzy turned to face Gunnar. "You sure you want to find him?"

"Why wouldn't I be?"

Fitzy shrugged, noticing that Patricia was sunk to the floor in the corner, practically trying to melt through the floorboards, her face white. "He's a dangerous man. Sometimes with dangerous men it's better to just leave them be."

Gunnar raised his eyebrows. "That's not my way."

"Well good luck to you then. You'll be needing it."

"Tell me, what is it that makes him so damned dangerous? Why is everybody so scared by this man? He's hiding from me like a child."

"He's outgunned, not stupid. You'll see him when he wants you to. And then you'll wish you hadn't."

He was not sure what he was doing, only certain that he was enjoying poking at Gunnar's ego, and that having him nervous about Conlon may be profitable at a later stage.

Gunnar looked at him in silence for a few seconds. Then, calmly, with an even tone, he said, "I'm gonna kill Conlon slow. I'm gonna cut off his balls and feed them to him. I'm gonna kill his mother, his friends, his woman, and make sure he sees each and every moment of suffering and knows there's not a damn thing he can do about it. And then, when I'm good and ready, I'll gut him like a goddamn fish and he can bleed out in agony. And I'll watch and laugh at him. Then we'll see how dangerous he is."

Fitzy nodded. "We will."

And then Swaney was there. He had appeared silently, with no fanfare or fuss. He walked into the room slowly, his eyes taking it in. Fitzy was shocked at how ordinary he looked; small and gray, wearing a dark suit and clutching a hat in one hand.

He nodded to Patricia, then turned his gaze on Fitzy.

"Mr. Fitzgerald."

"Who are you?"

"Mr. Swaney. Aside from that, you know exactly who I am."

"I do. What I'm wondering about is what it is that you want?"

"You mean why are we having this conversation? That is the right question, Mr. Fitzgerald. So, I could end this today, here and now. With one bullet."

He paused for effect, took a few steps around the room, barely able to hide the distaste wrinkling his features. He looked at Fitzy again.

"And then the city is mine, as soon as I can claim the other half from Mr. Xavier. But what would I do with it? Stay here, never go back to Boston? Deal with these little rotten people in their hovels, and the English lording over all of you? That is not acceptable to me."

"So I'd be guessing you have a better idea."

Swaney grinned for the first time. "You see? We've only been together for a few minutes, and already you know how I think."

"Sure we're both businessmen, aren't we?"

"We are, Mr. Fitzgerald. And that's why I believe we can work together."

"I think you mean I can work for you."

"I understand you have your pride. You've made yourself a powerful man here. And you still will be—on a much greater level—with my backing."

"Your backing? I don't need any bleeding backing."

Swaney was calm, unruffled. It was as if, though he heard Fitzy's words, he was assured of their utter meaninglessness.

"You have a choice to make, Mr. Fitzgerald. Your world is changing around you. Either you can accept my proposition, or you can die. Not today. I will let you walk out of this room. But soon, your life will end. Gunnar here will see to that."

Fitzy looked at Gunnar, who was grinning at him.

"What is your proposition, exactly...?"

"You'll maintain your current position. Your men will answer to you. But you will answer to me. I will provide for you—guns, drugs, anything else you may need. The British Government is likely to make opium illegal in the near future, did you know that? A businessman should know such things if that's part of his business. I will take a percentage of your profits. And the girls. I'll need you to keep supplying the girls."

"I don't really see what's in it for me, Mr. Swaney."

"No? Maybe you're not listening properly. Your profits will increase with my guidance. Your organization will become more efficient. But more than that, you and your family will live long lives. Did I mention your family? You have, what is it, six children? Seven? And that lovely wife. Gunnar has developed a fondness for her, haven't you, Gunnar?"

The big man was playing with his moustache and now he winked at Fitzy.

"Such a fondness in fact that he was almost offended to learn that you and this—" he gestured at Patricia, whose eyes were moons of fear "—lady were here together."

He turned to Gunnar. "Would you like to restore

Mrs. Fitzgerald's honor, Gunnar? The old-fashioned way?"

Gunnar ceased twirling his moustache, nodded curtly, and walked around Swaney towards Patricia.

Fitzy could see what was about to happen. In truth, Fitzy had seen worse, had ordered worse. But this was Patricia. His Patricia. And yet he was frozen. He could not even speak.

Patricia was screaming and kicking, burrowing into the corner of the room like an animal, tears streaming down her face.

Gunnar chuckled.

He wrenched her up by her hair, then clamped one big hand around her throat. He squeezed and both her hands scrabbled at his wrist and fingers. His arm was so long that there was no point in her trying to reach his face or chest.

He chuckled again and lifted her off her feet. She was making long hacking coughing noises and her feet were flapping and knifing at the air and the wall behind her.

Suddenly Gunnar lowered her and buried a left hook into her stomach. She yelped a scream and he smacked her head back into the wall, her hair in his fist.

Fitzy realized that he was keeping her standing.

Then he hit her. Three, four, five huge punches until she flopped sideways, her face a bloody ruin. Gunnar crouched and hit her again and again until the sounds his fist made were wet splashes and the pond of her blood was soaking the edge of the rug in the center of the room. Then he stood, picked the sheet she had been wrapped in from the floor and wiped his knuckles off on it. He took his time over this, scrutinizing his hands as he smeared and buffed with the fabric while Swaney and Fitzy watched. When he was done, he tossed it behind him. It twisted into the blood and Fitzy could not turn his face away as it was consumed by crimson.

Patricia had not moved for some time.

Gunnar had crossed the room again and now stood in the doorway behind Swaney, arms folded, like a bored child.

"So, Mr. Fitzgerald," Swaney said. "What do you think?"

11

ON THE MORNING CONLON VENTURED OUT AGAIN, HE exercised some in his room. He shadow-boxed in the mirror until his body was filmed in sweat and his fists were blurred lines of flesh in the glass. Then press-ups and sit-ups, lunges and squats, and finally the stretching the Major had taught him. After, he had that feeling he remembered from training when he had been a fighter; a glow from his muscles, a feeling of elevated athleticism. He felt strong.

He washed, dressed and went downstairs for a light breakfast.

The nuns were already gone, which made it easier. He did not want to see Sister Maude and that look in her eyes when he told them he was going out. He was generally confused about her, in fact. The way she made him feel, the connection between them. What he was meant to do about it.

He knew he was meant to do nothing. He was meant to bury his feelings and respect her vow. But the longer they were around one another, the better they got to know one another, the harder that became.

He could feel Sister Diana watching them now, when they spoke, and he felt an obscure guilt whenever he sensed her eyes on him. He had to remind himself that he had done nothing, said nothing, even, to feel guilty about, and that all this was ridiculous. Most ridiculous of all, perhaps, was allowing something like this to distract him when there were dangerous men in his city, looking for him, hunting him, wanting him dead.

It was a sign that he had been in this house for too long; cabin fever. He needed to get back to the dirty streets and start putting some plans in motion. He was always better when he took the initiative, and that was just what he intended to do. He wanted these Americans worried about him, afraid of him, desperate to find him.

He had some black tea and toast, heavy with strawberry jam and butter, made sure he was armed—his pistol hard and heavy in the waistband at the small of his back—and wheeled Father Brailsford's bicycle out of its parking spot beneath the stairs and through the hall. He had asked the priest if he could borrow it the night before, and ended up in a twenty-five-minute conversation on bicycles, which Brailsford regarded as just about the peak of Western civilization.

It was the longest single conversation the two of them had ever had, and Conlon noted Brailsford's love of his own voice, his expectation that others would respectfully remain quiet and listen when he spoke. He was grateful for the priest's hospitality but was finding it difficult to warm to the man. The deference of everyone around a man would inevitably change him. He had seen it in the old days, with the gangs. He had seen it in the army, where Officers and even the odd sergeant-major could become monstrous when they had tasted a little too much power. But he had never considered that he might see it in the church, too.

Still, Brailsford had enough to bestow his favors with self-consciously underplayed casualness, and he had acted as if allowing Conlon the use of his bicycle was a trifle, while nonetheless emphasizing how much he loved the contraption.

Conlon had not cycled a bicycle since his time in the British army, and now the smell and feel of the machine excited him. He also suspected that the Americans would not be looking for a man on a bicycle, because, well; who would? With that in mind, he opened the front door, prodded the bike over the step and went out into the bright late morning, ready for whatever awaited him.

After visiting a tenement on the quays on the edge of the Monto, he was redirected by an old man to another tenement on Mountjoy Square.

The ride into town had taken him almost an hour, but from the Liffey to the Square was a little over a minute, and it was enjoyable to race along the street in the sun. He left the bike by the railings and climbed the steps to the door squinting up at the building. It was a big old Georgian townhouse like every other building on the Square, proud and beautiful, its windows reflecting the green park behind his back, trees sashaying in the breeze, the odd mother or nanny with small children on the grass. The door had been painted red, and, as in most tenements, it was closed over but unlocked.

The hallway beyond was a muted mint green, paint hanging off in large leaves, cracks spider-webbing across the ceiling and porticos. It was empty of any life. He began to ascend the stairs. He could hear the odd voice behind a door, the rattle of china, a splash of music. On the third floor he finished his climb, and knocked on one of the doors.

A man answered, wearing only a pair of shorts, his body muscular and toned. He squinted at Conlon for an instant, face a mask of outrage to be disturbed. Then it broke into a smile. "Tommy! Tommy bleedin' Conlon, howya doin'?"

He came out across the threshold and grasped Conlon's hand.

Conlon nodded. "I'm well, Finn, I'm well."

"You look well, so you do."

"You look good, too. When did you fight last?"

"Ah last Saturday. Some Belfast gobshite with big hands and a big mouth and a glass jaw. First round I knocked him out. Bye bye, bud. It's like they think that just because you're from Belfast, you're a good fighter, these days. Load 'a bollocks. How about you? When did you last put in a few rounds?"

"Years ago now. You were probably there."

Finn looked thoughtful. "Daniel O'Dowd?"

Conlon nodded. "That's the one."

"Third round, that was. He was a tough lad, O'Dowd. I remember him taking a lot of punishment. You dropped him with a beautiful kidney shot. He was walking funny for a month."

They laughed.

"What happened to him?"

"Last I heard he'd gone to America. Probably fighting somewhere that smells of beer and piss right this second, wha?"

"Rather him than me."

"Ah I don't believe that Tommy. You must miss it. That feeling."

Conlon shrugged. "Sometimes. I still get the odd bit of action."

"So I've heard, yeah. So, how'd you find me?"

"I went to the old place. One of your old neighbors told me the address."

"Ah fair enough. I'd invite you in, but the place is trashed. Can I do something for you? You're not looking for a place to hide out?"

"You heard?"

"Heard your name around alright, yeah. Doesn't sound the best, Tommy."

"It'll blow over. I've been in worse situations."

"I heard about those as well. We all thought you were dead."

"Yeah, sorry about that. But if it's any consolation, I'm not."

"That's consolation for sure. You'll have to come down to the gym. We can have a bit of sparring. Finally get to beat the head off you."

"You couldn't beat the head off me with four arms, you were always too slow."

Finn guffawed at that. "Compared to you, yeah, I was and all."

"But you're right, I'd love to come down to the gym. I do need a favor, though."

"Ah go on then."

"Just the whereabouts of a mutual friend."

"You're not goin' to beat this mutual friend to death, are ye?"

"I wasn't planning to, no. But if things get tricky..."

They laughed again.

"Who is it, then?"

"Devereaux."

————

FINN'S INFORMATION led Conlon into town and to a flat above a barbershop on Hawkins Street. Conlon left the bicycle leaning against the gates to Leinster Market, and walked through the laneway itself.

When he was a child, his memories of the market were of butcher shops filled with purple, marbled slabs of beef and lamb and the carcasses of birds his mother could never have afforded, the mounded sawdust from the floors fascinating his boy's eyes. But now there was a greengrocer selling plump apples and lettuces from a cart by the front door at one end, a furniture shop where rickety chairs were piled in pyramids in the middle, and a little pub at the other end. Children sat playing with dice near the furniture shop, and a woman chatted with a man outside a cobblers.

He had always loved the way the lane dipped under the buildings at either end, like some sort of magical underground river, and he found that he still took pleasure in this feature.

The barbershop under Devereaux's place was busy, as was the oyster bar next door. Conlon looked up, surveying the landscape before entering. It must have a nice view of the Theatre Royal, splendid across the street as it was, he thought. And otherwise, it was central and close to everything. Devereaux was perhaps Xavier's best and most persuasive fixer and advisor. He had been Conlon's first introduction to that world, and he had always seemed to be everywhere all the time, and this made that much easier to understand.

He found the door and made his way inside and up the dingy stairs.

He knocked and listened for movement within. It was still the early afternoon, and potentially Devereaux, a man who did most of his work after dark, might still be in bed.

Finally, the door opened and there he was, blearily peering out through a crack, a gun in his hand. "Thomas?" he said.

"Jordan," said Conlon.

Conlon was ushered in and waited in Devereaux's opulent sitting room while the man dressed and readied himself. Meanwhile, Mrs. Devereaux emerged. Conlon had not known that she even existed. She was well-dressed, middle-aged and pretty, with a jolly little smile in her cheeks and flashing eyes as she said hello to Conlon, and asked him would he like tea, or something a little more interesting.

He laughed at that. "It's too early for interesting. Tea would be lovely, Mrs. Devereaux, thanks a million."

"It's never too early for interesting, Mr. Conlon. Are you a colleague of Jordan's?"

"Eh—I used to be."

Did she know what her husband did? She had to, surely. She was rattling around in the kitchen, preparing their tea, and now her head was visible, leaning back through the door to fix him with a glare. "You look like muscle. But you don't seem like muscle. So what are you?"

So she did know.

"I was a boxer. In a more interesting life."

"That does explain it. So what do you do with yourself these days?"

"I find people."

"I beg your pardon?" Again her head appeared in the doorway.

"People come to me to help them find their loved ones who have disappeared."

"Oh. Does that happen often?"

"You'd be surprised."

She was out then, with the tea, and sat across from him on the settee.

"This is a nice flat," he said.

"Oh, it can be awful noisy, so close to Sackville Street and Trinity and the crowds from the theatre, but Jordan loves living at the center of everything. I've become accustomed to it over the years."

Jordan was there then, and he sat on the settee beside her and was silent as she poured tea for all three of them. It was odd for Conlon to see him in such a domestic setting. He had always seemed like some rare exotic bird Xavier had captured. But now Conlon could see that was just a persona he had created and successfully inhabited. And now here he was, sipping tea on a gaudy settee in his living room, a prim little grin on his face as he watched his wife.

Then he said to Conlon, "So Thomas, how can I help you?"

"I need to see Xavier."

A hint of a smile. "And why do you need to do that?"

"Don't act as if you don't know."

"You have some people out for your blood."

His wife, whose name he still did not know, remained deadpan through this exchange, sipping her tea.

"I think those people should be a concern for Xavier. And Finch, and yourself."

"You're suggesting you have intelligence we may be interested in?"

"I'm sure you know everything I do, Jordan. But I do think we can help each other here."

"How so, Thomas? How can you possibly help us, on the run from these people, as you are? Extremely dangerous people, by all accounts."

"All I need is some information, and I can hurt them."

Devereaux looked at him quietly. "Go on."

"They're aggressive. They've moved in on the city, and Xavier will know that it's only a matter of time before they move on him."

Something in Devereaux's eyes made Conlon pause.

"What?" he said. "What's happened?"

Devereaux chuckled. "We believe—people tell us, rather—that their bossman, an individual known as Swaney, paid a visit to Fitzy yesterday evening and laid out his intentions."

"Which were?"

"Fitzy is now his employee. Dublin is to be controlled from Boston."

"You know he'll come for Xavier sooner or later."

Devereaux nodded.

"You know how well-organized they are. Ex-army,

most of them. Well-funded, good weapons, trained, disciplined."

"Why do they want you dead, Thomas? What exactly happened?"

"They're shipping girls across the ocean, selling them in America. I've been looking into it."

"They tried to stop you...?"

"They did. With a pistol."

"Ah. The dead man on Capel Street. That was you."

Conlon nodded.

Devereaux said, "Frankly, I'm doubtful that even somebody with your unquestioned gifts can take these gentlemen on. They seem formidable."

"You've never seen me off the leash, Jordan. And I don't propose to destroy their organization. I propose to create enough of a distraction to allow Finch to do what he does. Any damage I do to the other side can only help you."

The reference to Finch, Xavier's feared enforcer, prompted Devereaux to look at his wife, who suddenly spoke.

"What do you need, Mr. Conlon?"

And Conlon suddenly understood—that while Devereaux was smooth and charming and looked the part, she was the thinker here, the strategist—she was the one with Xavier's ear. And that when she had acted as if she had no idea who he was a few moments earlier, she had been acting, feeling him out, studying his responses.

He looked at her. "I need to know when and where they're moving the girls. I need to know where they're based, who this Swaney is, any other names of interest."

"And in return, what do we get?"

"I'll make trouble."

"What kind of trouble?" she said with obvious relish.

"The kind that involves lots of guns and fire and blood."

Both of the Devereaux grinned at this, and Conlon felt a strange nausea growing. Sitting here with these people, plotting violence like this... The smiles they wore at his words, and even the fact that he had chosen just those words in order to excite them...he felt sick. This was a world he hated, and one he had tried to escape. But here he was anyway. And the two grinning ghouls sat before him, their souls blackened by decades of ruined lives and compromise and eternally expecting the worst and being proven right—he could barely stand to look at them and think of what too much time around these people might do to him. His conversation with Sister Maude the other night had been niggling at him, and now it was as if it had opened up a hole in his stomach. Suddenly he felt an extreme pressure. He needed to be out of this room.

Mrs. Devereaux said, "That sounds like it might be worth watching. We do know a few things. They haven't got that many men. There are more coming, but at the moment they've hired some men back from the War to supplement what they have. We're working on exploiting that. Swaney is staying in the Shelbourne. He has a lot of security, and you wouldn't get out alive."

They looked at one another. "So what do we do now?" Conlon asked.

"Anything we think might benefit you will be behind the bar at Yates' over the next few days. After that you're on your own."

Conlon nodded. "Thank you." He finished his tea and stood to leave.

Mrs. Devereaux looked at him. "Whatever you're going to do, you need to be quick about it. We have plans, and they won't wait."

"Fair enough. I'll do my best."

Devereaux made to stand, to see him out.

Conlon held up a hand. "It's fine, Jordan."

As he reached the door he turned and said, "Just one other thing. Keep your people out of my way. And thanks for the tea. Bye now."

After that, he cycled out to Sandymount, bought a paper and ate a sandwich on the sand, half reading, half watching the waves. He had taken off his jacket and sat upon it, shirtsleeves rolled up.

The paper was filled with misery—the War, Spanish Flu, stalemate for Irish politicians in Westminster. He lay it down, chewing his beef sandwich and tracking the progress of a couple walking close together along the water's edge.

Here, in the quiet and the sunshine, it was hard to credit that there were men in the city at his back intent upon his death; hard, too, to believe that anyone would want to steal and sell young women across the ocean. But if he knew anything it was that people were full of potential acts that were hard to believe, and that it was better to expect them to disappoint you than to be surprised by something banal and predictable.

But he had felt the need to come here to clear his head, to cease thinking about these things for an hour or two, and so he closed his eyes and tried to calm himself, to let such thoughts float away.

There was virtually no wind now, and in the stillness, the heat began to creep upwards. Having quieted his mind, he eventually lay back and after ten minutes or so, he dozed off.

When he woke, it was evening. He walked into Sandymount village and sent a telegram to his friend Mossy, asking that he get himself to Dublin as soon as possible, and install himself in the hotel in Drumcondra they had used the last time they had seen one another. His telegram promised Mossy some more action, which he knew would be something the big man would be unable to resist.

That accomplished, he headed back out on the coast road towards the priest's house.

————

THE CONVERSATION over dinner that night took a theological turn, and Conlon was quiet, listening to Sister Diana and the priest argue scripture.

The dining room was the most somber in the house, all varnished wood and deep, cardinal reds. Only one religious icon here, although the huge dinner table did remind him of an altar, covered in its thick white table-cloth. All that was missing was the scent of incense, the rote chanting of prayers.

The priest ate well, at a time when Conlon knew so many in Dublin were starving, and though he appreci-ated what the old man had done for him, that level of hypocrisy was one reason why he loathed the church. Another was the patronizing tone this man of the clergy again adopted, one Conlon had heard from priests before—a tone of amused condescension, of an old man laughing at those younger, and more female than himself—and although here he knew that was partly the wine, still it infuriated him, and he bit his tongue to avoid uttering something controversial or rude.

Sister Maude was mostly silent, too, although she broke in on a few occasions to challenge a statement made by the old man, tipsy on red wine and chuckling to himself as he debated. Conlon liked to listen to her, revealing her sharp mind in knife-like cuts of wit that the priest missed, her thoughtful contributions balancing her devotion with some common-sense attitudes he enjoyed.

He realized that must have been staring at her when he caught Sister Diana watching him.

The conversation was a pleasant diversion from his nerves. He had never been good at waiting on others. Waiting to get this information from Devereaux felt like torture. He knew the girls were out there somewhere, right now, probably still in Dublin. And yet he could do nothing, was dependent on other people to supply crucial information.

Part of him itched to go, out into the city, and see what he could discover, just with his questions and his face and his fists, in the right pubs, the right living rooms. He had a feeling that might lead him right to the girls. But he also knew that it was far too dangerous at the moment, that if the wrong person spotted him, then he would be dead in seconds, that he could bring ruin on the sisters, and his mother, and Theresa.

In his life, he had made enough stupid choices based on his need for action and his impatience. People had suffered for this. He had suffered. People had died. He was determined that this should never happen again. He was determined to focus, and do what his training had shown him, to do what the major had said —to breathe and let it pass him by and then, calm, decide what his best course of action was.

And of course that was to go nowhere, to wait, to wait, to stay as safe as he could and wait. So he stayed in his seat and waited, saying little, watching Sister Maude, listening to every word that was said but saying virtually nothing himself.

———

IT TOOK him a long time to sleep that night, which was not like him. Most nights he was sound asleep within three minutes of lying down. He had learned not to question or second-guess this; he had acquired this habit in the War, when sleep was irregular and consistently disrupted by the hellish hailstorms of shells and gunfire, among other things. He believed he could sleep anywhere, in any conditions. But apparently not in a comfortable single bed in a dark, pleasant, warm bedroom, on a quiet night after a nice meal. After that he lay there for an hour or so, mind racing, wide awake. Something was always wrong; his feet felt confined. Or he could not make his arm accept sleeping on his side. Or the pillow felt coarse. Or his shin itched.

Sleep finally came, although later he would muse that he had had no idea what had prompted its arrival. And then, at some point in the night, he came awake. And his door was open and Sister Maude stood in the doorway.

In his bewilderment, for a moment, he believed that she had come to him, finally, wanting to come into his arms. But then the last of the sleep ebbed away and he saw that she was in her habit, that she was carrying a lamp, and that her face was serious, and that she was saying something to him.

"What?" he said, his voice husky with sleep.

"Oh, I'm sorry to wake you, I'm sorry."

"It's fine. What's wrong? Is something the matter?"

She came and stood by the bed, hesitant. He was suddenly acutely aware that he was sleeping in just his undershorts, and that her eyes were on his chest and shoulders.

"Give me a minute, please," he said, and she nodded and left the room. He dressed quickly, a little rattled by all this.

She was waiting on the landing, and wordlessly she led him down the stairs and into the echoing kitchen, where she silently began to make tea while he sat, rubbing his eyes, his socks rolled in a ball in one fist, feet still bare and chilly. The burble of the water pouring, the kettle's strangled hiss; they sounded huge, frightening against the silence. She placed a mug before him. He had already fetched the milk and sugar. They helped themselves as she sat, facing him.

It had been a few minutes since either had spoken, and now it was almost as if neither wanted to break the silence. Instead they could just sit here all night, looking at one another and enjoying the orchestra of the ritual of making tea; the clicks and clatters and splashes and sighs.

She eventually did speak, and a part of him felt disappointed.

"I'm sorry, Thomas. I couldn't sleep. Something was in the back of my mind all night and it finally came to the front and I couldn't wait, I had to tell you."

MICHAEL NOLAN

"What is it?" he asked, not whispering, but quietly.

"Those men...the ones who broke in to the Convent...do you remember?"

"Yeah," he said, realizing that he had not thought of those men in days, that he had, for all intents and purposes, absolutely forgotten them. Sloppy of him. He had been sloppy on this case from the start; not doing his job all that well. And the main reason was sat across from him right now.

"Well, we were wondering why they broke in, remember? What they were looking for, what they were doing. Were they just trying to scare us, or was it something else."

"I remember. We weren't really sure."

"No, we weren't. But I've thought of something."

She nodded to herself. "We thought that they hadn't taken anything. Because nothing valuable was taken. The china was all there, what little money we have— they hadn't touched it. But what if they were looking for something else?"

"Like what?"

"I've been trying to figure out for days."

He drank some tea and watched her.

"So I went back to the convent and looked around, to try to jog my memory. The area they were in when I saw them and the rooms around that...what could they be looking for?"

"And did anything occur to you?"

"No, no. It just seemed strange that they'd even be in that area of the house. And then tonight it just came to me."

"What did?"

"Keys. There's a cabinet full of keys."

"Keys to what?"

"All of the buildings we use, the ones the Sisters run, some of the local churches and shelters."

"Why would they be after a key?"

"I don't know. I'm not even sure exactly what keys are there, or if any of them have been missing..."

"But it's better than nothing," he said.

"It has to be, doesn't it?"

He nodded.

"The keys all have names on them. There must be keys to forty buildings in that cabinet. And maps, of the city, and plans, the kind that architects use. Everything you might need if you wanted to use a building."

"Who would know what keys are there? Is there any kind of record?"

"Mister Devlin. He's a caretaker for us, looks after the properties, as far as I know."

"Right so. In the morning, I go see this Mister Devlin."

She stood. "I'm tired. I think I'll get back to bed."

"What would I do without you, Maude?"

"Ah, I think you'd manage fine. Good night."

"Night."

———

Sister Diana supplied him with the address and a letter of introduction. "Mister Devlin is a particular man," she said. "He likes to do things in the proper manner."

Conlon cycled again, his cap down low on his head. Devlin lived in Bluebell, an area Conlon didn't know on the Southern edge of the city, where the housing dissolved into countryside, walls and windows gradually fading from the roadsides as he peddled along, overtaken by hedgerows and farmland. He had to stop and ask an old farmer for directions and finally found Devlin's cottage, sunk among brambles and oak saplings a half mile back from the road.

He was a squat middle-aged man, in shirt-sleeves when he came to the door. A wireless crackled behind him in the house, the backlit face of a woman glimpsed in a doorway. He read the letter from Sister Diana with the aid of a monocle, nodded and shook Conlon's hand, and then spent ten minutes readying his horse and cart to take them both back into Dublin.

Conlon lofted the bike onto the back and climbed up alongside the older man, who spoke little all the way back into town. That was fine with Conlon, who enjoyed the sun on his bare arms and the opportunity to run his eyes over streets and corners he had never seen before.

When they reached the Convent, Devlin tied up the horse and took Conlon inside, greeting the nuns they encountered on their way through the building with a cheer and smile of which Conlon had doubted him capable.

Within seconds of opening the cabinet, Devlin knew which key was missing.

"The old Choristers Hall on Francis Street."

"Not far."

"Not far, no. A five minute walk, I'd say."

"What kind of building is it?"

"It was built as quarters for the choir for the Cathedral but they never used it. Big rooms, they were meant to be dormitory rooms with many beds, but it's always been empty."

"So it could accommodate a fair few people?"

"Oh yes, yes it could."

"How many, roughly?"

"Up to a hundred, I'd say."

Conlon nodded. That had to be it. And instantly he was wondering, how much time did he have? Would the girls still be there? And he knew before this thought process was even completed that he was going; now, today, this moment. He had to check it out, poke around, just on the off chance that the kids were still there, that it wasn't too late.

He thought about Francis Street, its layout, and looked at Devlin. "Have you got any other buildings on Francis Street? Close to that one?"

"Aye, we've an old house three doors down. Used to be office, but it's been empty these last fifteen years."

"Can you get me in there?"

Devlin looked at the array of keys and flicked one off its hook. Then he looked at Conlon. "I can. Shall we?"

————

IT WAS as Conlon had expected; a three story house, the ground floor occupied by a small barbershop. As they passed the window, Conlon saw two men in chairs, one being shaved, the other chatting while a stocky barber cut his hair scalp-tight. He could virtually smell the hair oil through the glass.

Devlin opened the door to the side of the shop and they were in the musty, dour flat, moving up the stairs to the landing. Trooping up two more landings through echoes and clouds of lint and fluff until they were at the attic, Conlon was silent and grim faced. He could feel it now. The proximity of it. And he was preparing himself, on some level. Men would be trying to kill him in a few moments, and he desperately needed to quiet his mind and be alert and focused.

The attic had a couple of dormer windows out onto the roof. Devlin said, "Well, you've seen the house..."

Conlon said, "I need to get onto the roof."

"Now why in heavens name would you want to do a thing like that?"

"I need to get into the Choristers Hall. But there may be people there already, so I can't be going in by the front door."

"What sort of people?"

"Bad people."

Devlin made a face at that; an expression in the no man's land between pain and annoyance crossed his features, although he did not reply. Conlon was the one to speak, realizing that the man needed some explanation, that this was all too unusual for him.

"Listen Mr. Devlin. This is my job. The sisters hired me to find some people who went missing. If those people are anywhere, then they're in the Choristers Hall."

"But they're not alone."

"No. So I need to go and poke around and see what I can see."

Devlin nodded. "Is there anything I can do?"

"Wait for me here. If I'm not out in twenty minutes or so, get onto the police for me. Ask for a Detective Barry. Tell him where I am. He'll know what to do."

"Are you armed, son?"

"I'm not."

"Now, that seems a bit cavalier considering your line of work, doesn't it?"

Conlon laughed, a genuine laugh of surprise and amusement. "It does at the moment, yes. But I wasn't expecting today to take this turn when I left the house this morning."

"You look like you might be able to handle yourself."

"I've been in the odd scrap."

"Well, good luck. And God bless."

Conlon nodded. Devlin moved to the window and wrenched it open. The sounds of the city were in the room with them again, the sooty smell of the rooftops.

Conlon stepped out, carefully picking his steps, watching his feet upon the roof slates. A pigeon exploded away into the sky. Looking through the window he nodded at Devlin, semi-visible in the gloom of the attic, and then he moved off, along the roof towards the next building. He had to jump down onto the rooftop, a smart ten-foot drop, but then it was easier, a flat concrete surface, two chimneys propping up the sky, bird droppings staining it like the clouds had been dripping onto the roof for months. There were skylights here, and he hunkered down and approached the first slowly.

Peeking over the edge he saw a room below full of junk—furniture piled and jammed into corners; jagged mountains of desks and chairs and bed frames, jumbles of curtain and sheets, all of it hung with shivering cobwebs and dust. Moving around that one, he stayed low and crossed the rooftop to the other skylight. This one was cracked in several places, and shone a patch of willowy light down into an empty attic, bare floorboards dull with grime. He searched for a door and found it a few meters away, a hatch fastened with padlock which had been left open, hanging disconsolately from the latch. He discarded it and slowly, carefully prized the door upwards. With it open he lowered his head and listened for any activity, voices, movement, anything. He waited one minute and then he dropped his head into the space and looked around. The room was deserted. A ladder was propped against the wall nearby.

Sitting back, he removed his shoes, quickly tied the laces together, then hung them around his neck like a scarf. Then he levered himself into position and dropped silently to the floor. His metatarsals stung and he stayed crouched down for a moment, listening again. Then he was up, moving across the room, shoes still hung around from his shoulders like some odd neck-lace. The door was unlocked and he tested the handle for noise before he opened it.

He came out onto a tight, darkened landing, light filtering dimly up from a source a few flights below. Sounds also; voices, he thought. He paused, listening, and then he began to descend. He took each step with a fastidious deliberation; lowering his toes like a dancer, feeling for weaknesses in the wood which might emit a cry of alarm. He tried to stay to the edge of the steps, aware that the wear, and thus the more likely noise, would be in the middle. On the next floor, the door off the landing was open.

Inside was a large room, beds arrayed on either side of a central aisle. Like the military barracks he had slept in in England, France and Turkey. There were large windows along one wall but they had been blacked out. Heavy curtains were draped over each, so that the only, feeble light came from a set of lamps, one at either end of the aisle.

Three young girls were lying on the beds at the far end of the room. They looked up when he came in and he froze, his eyes taking in details while they in turn studied him. He put a finger to his lips so that they would be quiet.

Each of them was chained to their bed, and looking around, he saw chains by every bed, piled on the floor, strewn across pillows. The girls wore dirty clothing; street clothing, though their feet were bare. Bowls and cups sat on the floor by their beds, alongside buckets which he could smell as he approached. They looked unwashed, tired, their hair lank and greasy, eyes glassy. He wondered if they had been drugged—he had seen that deadened look in their eyes before, in opium users.

He gestured quiet again as he crept closer.

"Who are you, Mister?" one of them whispered.

"I'm goin' to get you out of here. How many men are there downstairs?"

They looked at each other. "Three or four, I think."

"Four," another said.

"Are they armed? Do they have guns?"

The girls shook their heads and shrugged.

"I don't think so. Don't go down there, mister. They'll kill ye."

He nodded. "The keys to these chains are down there."

The girls all looked at him, eyes wide now. He forced a smile. "Don't worry. I'll be back."

"Who are you?"

"Sister Diana sent me."

At that, all three made something of the same face—

everything made sense. Her name carried weight with them.

"I'll be back," he said. "Stay quiet."

He crept across the room, trying to come up with an approach. Four men in a room downstairs. Armed— probably. Trained—more than likely. He knew neither the geography of the room or the positions of the men. Nor even, with any certainty, if there were definitely four of them. The best course of action would be to create a diversion, but even then he was wandering into their environment, blind.

He stopped where he stood, and knew exactly how to handle this.

He crouched and put his shoes back on his feet, tying the laces and stretching his thighs and calves as he stood. He turned back to the girls, picked up the lamp from the floor, and carried it across to the doorway. He did the same with the other lamp. The far end of the room was lost in the blackness.

He pulled a chain from the nearest bed, admiring the weight, and wrapped the end around his fist. He would make them come to him. They would fight on his terms.

He tossed both lamps down the staircase and heard the metal clatter and glass shatter on the landing below. The oil from one sprayed onto the wall and the flames jumped hungrily after it, then climbed, throwing some dancing light into the dark room where he crouched by the doorway. One of the girls whimpered.

Voices raised from below, shouts—three voices, perhaps four. At least one of them—no, two—Ameri-can. They put the fire out quickly and then they were coming up the stairs, at least two of them, a rumble of shoes on the wood, scuffs and one of them saying loudly, "What the hell is going on?"

The first one was already in the room before he realized that there was something wrong, and he stopped. Conlon could see his silhouette in the dim light of the doorway and he sprang up and swept the chain around the side of his head.

Conlon had always been trained to punch through a target and he did the same with the chain, swinging from his hips as he would with a punch. He could hear the metal in the air, feel it moving in the blackness. It took the man like an axe into a tree and he cried out and went down heavily, onto a bed and then sprawling onto the floor in a mess of limbs and blood.

The second one was in the doorway now, too, and he said, "Tierney?"

Conlon stayed low and circled to his side, then whipped the chain at his knees. He screamed—a gargle of high notes—when it smashed into bone and scissored over, and Conlon groped over him to deliver two sharp, horrific hooks to his head. He went still. Conlon stepped over him, and found the first one, moaning on the floor. He hit him three times before he went quiet.

Now Conlon stayed low, waiting. If there were two others downstairs, they were doing the same thing.

There was perhaps one minute of silence before he heard a moaning floorboard. And suddenly there was a man coming up onto the landing, shooting at the darkness.

The girls screamed as three shots were fired into the room. The reports echoed, the muzzle flashes giving Conlon a flickering picture of the scene. The gunman was half crouched in the doorway, firing out of hope, his eyes wide with fear. The girls screamed again and again.

Ducked down as low as he could get, Conlon hefted the chain in his hand, then rose up slightly and threw it like a ball, from over his shoulder. It opened up as it traveled, but that meant that some of it would catch the gunman, and some of it did, a strand of metal smacking him in the teeth. Conlon was already coming, launching himself off the bed and through the air so that he smashed into the man's torso, his shoulder battering into ribcage. The pistol skittered away across the floor. But the man had been reeling from the surprise chain to the face and, off balance, he toppled over backwards, his fingers grappling with Conlon's body; and they both went over, sliding and banging into the stairwell, Conlon simultaneously trying to smash the gunman in the face and to grab a banister and arrest his descent.

The man kept on scrabbling for him, fingers on him, against the walls, and they bounced off a wall where the stair turned together. Conlon took advantage of the impact, jackknifing and kicking with both legs so that the other almost flipped off him and then pinwheeled down the rest of the staircase, head and legs beating against the wood.

At the bottom he lay still.

Conlon pulled himself up, conscious that there was still at least one man left. He went back up the stairs, carefully, gingerly, and after a quick search along the floor, he found the fallen revolver. He thought he had counted four shots altogether, which gave him two to work with. He had to assume that the man downstairs was also armed.

He said, "You all well, girls?" and they went quiet to hear his voice.

Then he was back on the stairs, taking his time. He started talking before he got halfway down.

"Right, so," he said. He wasn't shouting, but he was projecting, ensuring whoever was crouching below, waiting for him to stick his head out could hear every word. "I've got your man's gun. So when I get to the bottom of these stairs, you and me are gonna have a shootout, right? A proper gunfight." He took a step. "And maybe you shoot me, and that kills me. Or maybe you shoot me, but I'm still alive, and I shoot you, too. Or maybe I just shoot you, and you're fuckin' dead."

Another step.

"I've been in a few gunfights. I'm still here. How about you? You ever been in a gunfight?" A step. "Or maybe—just think about this—maybe you just walk away. You're fighting me so that those little girls upstairs can be sold and used like meat. Is that worth dyin' for?" Another. "I don't think so."

Another. He could see a foot or so of the floor in the room on the next floor down. There were windows there; it was bright. The body of the gunman was on its back half on the stairs. His head was twisted at an unnatural angle, like a broken toy.

"So when I come off these stairs, I'm goin' to kill you. Or you can walk away, now."

A step.

A voice from downstairs. "Who are you?"

Irish, a Dublin accent. "I'm Thomas Conlon. You might have heard my name. Your bosses are looking for me."

A pause. Conlon took another step. "You tell them it was me. That might make it alright."

Silence. He began to step, then stopped when he heard the man speak again.

"I'm goin'. Don't you come down and shoot me in the back or nuthin'!"

"I won't. Toss your gun to the bottom of the stairs so I can see it, now."

It came, with a ringing, metallic clang.

"Go on, then."

"I'm goin'."

Conlon waited for a minute before he finished his descent. He picked up the gun and put it in his jacket pocket. There wasn't much here—a table scattered with cards, some glasses and a bottle of Jameson, together with overflowing ashtrays; a rusting bicycle propped dolefully in a corner; a paper bag with some bread and a couple of apples on a chair. On a bureau by the window he found a large map spread out to take the light. Pages of notes scrawled in pencil sat atop its fold, and a ring of keys weighed it all down. He wrapped the notes in the map and pocketed the lot, then hurried back up the stairs.

The girls were standing, whispering to one another in agitation. Using the big ring of keys, Conlon began to unlock their chains. But as he freed each one, they stood nearby, quivering and looking over their shoulders and plainly terrified.

"You can go," he said over his shoulder, searching for the lock. "Girls, I said you can go now, get out."

Neither spoke then, just adamant shakes of the head at him.

He realized that they were afraid, afraid to chance leaving without his protection.

He finished unlocking the last set of chains, and looked at them.

"Alright, so. Do youse all have anywhere to go?"

The girls looked at each other. They looked lost, and so young.

He said, "I've got a place for you. For a while anyways."

He led them down and out the front door, looking around to make sure there was nobody watching or following.

Devlin was waiting in the hall of the building where Conlon had left him, and he gave a rare smile at the sight of him.

"Are you alright, son? I heard shots."

"I'm fine, thanks." He had been here before—how did you hope to communicate what had just happened in the other building; the terror, the beautiful simplicity of it, the death, the way it all felt so easy to him? He could not, not to somebody he barely knew, not without betraying himself and the men he had killed. So he said little, made light of it, and honored it only inside.

The older man's eyes took in the girls. "You found what you were looking for, I see."

Conlon retrieved his bike from the cart, and they shook hands and Conlon thanked him for his help. Then he took the girls across the South side of the city to a house on the edge of Ranelagh.

They were quiet during the walk, and he was paranoid, eying every strange man they saw, the girls walking behind him and occasionally murmuring to one another, but otherwise silent.

Their destination was a fine Georgian Terrace, and he had only visited it a few months before, successfully finding somebody for the owner. When he knocked, one of her girls answered, recognizing him instantly. He was ushered inside, and he beckoned the girls to follow him.

Ruby came down the stairs then, dressed in a robe and a fez, and he had to smile at the sight of her, her confidence and eccentricity undimmed, her smile of pleasure at seeing him bright and sincere.

"Tommy, I didn't think we'd be seeing you again so soon!"

"Well, you said to call in if I ever needed something, Ruby."

Ruby's eyes were already taking in the three girls, and when they came back to his face, he saw that she understood.

"You have some waifs for me," she said.

He nodded. "They've had a hard time."

Ruby was amongst the girls now, inspecting them. Their eyes were wide at the sight of her, her color and vivid spirit.

"I can see that," she said. "And if they've needed your help, I can imagine it wasn't pleasant, wha?"

He laughed. "No. It wasn't. Do you have any space, then?"

She looked at him. "I'm only after letting some of my girls leave, so you're in luck, Tommy."

The girls were looking at him now, confused, unsure of what exactly was happening.

He said, "Ruby used to work in the Monto. But she got out of there, and now she runs this place, and helps girls who want to get out, too."

He didn't add the details they didn't need—that Ruby had married into money but that her husband had lived only weeks past the wedding, leaving her an extremely wealthy woman; that she had hired him to find one of her girls who had been abducted by an obsessive old client of hers; that this was perhaps the last chance they would have to escape the future that had until recently looked so bleak.

Ruby said, "Darlings, I'll teach you how to dress, and speak, and this time next year you'll all have either husbands or positions. No time begging in the street, no time on your back except the times you want to spend on your back. How does that sound?"

"That sounds...lovely," one of the girls said.

Ruby smiled. "Cleo," she called. The girl who had answered the door returned. "These lovely lassies will be in the room on the third floor. Can you show them the way, darling? I think they'll need some clothes and maybe a bath, don't you?"

Cleo smiled. The girls looked at Conlon. He nodded. "It's alright. You'll be safe here. I trust this lady. I'll come back and see you in a few days."

And he watched them move off, up the stairs, the beginnings of smiles on their faces, for all that they kept looking at him as they went.

Ruby looked at him. "Are you well, Tommy? I've been hearing your name from bad mouths."

"You know me, Ruby. If I see a wasp nest, I just can't not poke it."

"That's what I was thinking, alright. Do you need a place to stay?"

"No, I've got one. Thanks for the offer. And for the girls."

"Anything for you, Tommy."

"Well...you can do one thing for me. Call Detective Barry and tell him to get himself along to this address." He handed her a piece of paper. "He'll have an idea of what he's going to find, if you mention my name."

"I'm sure he won't like it, then?"

"You never know, Ruby. It takes all sorts."

And with that he left, and cycled back through the evening sun to Father Brailsford's place.

12

GUNNAR GOT AS MUCH INFORMATION FROM THE IDIOT
who had run away from this Conlon as he could. He
questioned him for two hours, as if it was a normal
conversation. Gave him tea, lit his cigarettes, played
friendly. Then he strung him up and beat him for an
hour, still asking questions.

He beat him until the man was unrecognizable, his
face a mush of bruised flesh and cuts gouged into bone,
one of his eyes an inch or so lower in his face than it had
been earlier in the day. Then he slashed his throat and
idly watched him bleed out, listening until the
streaming splatter of gore become a whispered, gentle
dripping.

He had learned of the entire chronology of the inci-
dent, in as much detail as the imbecile was capable of
summoning. Gunnar had memorized it. Then he visited
the Choristers Hall but the Irish Cops were there, and
he had to wait until they had taken away the bodies in a
wagon before he could break in.

He did that, and walked around the space, picturing

the events, playing it out in his mind. He was trying to understand the way this Conlon thought, the way he operated, his strategies and impulses.

He stood in the attic staring at the skylight through which Conlon had entered for at least ten minutes. He thought like a soldier, Gunnar realized. He had planned this and executed it, utilized his environment to best advantage, and taken away the only edge his opponent had.

Even then there had been a risk. He had faced four men, armed with guns. And by the sound of it he had been unarmed. Even the gambit of forcing them into darkness to fight him had been supremely risky. But he was good enough to make it work, to scare them and take them out one at a time so that the last one was terrified of him, and fled to face Gunnar rather than face Conlon.

He was an even more resourceful opponent than Gunnar had thought. So unexpected in this place. So inconvenient. He took risks. Coming in through the roof was a risk. But it had worked. He was lucky. But luck ran out. His would, soon.

And then it was more than luck, he knew. He felt something rare, for him, when he thought about Conlon. He felt anxious. This man was skilled. This man was trained in violence, and was evidently very good at using it. Gunnar would have to be careful, and be on his game, if he was to emerge from this situation as he had entered it.

Gunnar thought about what he knew of Conlon. He had to go deeper. There had to be a weakness, a way they could find him, and get to him. He was on some level, soft. He had let the last man go rather than killing him. But then he could see that Conlon had been sending a message, to him, to all of them. He wanted Gunnar's men to fear him. And he knew that it would work, too.

He must know what kind of men he was up against. Hired men. Hired men were fearful when it came to such things. They were there for money, they weren't believers, they weren't there for religion or country. Money.

That made them easier to spook. They would hear that one men had beaten four of them. He was being built up already, that one man. Only Gunnar's soldiers and the ex-Pinkertons would be skeptical of all this. But even some of them would have doubts. Their experience would tell them that any man who takes on four other men is either insane or special in some way. And they, too, would begin to fear him.

So Gunnar had to control the message. Conlon had let the last man go because he was soft, because he was lazy, because he was injured. That was what he would tell them.

Conlon was hiding from them because he was afraid of them, he would say. He was afraid to come out and fight them. Conlon was weak. Conlon was human. Conlon was just an Irishman, washed out of the Great War with shell shock.

But he needed more to go on if he was going to find him. More if he was going to beat him.

———

GUNNER HAD BEEN to two boxing gyms before he found the right one. This was on the northside of the city, with which he was far less familiar. Xavier's turf. It was near a church—as apparently everything was in Ireland. A five-minute walk from the Liffey. A poor area; one of many. Some of them jumped with lice and stank of shit, the children had bodies smeared with dirt. It was like something from the dark ages.

He wondered as he walked up if this was where Conlon came from. Some of the toughest men he had known came from places like this. They had fought all their lives. It became second nature. Not Gunnar, no. But men he had known. Some men he had killed.

He was carrying a duffel of his gloves, some shorts and a pair of boxing shoes, and he came in and acted all stupid and American, said he was staying in Dublin for a few weeks, and needed a place to train, and was it members only? And he could pay any fees, no problem, and yes he had fought in America, and yes he was happy to spar. He said his name was Joe.

There were posters on the walls, he noticed as he changed. Yellowing squares of paper, bisected by fold lines and peeling at the corners like dried-out stamps. Bills advertising bouts, mostly. The odd photograph of a young fighter, staring at the camera with all the sullen glory of youth. Lists of Irish surnames, stupid boxer nicknames, dingy venues. Paintings, too, clumsy renderings of anatomy and male profiles daubed in crude colors. And there he was—Tommy Conlon. On the Undercard of a fight, five years earlier.

It had been a few years since he'd been in a gym, and he wasn't in the kind of shape he would have been in his fighting days, but the rush of memory which surged over him upon entering the gym got him through the first half hour. It was brought on by the smell, mostly; the pungent glue of raw sweat, leather and oil, the faint medicinal odor underlying all else.

He remembered the routine...stretching for ten minutes, then jumping rope for fifteen, then shadow-boxing. Huffing and puffing after the rope, he loosened up a bit during the shadowboxing, his frame finally starting to feel like the one he remembered.

He had been good but never great, which meant that he would win in a fight with ninety-nine out of a hundred men in the street. Great was something he had brushed up against in the ring once, when had encoun-tered a colored fighter from Alabama by the name of Williams. Williams had been at least three inches shorter than him, and Gunnar estimated he had a few inches in reach over the man. But Williams had been a ghost to him. Gunnar had only laid gloves on him a handful of times over the three rounds they shared a ring. Williams was always moving, always ducking, always bobbing. Gunnar would spot him and throw a jab, but Williams was already a foot away from where the jab had arrived, and Gunnar had a glove cracking his mouth while his fist cut only air.

Three rounds of this. After two he was exhausted; hanging on, though his coach didn't know it. In the third, Williams read his body language and the weak-ness in his attempted shots, and cut loose with a fusil-lade of punches from all angles. The shots weren't hard —he had taken much, much harder—but there were so many, coming at him in such a sustained manner, that he couldn't take it, and meekly fell to the canvas when Williams found his chin with one solid uppercut.

As he climbed to his feet after being counted out and he and Williams shared a respectful embrace, he thought to himself that Williams would surely become one of the greats, that he was the greatest he'd ever fought.

Two years later, Williams was dead, shot by his girl-friend's husband in a backyard in Memphis. Not quick enough to dodge a bullet, then, Gunnar had thought.

Gunnar wondered how good Conlon was. Would it even matter? He was a much smaller man, and the advantage Gunnar held in that regard would give him greater destructive power and range if it should come to that. Not that it would. He would take Conlon dead in the pub, knifed by one of their dumb Dublin contrac-tors, as long as it meant he was dead.

After shadowboxing, Gunnar worked the heavy bag. He had forgotten the hypnotic pleasure of it, the report of the impact in either fist as he hammered it, the way it shuddered away from big hooks. His footwork was bad, he knew that, but if anything he was stronger now than he had been back then, and his power punching was transformed. His big shots rocked the bag with flat hollow thud after flat hollow thud.

He worked until sweat was dripping from his fore-head and gleamed upon his shoulders. He came back the next day and did the same thing. By the third day, the old trainers were nodding hello to him. On the fourth, two of them came to chat to him about boxing in America; the conditions, the money, the quality of the opposition. He was as helpful as he could be, and he even enjoyed the conversation once he had abandoned any hope of learning about Conlon today. This was groundwork; he saw that—gaining their trust, becoming invisible through ubiquity—so that when he asked for information they would hardly notice.

It took a week of training before he got what he needed. In that time, he had relaxed into the life of the gym. He enjoyed his time there, training even. The simplicity of it.

He had one of the older men—the one who was enamored of his own voice than anything else, whose life was empty enough he spent most waking moments at the gymnasium, even though he held no position there, the one who would talk on and on about fights he had seen, the correct way to throw a cross, when to retire—chatting as he prepared to warm up, chatting all through his warm up, chatting after the warm up.

Turner, the others called him. Turner could talk for Ireland. Gunnar gently directed the conversation around to the Dublin fighters whose names and faces cried out from the walls of the building. Then there was no stopping Turner. This was his subject, the object of intense focus throughout his adult life, and with a willing audience, he was unstoppable. Gunnar didn't even need to prompt him; he came to Conlon all on his own.

Before that he recited names, recounted the action of fights, even pantomiming the odd combination. He had been a fighter once himself, a few decades and a lot of pounds ago, and still he could move the right way.

He was in a sort of list when he mentioned Conlon — "the best I've ever seen" —and Gunnar was tiring of his constant self-mythologizing, but still alert and awake enough to ask him for more details on a few random fighters so that it might not appear too strange when he did the same for Conlon.

This list of the best he'd ever seen consisted of a

string of fighters whose main quality seemed to have been their courage and toughness.

"He could take a beating, so he could," Turner would say, or, "The bravest lad in Ireland." Gunnar wondered if Dublin—or Belfast, which Turner allowed perhaps even surpassed this city as a producer of fighters—produced any other kind of boxer, or was it all just toughened dullards, who led with their faces.

Turner answered that question for him. Turner didn't even know if Tommy Conlon was tough or brave. He'd only seen him get hit a handful of times. He was, apparently, the fastest fighter Turner had ever seen, like mercury in the ring, whipping punches at opponents in devastating flurries that ended most bouts in the opening two or three rounds. And he wouldn't be slapping people the way some fighters with fast hands did, no; he had thunder in his fists, ending every fight with a knock out and gaining a reputation early. Something scary about him, and his opponents all felt that.

Gunnar asked what had happened to him, why hadn't he heard of him, if he was so good.

"He was that good, so he was. There was talk of bringing him over to America. Everyone thought he'd make world champion. But there was some trouble and he went off to the war."

"Trouble?"

"Ahh, he got involved with some young one, belonged to a gurrier. He had to leave the country."

"He die? In the War?"

"Not at all, he's back in Dublin now. Doesn't fight anymore though. Not in a ring, anyhow."

"Undefeated, then? That's something to be proud of."

"'Tis. I've heard some say that he never faced any real opponents though. Sure how d'ye know if a man can take a punch if he's never had to take a punch?"

They talked for a while longer but Gunnar felt he had what he needed. Conlon was fast, strong, in and out. But Dublin boxing was a world of amateurs. There was virtually no professional boxing in the city. To move up to that level, boxers went across the water to England or across the Atlantic to America. The reputation the Irish had as fighters mainly came from emigrants, second generation Paddies in New York and London and Philadelphia. Conlon hadn't even gotten that far. His reputation rested entirely on a series of amateur fights years before. He had been good, yes, great—perhaps. But also untested. He had never been hit by somebody who could hit.

Gunnar and his people were going to hit Conlon like they had never hit anyone before. They just had to find him. He had an idea about that, too.

13

CONLON MET MOSSY OFF THE TRAIN, AND THEY SHOOK hands on the platform. Conlon had watched him disembark; this big bearish figure filling up the doorway of the carriage, and taking the steps down in one little hop, surprisingly light on his feet. Mossy had grown a beard, and it made his eyes gleam brightly between two thick masses of wiry blackness, giving him a lunatic air that was in keeping with some of the excesses in his personality. People swerved him on the platform, his size and general air of hirsute anarchism disturbed strangers at a glance.

It made Conlon laugh. "You look like the farmer you are."

"Ah, I can't be arsed with shaving anymore. I've no wife to be concerned with me face, so who cares how I look?"

They took a horse and cab from the station and Conlon explained the situation as they went.

Mossy's interruptions were all outraged. "Nuns, Tommy?"

"They're not selling little girls!"

"Fuckin' Yanks!"

Before they had even arrived at Father Brailsford's, Mossy said, "Well, you don't have to convince me. These boys need to be put down like fuckin' dogs. What's the plan?"

Conlon had known this would be his answer. Since returning from the trenches, Mossy lived a life of listless tedium on his family farm. He was a machine built to destroy, and incredibly good at it. He realized that Conlon would give him an opportunity to do what he was good at, and though the legality of it might be questionable, the morality of it would not be. He trusted Conlon. And Conlon trusted him. They had saved one another countless times in the War. And so Conlon had resolved only to call on his friend when he knew that there would be blood, and when he needed somebody who would not hesitate or question what they were doing, somebody who would kill happily and risk his life as if it was nothing. And that was Mossy.

"Well, I think I know where they're going to put the girls on a boat."

"And we're going there?"

Conlon nodded.

"And we're going to get these girls back?"

Conlon nodded again.

Mossy made a face of serious appreciation. "That sounds like a fine way to spend an evening."

Conlon laughed. That was the other thing about Mossy; he always made Conlon laugh.

In the kitchen at Brailsford's house, Conlon and Mossy talked things over. He had been a different man around the nuns, much to Conlon's amusement, and they had been pleasant but businesslike with him. Brailsford was out getting fed in some house in the Parish, as usual, and after a light tea of dressed crab and butter on brown bread, Conlon spread out the map he had taken from Choristers Hall on the dinner table, and explained the beginnings of his plan.

From the markings on the map, they were putting the girls on a boat at Queenstown. Conlon had already asked the priest and nuns if any of them knew of a place —any place—in that neck of the woods which was quiet and away from busy, prying eyes.

While Brailsford had made his excuses and left, Sister Diana had gone off to check on something but eventually told him that their order had a retreat on the Saltee Islands which was currently mostly empty, and would easily cater for a large group of people.

So they needed a vehicle large enough to transport all of the girls to Wexford from Queenstown. Conlon had been thinking of ways to steal one from the navy, but they would have enough problems getting the girls away from the Americans and out of Queenstown without having to do with the British authorities after them. And there existed the strong possibility that the Americans would be arriving in their own truck, and that all he and Mossy would need to do would be to liberate it from them.

There were too many unknowns for his liking at this stage. Too many elements he could not see or predict, too many things that could go wrong. He needed to be on the ground down there, he realized, to see how the place worked, before he could plan this properly. And they only had the shortest of windows, he knew. The girls might already be on a boat, already be somewhere upon the ocean.

They decided to leave the next day.

———————

GEAROID CAME WITH THEM. They had agreed that they would need another man, and since he could drive, and was intelligent and brave enough; and due to his ill-feeling towards the Americans, Gearoid seemed the best choice. Mossy looked him over, asked a few questions and nodded at Conlon almost instantly. He had been in a few fights—although nothing of this magnitude—and he would do what he was told. That would be necessary.

They took a train down in the morning, the sun bending light through the windows, Mossy snoring softly, asleep where he sat, Gearoid all twitchy nerves. Conlon closed his eyes and tried to rest.

At Mossy's feet lay his rifle, still wrapped in sheet, and a rucksack with the homemade explosives he had spent the night before concocting. He had explained to Conlon that he had perfected a "recipe", and that the substances were safe to transport as long as nobody set them alight. This meant of course that whenever Mossy lit a cigarette, Conlon watched him with tightly held breath.

Mossy loved such pointless risk. He had not felt that way during the War, when surviving each mission and indeed each day had seemed its own small miracle, but since their return home he craved that thrill, the sense of peril coating everyday life like a choking moss. He was addicted to it, it seemed. And so he went out of his way to put himself in foolishly dangerous situations. He started brawls. He literally played with fire. He took explosives that might prove useless on train journeys just to see what would happen. When Conlon questioned this, all he did was laugh.

Queenstown was crawling with Americans almost from the instant they left the station. The US Navy were in town on their way to the War in France, and sailors seemed to be in every shop and café, eyeing women on street corners, and smoking on walls by the harbor. The place rang with their broad, loud voices. Out in the bay their vessels sagged squat and hard in the water, studded with guns, busy with men readying for combat.

Conlon and Mossy squinted at one another while Gearoid tried not to gawp at it all. They wandered around the town, pretty, with fine views of the ocean and colorful houses up high above the harbor, and sought places where a bunch of Dublin street children might possibly be concealed by a band of armed men.

The main areas of interests were the warehouses near the docks, a few of which appeared run down and abandoned, and an old factory near the far outskirts. But once they had checked these more closely—breaking locks and smashing windows to get inside—Conlon realized that only one of them was a real possibility. The others were too small or would be too difficult to access. They were also perhaps a bit too far from the docks.

Mossy watched him ruminate on this.

"What're you thinking?"

"They could have gone already. I can't see where they'd stay. With that many girls..."

"Maybe they don't stay, ha? Maybe they just drive right up to a boat and get onto it."

"Like we did."

"Yeah, some of them are ex-military, ye said?"

"I did."

"That's what I'd do."

"That's what I'd do, too."

They looked at one another.

"Gonna be hard to get them off the docks," Mossy said, unable to conceal the excited anticipation in his voice.

Conlon nodded. "We need to go."

Mossy paid a visit to the Harbormaster's office to establish which vessel was bound for America. There were only two which were not military, and one of them was anchored off out in the bay. So they focused upon the other, the *Gibraltar*. It appeared dormant. No men were to be seen, no crew, no cargo, no activity of any kind. It was a great, pale hulk shifting slowly in the water; frightening in its stillness, rust angry in patches on its hull.

Conlon studied it for a minute or so, and then he looked at the others. "That's it."

Mossy nodded. Gearoid said, "How do you know?"

Conlon faintly shook his head. "I can feel it."

"When?" Mossy said.

"It has to be today. Tonight, probably."

He looked around. The docks were quiet, the early morning activity long faded, the American vessels far out, the warehouses locked up and silent.

Mossy grinned. "Where do you want me?"

Conlon pointed down the harbor. "They'll come from that way. Find a spot up high, on a rooftop."

"Any signal or just the usual?"

Conlon smiled at this. The usual meant as soon as the shooting started.

"Ah, I think you'll know. If you could attract the US Navy's attention that might help us."

Mossy said, "Oh, you're making this better and better, Tommy. It's just a shame I won't get to use my dynamite."

Gearoid's eyes could not have been any wider.

Conlon said, "I'll handle them down here, but you'll need a gun, and be ready. You have to get into the truck they're driving and get us out of here as quick as you can."

He looked at Mossy. "We won't have time to wait for you."

"I know. I'll meet you there."

"Are you sure? The US Navy might be after you."

"Let's hope so."

Conlon laughed at this, and nodded and he and Mossy shook hands. Then they both shook Gearoid's hand, too, to settle him down.

Gearoid said, "What's the plan? Is there a plan?"

Conlon had forgotten; though he and Mossy had a sort of shorthand, having worked together countless times, this would all seem a bewildering and terrifying blur of scary possibilities to Gearoid.

"They'll drive in with a transport of some kind and maybe an automobile or two as well. And a few gunmen."

"What's a few?"

"Six or seven."

"Could be as many as ten, twelve," Mossy said, grinning again.

Conlon shrugged. "We only need the transport. It'll probably be a lorry of some kind. We wait here. Mossy is on high ground. Once it starts, he'll take them out from up there, and provide some cover for me and you. If the Navy gets attracted by the noise, we'll slip away easier."

"They will," Mossy said.

"What are you going to do? Do we hide?" Gearoid said.

"Nothing fancy," Conlon said. "I walk up to them and I start shooting. Then Mossy joins in. If you're together enough to do something before you have to drive, then shoot some of them. That'll help. If you're not, that's fine, I'll take care of it. Just make sure you're ready to drive. Can you handle this, Gearoid?"

"Yeah, yeah I can."

"Right so. We'll sit."

He nodded to Mossy, who, with one eyebrow exaggeratedly raised, made his way off, his rifle hung loosely over his shoulder, still wrapped up. Conlon and Gearoid walked up the edge of the dock and finally sat, looking out to sea. Conlon kept his back to a huge steel bollard, so he was looking directly at the *Gibraltar* and the road onto the dock. Gearoid sat with his legs swinging over the water. They talked little as the day faded into night.

Around eleven, there was movement on the *Gibraltar*. Conlon saw men on deck. Voices carried across the water to them, scraps of sound with no words attached. And then, eventually, a deep rumbling noise, too, becoming rhythmic and continual. The engine.

"It'll be soon," Conlon said to Gearoid. He knew that nearby, Mossy had become still and ready.

"I'm scared, Tommy, I'm scared," Gearoid moaned, with the sense that the words were involuntary.

Conlon looked at him. "I know you saw your friends die, and it was bloody awful. This will be different. I know you don't really want to hurt any of them. Neither do I. But they want to take those girls across the sea and sell them like cattle. We could ask them nicely, but before we'd finished talking, they'd have shot us both. So we have to do this. I'll take the lead. Stay behind me and to my right. Don't shoot me. Getting shot hurts." He chuckled to break the tension, and Gearoid chuckled, too.

"Once Mossy starts shooting, they won't know which way to turn. I need you to keep an eye on the *Gibraltar*. If any men come up the gangplank, you put a bullet in them, ok? It'll all be over in twenty seconds. I'll get in the truck, then I'll call for you. And you need to drive. Can you do that, Gearoid?"

Gearoid nodded.

"It's alright to be scared. It's normal to be scared."

"You're not scared."

"Yes I am, every time. But once it starts, that goes away. You do the things you have to do to stay alive."

Gearoid nodded. He looked as if he might be sick.

Conlon said, "Check your gun. Take deep breaths. We'll be fine."

They heard the truck before it appeared around the far corner. Conlon stood, keeping slightly bent. He had the pistol in his hand, which was in his coat pocket, concealing it. He took his cap off, and folded it into the other pocket. Gearoid climbed shakily to his feet. Conlon put a hand on his shoulder and nodded. Then he returned his hands to his pockets and set off, still keeping low, following the line of the dock towards the *Gibraltar* and the truck, just pulling in, it's engine a flat petrol growl in the night.

Men were on the dock now. A handful had come from the vessel, and at least three had climbed from the lorry. Their voices were raised above the noise. They sounded jolly; inimitably American.

Conlon counted. He saw seven by the truck. At least one more behind the wheel. Probably one in back with the girls. And a few on the deck of the *Gibraltar*. They would be armed, though he could see no guns yet. He stayed bent low, and then when he was too close for that to work and he knew one of them might see him any moment, he put a little bit of whisky in his walk, and staggered along.

He heard them go quiet, just as the driver turned off the engine. He saw hands now, dipping into their coats, heading for waistbands. He was too far away still; he needed to be closer before he did anything. He hoped Gearoid was smart enough to keep his head down behind him.

The men were silent, watching him. Then a voice from one of them, "Hey mister. You need to stay away from this dock."

Ten more steps, Conlon thought.

He said, "Wha d'ya mean? Are youse yanks?"

Five steps.

"Mister. Don't come any closer."

Guns in at least four hands now, their eyes narrow with suspicion. In that second, the yellowness of the light, the grumbling sound of the *Gibraltar*'s engine, the cool kiss of sweat at the small of his own back all crystalized for him, and suddenly he had the gun out of his pocket and he fired four shots in rapid, startling fashion, shifting targets as he moved, so that in perhaps a second, four men were down.

It must have looked easy; smooth. He raised the gun, fired, shifted it slightly, fired, shifted again, fired; and then turned and fired one last time. All in just over a second. Four men hit. Then Mossy opened up, the flat crack of his rifle echoing down onto the dock and the water every few seconds, his usual, stunningly consistent rate of fire, and Conlon was running, bent low again, as the Americans began to shoot back.

Bullets kicked up stone behind him, and he rolled and came up shooting. One of the Americans ducked behind the truck, and Conlon crouched and sought to take it all in at a glance.

Rifle fire from the *Gibraltar*, Mossy was returning that. There were three or perhaps four Americans on the dock and alive, all behind cover. At least two behind the truck, one behind a bollard, and the fourth crouched inside the gangplank. The driver of the lorry was still in the cab, too, presumably armed.

Gearoid was crouched behind his own bollard, and Conlon was unsure if he'd even fired a shot yet.

A lengthy gunfight only increased the chances of one of the girls getting hurt. He waited for the American behind the truck to move and as soon as his face came into view, Conlon shot him in the head. He went over sideways.

Mossy's rifle barked every two or three seconds. Conlon stayed low. They had only a short time before others started to arrive—the American Navy, the Brits, the police—yet he could feel this at a stalemate already.

These Americans were soldiers, and showing it.

They understood cover and how to use it. He could see that already. He had taken them by surprise with his approach, but now they were digging in, and soon there would be reinforcements from the *Gibraltar*, despite Mossy's attentions. If he was going to get at them, and expose them, he was going to have to risk something that might lead to him getting hurt.

In the War, so many times he'd been in this situation; that feeling of teetering on the edge of defeat and his only option was a mad gambit, a dash into gunfire, a drop into a room full of armed men, a leap towards a sharpened blade. Each time he had done it. He had been different then...lost, careless, a part of him craving death. This was different. He had to save these girls. He could not do that with a bullet in his chest.

He looked around, thinking, desperate. He could think of nothing. But he always thought of something. Or he made something work.

Gearoid fired and one of the Americans responded. He knew what to do. He would have to run at them. Get around the truck and shoot them. Rely on Gearoid and Mossy to get the girls out, because he was bound to end up shot.

He looked at the truck. The American in the gangplank shot at him and the bullet whined off the rock. Lights were approaching, out in the harbor.

And then something exploded on the *Gibraltar*. He felt the intake of air an instant before the explosion and cringed instinctively, some sense memory from the war activated. Then the sky was retina-flash bright, a burn of hot air pulsed over him, the noise monstrous.

He moved.

The American in the gangplank was on fire,

screaming and slapping at himself. Conlon ran around the back of the lorry and the men there were bewildered and unprepared, reeling from the sensory overload of the explosion. Calmly, he shot both, then wrenched the door of the cab open and clambered up, gun pointed at the occupant. The driver looked as if he had been weeping, and his hands were up already.

"Out," Conlon said. "Run. Tell them Conlon says hello. GO!"

The driver exploded out the other door of the cab, and Conlon shouted at Gearoid, beckoning for him to approach.

Mossy's rifle was still firing, and Conlon realized what had happened. Mossy had noticed something on the deck of the *Gibraltar* and deliberately targeted it. An oil drum, a cache of explosives...something flammable. That was luck, and Mossy's experience. Mossy had got his explosion anyway, without even having to use his homemade explosives. He would be delighted, Conlon knew.

There was no firing from the *Gibraltar* now, but he could hear men shouting. The lights were closer on the water—the American navy had sent boats to investigate. Conlon took aim and fired in their direction, knowing Mossy would notice and do the same. He did, and an instant later one of the lights on the boats was snuffed out with a muffled pop.

Gearoid scrambled up into the cab, and Conlon nodded. "Let's get out of here."

Gearoid was breathing heavily, but he got the truck started right away, and they were off, turning in a tight loop back towards the way they had come. Conlon swung into the cabin and before he closed the door he held up an arm, saluting Mossy, somewhere off above them in the darkness.

Behind them, as they drove away, the noise of battle grew louder again. Conlon looked back, craning his head out the window. The muzzle flashes fluttered in the black, shadowed by the hulk of the *Gibraltar*. The gunfire intensified. The US Navy had come to investigate the gunfire, been fired upon themselves, and responded.

14

HE WAITED UNTIL THEY WERE A FEW MILES OUT OF TOWN before he signaled to Gearoid to pull over. They were on a long, straight, quiet road; and it was late now, so there would be virtually no traffic. The wind had picked up, and trees whipped back and forth overhead as Conlon creaked the door open and dropped down, then walked around to climb up into the back of the lorry.

He had to lift a tarpaulin cover away, and the girls were huddled in darkness. He could see none of them until he shone his torch into the murk. Twelve confused, frightened young faces blinking and squinting in the glare, silent in their fear and confusion.

"Girls," he said, gently. "It's alright. We came to get you away from them."

The girls all seemed to talk at once then—but entirely in whispers; weeks of terror and punishment having taught them well. It was a disturbing experience, standing in the darkness, the hissing of these frightened girls surrounding him.

He lifted his hands. "I'm a friend, I'm a friend. Sister Diana—you remember her?"

There were sounds suggesting they did.

"She asked me to find you. So here I am. Is everybody ok?"

They were ok. Tired and scared but unhurt.

"Good. We have a few more hours of driving, and then we'll be taking a boat for a little trip, but then we'll be stopping for the night and for a few days, alright? Try to sleep now."

He left the torch with them, but as he was about to climb down, a single, cracked voice asked, "Did you get the others?"

He stopped. "What others?"

"The other girls."

"What other girls?"

Again the torrent of whispers, and he caught only the odd word.

He held up a hand. "Please, girls. One of you tell me."

The deepest, most confident whisper asserted itself. He saw that it was the girl holding the flashlight. "There were other girls. They came in later. Before they moved us."

"In Dublin?"

"I think so."

The others murmured agreement.

"Do any of you know where?"

Shaken heads and negative sounds.

The flashlight girl said, "A warehouse, I think. They kept us in the dark, but it was big and echoey."

"We had to wear blindfolds when we left the cage," another voice insisted.

"How many other girls were there?" Conlon asked.

"Ten or twelve," one of them said.

The flashlight girls spoke again. "They were really young, mister."

"How young?"

"Some of them were ten or twelve. A few of them were closer to eight."

He closed his eyes.

———

THEY ARRIVED at Kilmore around midnight, and as Sister Diana had promised, a man named Dawson was waiting in a little shack near the quay, smoking cigarettes with a gas lamp by his feet. It was a still, close night here, the wind having blown itself out, and he was monosyllabic but smiling, seemingly untroubled by the hour or the strangeness of the party who greeted him.

The moon was high and the boats in the tiny harbor gleamed and flickered under its white gaze. The sea was a constant echoing void which seemed to surround them here.

Dawson shook Conlon's hand, shook Gearoid's hand, and made an awkward little curtsying motion at the girls, cap in hand. He said he would take care of the lorry, and led them to his boat—a fishing boat by the looks of it—which felt low and heavy in the water once all of them had climbed in.

The girls had been dozing and distant upon arrival, but the walk down to the quay and the scent of the sea in the humidity of the night seemed to revive them somewhat, and for the first time there was some excited whispering amongst them.

As it cut across the waves, Conlon let the boats sway and fall lull him. He was tired. That familiar euphoric post-battle fatigue setting in now. He closed his eyes and saw it all once again—muzzle flashes lighting the dark and bodies tumbling. And then the chilling news again —more girls. This was not over.

———————

THERE WAS a rudimentary jetty once they had made their way between crags and through the heavy, jerking waves that seemed to hang immediately around the island like a hard collar. Conlon groped for it in the dark and felt that it was stone, cool and slick with oceanic damp. The island was something you could feel more than see; its solid presence almost comforting from the uneven, manic sea.

When they were all ashore, Dawson took his lamp from the boat and, chuckling to himself, headed off into the island's interior. Conlon sensed Gearoid's look in the dark. He felt close to the young man now. Battle did that; bonded men quickly. They had suffered together, survived together. Nobody else would ever experience that fight as they had done; the quiet wait on the dock, the sudden violence, Mossy laying down death from a height, their joyous drive out of town.

They watched Dawson's lamp sway away up some sort of path, then they followed behind, bundled in a mass, the girls still audibly excited between them and the lamp's movement.

There were nuns awaiting them, tired eyes and comforting smiles for the girls; with tea and toast and butter in the large, draughty dining room. Exhausted,

Conlon and Gearoid sat apart, accepted the tea from the sisters, and wearily watched as the girls calmed down, their energy levels slowly dropping until one of the nuns—Conlon didn't know any of their names—shepherded the entire group out of the room and up the stairs to their sleeping quarters.

The two men sat up for another hour or so, silent, allowing their systems to flatten out the adrenaline that still coursed through them. Conlon found himself thinking of Orla. He did that every day, anyway, but the proximity of death always brought her vividly to mind. On some level, in some far down, deep and childish, superstitious part of himself, he felt that she was waiting for him, that he should have died with her. That had been his impulse, that day, the day he had lost her. He had leapt blindly after her. Wanting to save her, hoping she might still be alive? Perhaps, to some extent.

But also...also throwing himself into oblivion because he did not want any life without her. And felt that if she were going, then he should go, too.

The Major had known this about him. The Major had seen that he was unafraid of death, however fiercely he fought to survive, and intuited that it had to do with a loss, a profound loss. And the Major had used this.

And now? Now he himself used it. Less often, of course. But his bravery, such as it was, came partly from an apathy. If he died, he would be with her.

This was the great unsaid when he had spoken to Sister Maude about violence and death; something he felt he could never say to another person. She was why he had never said the things any sane man would have said to Theresa. She was why he pursued women he could not keep, women he did not want to keep. And she was the thing he focused on now, to calm him, to still his mind and his heart so that he would be able to sleep without the cordite and blood in his head.

———

MOSSY ARRIVED EARLY the next morning. When Conlon descended the shadowed backstairs into the white glare of the kitchen, there he was, squinting and calm, a cup of coffee in his hand, at the kitchen table. He had walked most of the way, he said, and slept in a ditch. The nuns regarded him as if he was some holy man emerged from the desert.

Over porridge with strawberries picked on the island, the nun told them, to which Mossy raised his eyebrows in mock appreciation, he described the chaos that had followed their escape: the American Navy and the police battling the survivors on the *Gibraltar*; a general sense of mayhem throughout the town. Conlon knew him well enough to know that he had thoroughly enjoyed the spectacle.

They curtly discussed the detail of the firefight.

Halfway through this discussion, the noise level soared as most of the girls came into the dining room next door, chattering and laughing.

Mossy nodded at Conlon.

"This was a good thing," he said.

Conlon said, "Sure I told you."

"So what next. Are we goin' to finish these gobshites, or what?"

THEY LEFT the girls on the Saltees and returned to Dublin that afternoon. While Gearoid and Mossy played cards on the train, Conlon watched the landscape flicker by and tried to decide his next move.

So far it had felt like a cagey fight; everything on the outside. They had engaged the enemy but never outright, never quite face to face. Even the battle they had just survived—it had been what the Major had always called "bandit" warfare. A small group, striking hard and fast against a superior force, then escaping quickly. It had not been decisive. The enemy was still there, still strong.

Conlon knew that that face to face encounter would have to happen if this fight was to be won. He had been assuming that Xavier would be the one to land a decisive blow, and he knew he should check behind the bar at Kavanaghs, as Devereux had suggested, then contact Finch, and see if any coordination might be useful. They had to be planning a move against the Americans soon, if it was to be of any use.

And he knew that what they had done the night before would only mean that the Americans would double all efforts to find them and kill them. He felt no fear about this. Only a grim acceptance. He was in this now. He wanted it finished.

Conlon was worried that the Americans would be watching the trains, so, after disembarking, they made their way across a couple of tracks and left the station through a goods entrance, emerging out into the world via a side street. Mossy hailed a horse and cab for him and Gearoid, and said he planned on getting pissed in some pub "near the docks," then disappeared.

THERE WAS AN ODDLY celebratory mood when he arrived back at Father Brailsford's house, and it reminded him of years before, entering a pub after he had won a fight. The way people looked at him, the atmosphere of glowing admiration, people's eyes on his face, hoping to catch a nod from him...

The sisters knew what had happened, to some extent, and although they abhorred the violence, or said they did, at any rate, Conlon was acutely aware that this was why they had come to him. And he had done it. But he could not allow his eyes to meet Maude's. Not yet.

As soon as was polite, he escaped upstairs. He changed, and washed and rested a little, and then went down for dinner.

Father Brailsford seemed strained, his jollity forced and somewhat brittle. He made a few jokes that felt more like attacks. Conlon had a feeling he recognized from being around Xavier's people years before—the way innuendo was always aggressive; the way jokes were weapons if deployed correctly.

He looked at the priest as he sipped at his soup and saw something in his eyes that made him start. Could it have been fear? But then the conversation changed course; the sisters were pressing Gearoid for details of the girls and their reaction to the Saltees, and Conlon's attention was diverted.

They were just starting the main course when it happened.

He felt it before he was conscious of anything strange; a sense that something was wrong. This was a feeling he knew from the war—it was as if his blood reacted to something in the air, a drop in pressure, the scent of adrenaline; and he responded.

He was instantly alert. His eyes and ears reached out beyond the table, the room, further into the house. The chatter he had only seconds before been enjoying had fallen away and now all he was aware of was the view out of the window he could see by craning his neck and looking through the open doorway and into the kitchen.

It was twilight. A steely gray had stolen into the garden, and he maintained his stare, focused on the green bushes, almost blue in the lowering gloom, springing in the lazy breeze. And there it was—the flicker of a figure, keeping low, and Conlon was standing.

Sister Maude, ever alert to his movements, reacted. "What is it?"

"There are people outside." He felt alarmed enough that he did not care if he scared them. "We need to move."

The others at the table looked at him and at one another, a little baffled, unsure if he was joking.

Not wanting to shout, conscious that time was precious, he said again, with a hiss of intensity, "There are men outside. They almost certainly aren't friendly. You need to stand up and follow me immediately."

Gearoid was up and moving for the stairs in an instant. Conlon moved to the door and said over his shoulder, "Turn off the lamps."

A moment later, the room was dark. He peered out into the garden, which was still now. He needed to know how many there were, if they were armed. He wished Mossy were here, instead of in some pub somewhere in town.

The stairs creaked and Gearoid was back in the room. He handed Conlon his revolver, and his own gleamed in the dark. The presence of the guns affected everybody. Father Brailsford whispered and slumped against the wall. Sister Diana supported him.

"What are we to do, Thomas?" she asked sharply.

"You all go with Gearoid."

He looked at Gearoid. "Take them out the front door. Wait until you hear me start up. I'll distract them. Then go as fast as you can. If you see anyone, shoot them."

Sister Maude had her hand on his arm. "No, Tommy, no, they'll kill you..."

He took her hand gently. "I'm not that easy to kill, Maude."

"They followed me, they must have," she said with a cracked sob.

"It doesn't matter now. They're here for me. They're not interested in youse. Get out and keep going. When you get to a phone or the police station ask for a Detective Barry and mention my name. You can trust him."

"No, Tommy."

"Go. I'll be alright."

She was staring at him, her hand still in his.

"Maude," he said. "This is what I do. I don't want you anywhere near this."

He released her hand and his eyes met Gearoid's. He nodded and then he moved through the darkening house, mindful now of every sigh and moan of a floorboard, and took the stairs two at a time.

Upstairs he crept into Brailsford's bedroom.

He was wondering why they hadn't attempted entry yet, why they hadn't used a sniper, what they were waiting for. If he was lucky they were a reconnaissance team who had got cocky and decided to take him themselves. If these Americans did have the ex-army backgrounds he had heard about and seen evidence of the night before, then they wouldn't have been so clumsy.

He crept forward and inched his head up to look out the window down into the garden. One of them was climbing the big oak tree in the corner of the garden. One was lying in the grass, pistol leveled at the back door. He assumed there were at least one or two more he couldn't see.

Suddenly he felt the rage return; the feeling he had experienced on the island when he thought about the young girls and had wanted to return to the *Gibraltar* and massacre the lot of them. He needed to make a lot of noise. He needed them all focused on him so that Gearoid could lead the rest of them away.

He bit it down for a moment, and then he nodded and for once, he went with it—the fury and wildness in him. He would let it lead him for this moment and see what happened.

He stood, took a few steps back and jumped right through the window and into the sky above the garden.

The noise was ferocious in the evening quiet. The shattering glass was joined by ripping wood as most of the window frame was torn from the wall and jack-knifed to the ground below. He heard a gunshot jumbled up with all the other sounds as he fell.

He landed and rolled and came up firing, glass tinkling around him. The one in the tree took a bullet in the side as he turned in fright. He fell like a game bird; straight, heavy.

Conlon was moving already, his senses all exploding as he tried to take in the scene and process it.

Men were moving towards him. The one on the ground shot at him, and then another slammed into his chest with a shoulder and he lost his gun; spinning off into the flower beds. Two more coming; the one on the ground standing and yelling at them to give him a clear shot.

Conlon was surrounded. Four men, all but one unarmed, two of them much bigger than him. He understood why they had been so confident.

He felt that rage warm him, and he smiled.

"You should have let him shoot me," he said, and moved.

He feinted with a jab at the big one in front of him, and instead rolled under his own clumsy strike to piston a brutal uppercut into the man's throat. He went over backwards in an instant, choking and coughing as he kicked for a breath that would never come.

The gunman fired in a panic and the bullet whined off the house. Conlon had ducked and now, swinging up, he grabbed the gun elbow and wrenched the arm up and back, snapping it like timber. The man screamed, a sound almost as high-pitched as the ricochet.

A third had swung a wild punch at Conlon which grazed his shoulder, and followed it by groping for him, a big hand at his throat.

Conlon still had one arm locked behind the gunman's shattered limb, and now he whipped his free hand behind the other man and grabbed a fistful of his hair, then smashed him face first into the gunman. Their faces clacked together in an eruption of teeth and bone, their cries a mingled shriek. Conlon threw one to the grass and hit the former gunman in the gut, the kind of shot that would rupture something. He let him melt to the ground, then turned, took one calm step and stamped on the other one's groin.

The fourth one was scrabbling in the flower beds for Conlon's gun, but he realized that he had a problem when the noise of combat ceased, and he whirled, flinging a fistful of dirt and stone at Conlon. Momentarily blinded, Conlon groped at his eyes and the man charged him, swinging a wild haymaker at his head.

It hurt but Conlon had taken worse and he knew that the man's knuckles would almost certainly be in worse shape than his skull. He pivoted away as if in the ring, and squinted through eyes sore with grit. The figure came at him again.

Conlon slipped his punch and threw a raking hook to the body. He heard it crack ribs and retreated. Another man was in the garden now. He had come around from the front of the house and he stood for a moment, surveying the carnage, before stepping forward to stand beside the other one, raising his hands as fists in front of his face.

Conlon nodded grimly and stepped in again. He ducked the punch thrown by the new man and threw the same body hook at the first as before. The man cried out and slumped immediately, cradling his torso now. Conlon, still blinking, his vision still compromised, danced around him. The new fighter circled.

He was tall and lean, his movements quick. Conlon feinted and he covered. Conlon made to go left and he saw that off, moving his feet. He was a fighter then. And an overconfident one.

Counting on his Conlon's aggression, the man made a bold choice, launching a combination with a flickering jab and following behind it with a sharp cross.

Conlon leant away and then swarmed him; four unanswered punches and then a massive straight to his mouth to sprawl him back, stunned against the tree. Then Conlon ruined his knee with an angled stamp.

Turning, he ran through the garden and along the side of the house to the front. Gearoid and the sisters were huddled behind a bush and they screamed at him to hide. Brailsford lay dead on the path. Conlon skidded onto the grass and fell onto the seat of his pants, scrambling backwards for cover as two shots punched earth and scraps of grass into the air.

There was a sniper somewhere. That was the single shot Conlon had heard as he came out the window. In the back garden, the gunman had no shot. Out here they were in his field of fire somehow.

"You all alright?" he shouted.

"Father Brailsford's shot," Gearoid said.

The sniper fired again.

"Where are the shots coming from?" he asked.

Gearoid said, "Behind us somewhere."

Conlon flicked his head out, low down to take in as much as he could in an instant. The shot chipped stone from the house where his head had been in the same moment that he withdrew it, and he lay there, panting. There would surely be DMP here soon. The local middle class residents would be scandalized by a gun battle in the priest's garden.

Conlon retraced his steps to the back garden, past the groaning, twisted men on the ground, retrieved his gun from the flowerbed where it lay half-embedded, and crashed low through the back gate and into the laneway that ran along behind the houses, parallel with the road. It was unpaved and uneven, and little clouds of dust followed him as he ran along, a skittering of pebbles thrown up by his feet like rainfall.

The sniper would be either on the roof of the bank, looking down on the main road, or in one of the upstairs windows. They were the best elevated positions in the direction of the gunfire, and would offer a good view of the priest's house. Conlon had noticed them on his first few moments outside the house, when he was recovering from the flu. He had not, then, marked them as obvious potential spots he would need to attack over the next week or so—more that some idling professional part of his mind constantly played this game; looking for fields of fire, bottlenecks suitable for ambushes, high ground, etc.

But now here he was, racing down the laneway, bent over, with a revolver tight in his hand, fully intent on killing a man.

He was grimly determined to do this as quickly as possible; and if you had not known him, you might have read his demeanor and bearing as that of someone who was irritated by this inconvenience. All fear was gone. He was angry now.

The lane came out onto the main road about fifty meters from the bank, which was on the other side of the street and dominated a row of shops from its corner.

Conlon didn't pause or hesitate. He ran straight across the road and scaled the fencing between a shuttered butchers shop and a tailors. Finding himself in a yard filled with wooden pallets and crates, he moved through the space and hopped the back fence.

He was in another lane now. This ran along behind the shops and was wider and bore the marks of consistent use; deliveries came this way, staff left by the back doors, the shops left their rubbish in bins here, and there were the smells of the detritus of commerce— decaying meat, timber, oil. He looked around and took in the important details. Then, he moved again.

Keeping low, he quickly headed towards the bank.

The sniper made it easy for him. He must have deduced that his targets were not going to move out of cover and that the police would be arriving soon, and so he abandoned his position, and was walking out of the back gate, his rifle disassembled and in its case, when Conlon arrived at the back of the building.

He looked like a soldier; his hair shorn, eyes sharp and mobile, face brown with sun. He saw Conlon, their eyes meeting as if they were at a party, with a disarmingly casual slowness, and instantly went for a pistol.

But Conlon's gun was already in his hand, and he raised it, shooting the sniper in the head, once.

He went back to the house, but they were all gone. He stood in the gateway for a moment, baffled, not believing it. Father Brailsford's body lay still, arm folded over his face as if in a deep, silent sleep. The blood pooled around him had been trodden in, and footprints in red led up the path and to the street where Conlon stood.

The sisters and Gearoid were all gone.

He walked gingerly into the garden, around Brailsford, around the side of the house. All of the men he had fought in the garden were gone. He couldn't comprehend it at all.

His brain kept sticking on it. How long had he been gone? Three minutes?

More of them must have come. In a lorry? Why had they taken the Sisters? Why not just kill them?

He thought of Maude.

A wave of nausea rippled through him and he bent over and retched, the sourness rising onto his tongue. Hands on knees, he squeezed his eyes shut and gritted his teeth. The nausea passed, replaced by anger. Rage. He wanted to kill them all, every last one of them.

He had to move. He had to find Mossy.

The Americans wanted a war. They were soldiers. They thought that they knew war, knew what it was, what it meant, what it could be. Well, Conlon knew war. Conlon had seen its true face. Conlon had excelled at it. And since returning, he had only flirted with the warrior inside himself. He had been afraid to let him loose, afraid to unleash war back here, home, in this world.

But the Americans had pushed him, now. If the Americans wanted a war...well, Conlon was going to find his friend, a man who loved war and the desperate freedom it gave him, and then the two of them were going to give the Americans what they had been asking for.

15

THE ANGER SUSTAINED HIM ONTO A RATTLING, HALF-empty tram, and then the adrenaline began to drain and he was left with a hollow and uncertain sensation. He found a seat by a window but he was blind to the world; the light ebbing from the sky and the sudden gurgle and rush of night over the streets, the couples arm in arm on their way to dances, pictures, shows, the other passengers smoking and coughing and shaking newspapers. He saw none of it, his eyes glazed as he went over what had happened, what might happen next, what it would lead to.

Talking animatedly to another passenger, the conductor approached him and Conlon paid without thought or glance, an automatic gesture he would have no memory of minutes later. He was planning, yes, but also recriminating—what he could have done differently, mistakes he had made. And occasionally the anger would surge through him and he wanted to go straight to the Shelbourne and kill this man, their leader, whatever the consequences might be.

He did not.

Instead he missed his stop, jolting along with eyes only for the glass of the window, the tram interior reflected within, the black night beyond.

Once he had realized his error and disembarked, his walk was a short one. A pub off the Quays, still busy at this time, smoky and loud with chatter and laughing. He could hear that even before he had entered— muffled behind the wood and stained-glass of the door —and the sudden gush of noise when he opened it was startling.

Green and burnished brown was all he could see from the doorway; heads bowing in huddled conversation and thrown back, the better to down pints, a fog of smoke hanging in the room, the smell of oats and cigarettes and people.

He had never been here before, and he caught the glances a couple of the drinkers cast his way as he crossed the floor from the entrance to the bar. The barman, stout and white haired, his red face cross-hatched with exploded blood vessels took a moment or two to serve him, busy as he was entertaining two other men of a similar age in the corner.

"What can I get you, son?"

"I need to see Finch."

His poker face was excellent and never rippled. "Ah, I've never heard of any Finch. Will you be wanting a drink?"

"Listen, you are wasting time I don't have. I need to see Finch. It's important. I'm asking nicely."

"I told you—"

"You've been told to say that. I understand. But you

need to get me to Finch now or I'm going to start breaking things."

The barman gave an involuntary chuckle, more of surprise than amusement, at that. Then he stepped back and raised his eyebrows at somebody down the bar, then nodded at Conlon.

Conlon actually said, "Don't—"

He didn't want this. He had already spilled enough blood today. His knuckles ached. He knew there was more to come, probably much worse, and he was tired. He didn't want to hurt whoever was approaching right now, determined to hurt him.

He looked over. Two big men, the pub crowd parting to allow them passage. Typical Finch muscle. Conlon sighed and turned to face them.

One older, mid-forties perhaps, wearing a face lined with cracks and years, the other young and soft like a big baby.

And then suddenly the older one stopped and put out a hand to stop his partner.

"Tommy Conlon? Are you Tommy Conlon?"

Conlon nodded.

"Bleedin' hell, I thought it was you. Saw you fight many times, many times. You were something." He went to the bar. "Gimme that pen and some paper, Bobby."

He bent down and wrote something, the barman gaping at him, his young partner the same. When he was finished, he gave the paper to the younger man, who looked somewhat affronted.

"Who is he?" he asked.

The older man pulled him in close and hissed at him. "That is Tommy Conlon. He used to be a fighter, and if we'd tried to put our hands on him we'd both be on that fucking floor now. And Finch has been expecting him to show up. So you go to Delahoy, and you tell him Tommy Conlon is here. And you bleedin' hurry, right?"

The young man nodded and was off without a word. The older one looked at Conlon. "Sorry. Let's go in the back. You want a drink?"

"Tea if you have it."

"Tea we can do."

They waited in a little kitchen at the back, both sat on small, fragile wooden chairs, and the man, whose name was Jimmy, just wanted to talk boxing. Conlon was a little surprised, but he went with it, and after a short while, to his surprise, he had forgotten why he was there, and his rage, and he found himself enjoying talking to this man and drinking his tea.

Finch arrived perhaps twenty minutes after Conlon had asked for him.

He came in without any ceremony, placed his hand on Jimmy's shoulder, and waited for Jimmy to excuse himself before sitting on the same chair, his slight frame relaxed and casual.

"So, we've been waiting for you to get in touch."

"Whatever you've got planned, it needs to happen now."

"The Americans?"

Conlon nodded.

"Why now, Tommy? We've heard about a gunfight out by the coast near Bray. A dead priest is what people are saying, and another man nobody knows. Would you be knowing anything about that, now?"

"I hit them and they hit me back."

"Were you there?"

Conlon nodded again.

"How do they work?"

"Firepower and manpower. Send too many men. Have back-ups. If you're going up against them, Finch, have your people hit hard and get out quickly. Either that or send everything you've got and fucking destroy them."

Finch was watching him.

"It's not like Tommy Conlon to be so concerned with what the other side is doing."

"They've got my attention. They work like a military unit. Operations are planned. They're not that good but they have the guns and the numbers to use that. So you have to hit them hard when you hit."

"I understand. What are you going to be doing while I'm taking care of their soldiers?"

"Do you have targets?"

"We've been watching. We know most of the right places to hit. What about you?"

"The bossman."

Finch shook his head. "Be realistic, Tommy. He has a whole floor of the Shelbourne to himself. Armed guards all over it."

"Yeah, I've heard that alright."

Finch watched him levelly for a moment and then chuckled.

"Even you are not that good."

"Well, don't worry about me, then. How's tomorrow night?"

"Tomorrow night can be done. We'll kick off at eight, shall we say?"

"Eight. Just one thing. They have some young girls

somewhere. I'm hoping that they'll be in the Shelbourne but this man seems far too careful for that. Tell your boys to look out for them, will you? They'll be locked up, under guard."

"I can do that. Been nice knowing you, Tommy." Finch stood to leave. "I always thought I'd be the one who got to kill you."

Conlon laughed at that. "Eight tomorrow night. Don't forget now. I'll see you, Finch."

"Tommy."

———

MOSSY HADN'T RETURNED to his room yet when Conlon checked in on him. He was out carousing somewhere, Conlon knew, drinking his bodyweight in whiskey and more than likely clumsily trying to talk to a woman or a young man or expertly provoking some unsuspecting men into starting a fight with him so he could teach them a lesson.

The landlady of his boarding house—all pursed lips and silent disapproval—invited Conlon in to wait for him, and insisted he sit in the drawing room at the front of the house. She kept the lights low, and in the yellowing dimness, with nothing to read and nobody to talk to, Conlon found himself drifting off to sleep within a few moments of sitting down.

He fought it at first. His chin would dip and he would snap up and blink rapidly, as if to clear the tiredness away. Then less than a minute later, it would happen again. A blink would become a period without consciousness, he would wake and force his eyes to open wider than before—and then he would fall asleep again.

Finally sleep came properly; in an enveloping wave, and he went with it, let it take him.

———

GUNNAR COULD NOT SLEEP.

He hated this room. They had rented a big house on Mount Street and many of the American men slept there, sharing rooms, giving it the odd feel of a barracks —although the men largely came and went as they pleased on their days off, and it was not uncommon for Gunnar to return at night and find a bunch of them playing cards and drinking in the dining room.

Gunnar was in the attic, in what he was assured had been the servants quarters. A garret, they said. It had big windows and a nice view of the hills to the south of the city that the natives called mountains. On a clear night there were stars visible in the same direction, when the city glow had ebbed. But it had ugly patterns on the walls, and whenever a pigeon landed on the roof it was as if it was in bed with Gunnar. Each of its scratchy little footsteps echoed through his skull, the scuffs of its wings like his own pulse.

But that wasn't why he was awake. He had slept fine in this room many nights. He was awake because it was nagging at him. Conlon, again. Conlon.

He knew he ought to be happy. They had made progress, at last. Had hurt Conlon, had him where they wanted him, to some extent at least. The attack on the priest's house had been a success, and they had hostages, leverage. But Conlon had survived, had escaped. Conlon had faced off against six of his men and somehow, impossibly, he had won.

Gunnar had sent nine of them in total. And he had fought with himself over whether that was too many; was he being cautious? Had the men's silent fear of this mythic Irishman gotten to him? No. He knew there would be others there. They would need a driver, and they would need crowd control. A sniper, just in case. So he sent his boys. Americans. Ex-Pinkertons, ex-military to a man. And when they came back two of them were dead, their bodies in the back of the truck alongside the prisoners.

Donovan, the sniper, didn't come back at all. The others were all banged up—broken bones, ruined faces, internal injuries. Blood and bruises made some barely recognizable. Only the two who had stayed with the truck were untouched, and that was only because Conlon hadn't been aware of their presence.

Gunnar called the doc for them and then he went around as they were being treated, questioning each of them in turn, so that he would have a picture of what had happened.

At first it sounded barely believable—Conlon had jumped out of a first floor window and fought them in the garden, in the open. But they all told him the same. And they were terrified of him; he had torn through them like they were children, seemingly in a blind rage, a battle fury that had meant the fight was over in seconds.

Gunnar had listened and thought and planned. Sooner or later, he saw, unless he got exceptionally lucky, he and Conlon would come face to face. And though he understood his own capabilities, he was also beginning to see that Conlon would be an extremely difficult opponent. So he would need advantages.

Then, as he ruminated on this, another thing occurred to him—this was the first time he had heard that Conlon had shown any emotion. They all said he had been angry, insanely furious, even, which meant they had managed to provoke him. He could be gotten at, he could be prodded and hurt until he wanted to hurt somebody in return. That was good; that was a response Gunnar understood and could work with.

But still, Conlon was out there, alive. And he would be coming. It bothered Gunnar that he didn't know where or how or when.

The hostages. He hadn't even bothered to meet them yet. Nuns. They were a wrinkle he was unsure about. He knew that if he told Swaney, they would be dead. Swaney would see them as an unacceptable risk. But Gunnar saw them as an insurance policy. Something that might keep Conlon in check when the time came.

And thinking on this, Gunnar was struck by a new realization, something he had not thought before. He was approaching this all wrong. His pride was the problem. He was not accepting that perhaps Conlon was simply better at this than he was. Conlon was a soldier, and he could beat Gunnar in a war. And so far Gunnar had let him have his war, had allowed Conlon to fight his way out of every situation, because all he had needed to do was fight.

Gunnar had to change the nature of the conflict. Somehow create a situation in which Conlon had no clue they were still warring, even as Gunnar's fingers tightened around his neck.

Excitement began to bubble in him as he realized the possibilities of this. He thought, for the first time in days, that he may actually come out of this well. Very soon after that, he was asleep.

16

Conlon awoke the next morning, still slumped in the chair in the dining room. It was very early—the light had that pale glow that gave everything a fuzzy edge you only saw as day and night mingled. Someone had covered him in a blanket in the night.

The landlady came in as he was stirring, took the blanket without a word and brusquely folded it while she spoke in his direction.

"There'll be breakfast in half an hour if you'd be hungry."

He tried to reply but his voice was cracked and raspy. Eventually he whispered a thanks.

He began to eat alone in the room; tea and toast with butter, porridge made with milk and jam stirred in, a boiled egg and some bacon. Mossy, who always seemed as mysteriously light on his feet as a country priest, drifted in while he was eating and silently sat across from him, nodding mute thanks when the landlady placed food before him.

They ate, slowly and without speaking, as they had

done on innumerable mornings in France and Turkey and sometimes in places when they were unsure of where exactly they were, borders rendered meaningless by conflict. And Conlon thought that their friendship was defined by that—they were together in the hours before they would face death, they faced death together, and they were together in the aftermath.

And they had killed many men together.

It was odd to awaken and find that his troubles were intact within him, as if they had lain undisturbed inside a vault in his head as he dreamt. Whereas sleep washed good things away. When he had enjoyed a moment— the first time he had kissed Orla, winning his first fight, a day at Sandymount as a boy with his ma and da—that moment was held, lingering in his soul and imagination until he had fallen asleep. But once he had slept on it, the night and sleep and dreams stole some of it from him, and it was indelibly cast in a new form. It became memory, it became the past, and it could never be recaptured or experienced again.

But a bad experience...they seemed to rise up out of slumber fully armed, just as troubling and awful as they were the day before. It took a weight of time; of days, weeks, months and even years to wash the worst events away.

This was why some days he still awoke and felt something inside him break at the thought of Orla and having to go on without ever seeing her face again.

When they were finished eating and only the tea remained, Mossy said, "There a plan, sure?"

Conlon nodded.

"The bossman? In the hotel?"

Conlon nodded again. He felt odd about it all now. Strangely hesitant. Unlike himself.

"Right so. You alright?"

Conlon looked at him. Mossy knew him too well. There was no point in lying.

"They attacked the priest's house. He's dead. They got the women."

"The nuns?"

"And Gearoid."

"Jaysis. You sure this is the right thing? It's risky..."

Conlon shook his head. "We don't know where they are or if they're alive...we need to finish it. If I can get to him, I'll beat it out of him. It'll be grand."

Mossy was staring at him. "Or the minute we start to move they put bullets in all of them."

Conlon returned his look. "They won't be there. These people aren't that stupid. We get to him, we get in fast and I get it out of him, then we can move and get the sisters. You trust me, Mossy?"

"Of course I do, that's not the point here, is it, Tommy?"

"This needs to end. This is bigger than us and the nuns."

"Well, it better be a fucking good plan, then, hah?"

Conlon nodded. Mossy was right, he knew he was right, there had to be another way...but he felt trapped here. Violence was the only solution he could imagine. Violence would end all this, whether he survived, whether Maude survived, whether the Americans did— it would be over.

He knew violence. It was his servant. He could see no other way.

Mossy was thinking practically. "You'll be wanting me on a rooftop."

"I will. I'm thinking that he'll have a whole floor or at least a suite. If you can get up there early and give me some cover that'd be helpful."

"I'm not one to doubt your estimable abilities. But, there's an awful good chance that my position will do fuck all help to you. And you walk in there with no cover against God knows how many guns. This is madness, Tommy."

"It's our only move."

They looked at one another. Eventually Mossy nodded.

"Right so. I know better than to try to talk you out of somethin' you've set that thick head on. I'll go and have a look around, see what I can see. We'll need to meet."

"Yeah. Three at Trinity."

"Another day in this bloody pisshole."

"I think you're putting on how much you hate it because you love it underneath. We'll make a Dub of you yet."

Mossy laughed drily. "Well, it's never boring with yourself."

Conlon finished his tea and stood, trying in vain to rub creases and rumples out of the clothes he had just slept in. "I have a few matters to take care of. I'll see you at Trinity."

"You will of course."

Mossy watched him leave, eyes narrow with concern.

———

IT WAS A SCORCHING DAY, even this early in the morning. Dublin was hanging beneath a haze of smoke and sunlight. Conlon walked into town and then skirted the center, turning west before he reached the Liffey. It was busy; carriages and automobiles shared the streets with the odd gentleman on horseback, and bicycles wobbling over the cobblestones like baby birds. People were out, too, walking to work, to school, carrying post and goods for delivery, their hats shading their faces against the glare of the yellow sun above.

He loved mornings like this, normally. Normally they made him love his city. But not today. Today his city was hiding people he cared about and he felt a weight on his shoulders he could barely tolerate. Today he felt like the thing he had to do was going to lead to his own death and the deaths of other people he didn't want to see hurt.

He couldn't shake off this mood or these thoughts, and they were blotting out everything else. He had needed to get away from Mossy because he knew his friend saw through him, and he didn't want to answer questions or to argue about it. The only way he could function now was to keep going. Focus on what he needed to do, and get it done.

As he came into Smithfield, he needed to be more alert. There was a good chance they were still watching his place. He ducked into Cooney's and took a table near the counter. Flann, the owner saw him after a minute or two and came over.

"Where've you been? We've been hearing stories about ye."

"I'm sure you have. Anybody been looking for me?"

"A week or so ago, aye. Some fellas."

"Seen them lately?"

"I couldn't say for sure, now. You in trouble again, are ye?"

"I'm always in trouble, Flann. I seem to attract it."

"You go lookin' for it, ye gobshite. Life's too borin' for ye otherwise, ha?"

"It must be, because it keeps happening to me."

"What're ye havin?"

"Cuppa cha, please. And can I borrow a waiter or a porter?"

"Ye can have Sheridan. He's only fifteen, out in the kitchen."

"He can make a few bucks for two minutes' work."

"Alright, I'll get him."

The boy was there a minute later, wiping his hands on a grimy tea towel, mouth creased nervously. Flann had informed him who Conlon was.

Conlon told him to get his hat and coat, and gave him the key to his flat. He told him to take some paper with him to wrap what he needed to fetch. He told him what he was to get, where it would be, then he sat back and waited.

The boy was only gone perhaps five minutes, then he returned with a parcel of clothing wrapped in the paper he had taken. Conlon paid him and reclaimed his key and clothes, then he drank his tea. He asked Flann if he could use the toilet, and made his way through the door beside the counter, into a corridor of smudged gray with a strong smell of cleaning products; bleach and soap and dirty water. The toilet was behind a door at the end. Inside he changed out of his rumpled clothes, the same clothes he had worn when he fought the Americans in the garden, for a new shirt and dark trousers with a faint gray pinstripe. As he folded the shirt he had just discarded, he noticed a spray of blood on one cuff.

It was too hot for a jacket, and he was already rolling up his shirtsleeves as he went back out down the corridor, towards the café. He flicked his cap on, ready to go back out, and opened the door back into the café itself.

It felt odd and for an instant he was confused; why was it so quiet? Where had—

And then he knew, and he was turning and there were two men and two guns, one on either side of the door.

He was already moving; a boxer's instinctive reaction. He ducked under an anticipated blow and moved forward with rapid, skittering steps. The gunman panicked and shot at him. He felt the impact of the bullet as it slammed into his shoulder, but his momentum drove him into the gunman, and they went over in a sprawling heap, tables rolling away under their mindless, violent passage.

Conlon got in one-two-three punches in the chaos, but he couldn't swing from his hips, as he was sliding on his belly like a reptile. His shoulder already felt useless and leaden so that the punches were all thrown by his arms, and then there came a sharp impact to the back of his head; somebody was clubbing him with something heavy. He tried to roll, to face them, but strong hands were grasping and pulling at him.

His head felt hazy now, and another blow came and that was all he knew.

————

WHEN HE AWOKE he was tied to a chair. There was a sound coming from nearby but it felt echoey, at a remove. It took him a few minutes of dazed, confused semi-consciousness before he was able to determine what it was—voices...two voices...two voices speaking together. A conversation.

He had thrown up onto himself at that point.

His head throbbed. His shoulder and chest and arm were an inferno. Intense pain coursed through him when he tried to move.

Pain also at his wrists. He was tied. It felt like rope. But the shoulder...he had been shot. He remembered now. The café. It had to have been the Americans.

He kept his eyes shut, thinking. How tight were these ropes? So tight his hands were virtually numb, and he could not rotate either hand at all. He shifted his weight instead, testing the chair itself. It creaked like an elderly knee and a voice spoke from nearby, in English.

A few moments later there was a man standing before him. Conlon could sense him; he had heard his heavy footsteps as he strode across this small room. Now the light was duller, the man's bulk blocking the door or a lamp, perhaps, and Conlon could make that out even with his eyes closed.

"Tommy Conlon," the man spoke. "Don't disappoint me by pretending to be out, Tommy."

American. Conlon opened his eyes and looked up at him. A big man. Tall and wide, a thin smile of triumph spreading across his face.

"You're not the bossman, you're just the monkey. Why should I talk to you, when I can just wait for the accordion player?" Conlon said. His mouth was dry.

The American chuckled. He was playing this one

magnanimously, Conlon saw. He had won. He could take his time and enjoy himself.

"You Irish and your funny little sayings."

He pulled a chair across the floor and sat down easily so that they were face to face.

"My name is Gunnar. The gentleman I work for will be here in time. I think he might want to put a bullet in you himself, which would make you the first that I know of, and I've been with him for years now."

"So who are you? His secretary, is it? Typist? Make the tea?"

"I make things happen. I make people go away. I make people give us money. But these last few weeks, my business has been exclusively Tommy Conlon."

"Ahhh, sorry. I don't give autographs."

"I'm a little disappointed. I expected something more fearsome, or intimidating. And you? You're just some little scrapper, ain't ya?"

"Why don't you untie me and we'll find out, big man?"

Gunnar laughed again. "Oh, I'd like to. I really would. But the boss wants you. I can hurt you just a little bit, which I will, in time. But I'm a little scared that if I let you loose I wouldn't be of a mind to hold back and I'd just keep on punching until there wasn't too much Tommy Conlon left."

"I wouldn't worry myself about that."

"You're not afraid, Tommy, is that it? Tough guy right to the end?"

Conlon did his best to shrug, although his shoulder howled in protest and his bonds were so tight the movement was minimal. He was scared. Not of torture. And, for all that his life instinct was so tremendously powerful, death had always seemed, on some level, to be his way back to Orla. But he knew they had the sisters, and he was terrified of what would happen to them.

"Let me ask you a question I've been wondering about," he said.

Gunnar nodded. "Go ahead."

"How does it feel to make a living selling children into slavery? Young women? Fucking nuns? How do you sleep?"

"I really don't think about it."

"And that works?"

"They're weak. You have to fight for everything in this life, Tommy, you know this. These people are too weak for our world. You—you're strong. You take what you want. You just picked the wrong fight this time."

"With you? Not really a fair fight, is it."

"No, of course not. Life isn't fair, Tommy. You know this, too."

"You seem to think you know me. But you don't."

"I've done some research. I know you. I know about your fight career. You could've been a World Champion, I'm told. I know you fucked that up for a woman, and that got her killed. And then you ran away to the War. I know that you came back and caused a hell of a lot of trouble when you did, and that you find people now. But really you're a private dick. I think you miss the action, all the action—any action, and that gives you some. Day in and day out."

"That's all just facts. That doesn't mean you know me, or understand me."

"I understand that you've done some bad things in the past. And now you're making amends by doing good things."

"Bollocks I am. Life just happens and you respond and try to get by. Not everything is some fucking part of a jigsaw puzzle. You smuggle young girls to America and sell them into brothels because somebody was mean to you when you were a little boy, do you? Or because your ma was a whore?"

"You don't need to antagonize me, Tommy. It won't change anything. This is a done deal."

"I can't help it. I just don't like you."

Gunnar laughed at that, with genuine amusement. "It's funny. My men are terrified of you. They see you as some sort of unbeatable warrior. I didn't even tell the ones in the café who you were, because it would've affected them too much. And look, human after all. Here you are with a gunshot wound and a concussion. Helpless."

"They're right to be terrified."

Gunnar rolled his eyes. "No more threats now Tommy, only realities. Here's one for you. When the boss is finished with you, I'm going to cut off your head, and show my men what happens to unbeatable warriors who screw with us."

"You need to let the nuns go." And there it was. He had blurted it out, and shown his desperation. He saw no point in bartering or playing with this man.

Gunnar nodded. "You know I can't do that. The old one is useless to us, but it'll be painless. The young one is a pretty girl. I can use her."

He saw the feeling in Conlon's eyes at this, and chuckled dryly. "Think about that when you're looking up at that last gun, Tommy. She'll never see the sky again, that pretty nun. But she'll see a lot of ceilings, making her living on her back."

He was studying Conlon, who had made his eyes go flat and empty to hide his rage and was staring fixedly at the middle distance.

Gunnar tried to needle him further. "And it would never have happened if she hadn't met you, Tommy. You sealed her fate."

Conlon was trying to focus, trying to calm himself.

"Maybe I'll show her your head, before we put her on that ship. You can have a reunion."

Conlon opened his eyes and stared at him. "Here's my reality. You'll be dead before midnight. Most of your men will be dead. Your boss will be dead. If I'm alive, I'm goin' to beat you to death with my bare hands."

Gunnar looked back in silence. Then he sighed. "Tommy. We don't have too much time before the boss arrives. I need to torture you—just a little. But you don't have anything to tell me. You don't have anything I want. I have your nuns." A little chuckle accompanied this. "I have some girls to send back home. A little young, but that works, too."

"Just let them go." Conlon wearily shook his head. "It can't be worth the money, what you're doing."

Gunnar ignored him. "So I don't need to torture you. The only reason I have is to watch you suffer. You understand? I'm gonna hurt you just because I can."

Conlon nodded. "Let's get on with it then. You're a lunatic. You should be in Grangegorman. The sooner you're done, the sooner I get to kill you."

Gunnar sniggered at this and slipped a knife from his trouser pocket. Conlon watched it flashing under the lights and then he closed his eyes.

Gunnar cut him slowly across the chest. Conlon groaned under the pain. His skin opening like a seam ripping. So easily did he bleed. Gunnar reversed the angle of the first cut directly beneath it, as if he intended to draw a railway line in scar tissue. Conlon gritted his teeth. The pain was in hot waves. Two long slashes, blood cascading down his abdomen.

Gunnar laughed. Then, after a moment when he sighted it, like a workman addressing a screw with a gleaming screwdriver, he smoothly jabbed the knife into the bullet hole in Conlon's shoulder and Conlon passed out.

17

CONLON CAME TO SUDDENLY AND SAW MAUDE CROUCHED before him, the palms of her hands on his cheeks, her face crimpled with concern. Naturally, he thought he was dreaming. Hallucinating. Maude could not be here.

She was speaking to him, her lips moving, but he could not hear her. Her habit was gone. This was a dream. Of course. The noise in his ears, like waves on rock. A roaring. He squeezed his eyes shut and focused. Opened his eyes again.

She was still there.

"Tommy. Are you ok? Oh Tommy, come on, wake up, wake up. Tommy," she was saying.

"I'm awake," he said. His voice was soft, a whisper of pain. His eyes focused on hers and she moved her arms to around his neck and held his head against her.

"Are you ok? You're all bloody."

He shook his head. He felt still at a remove from his own body. No pain right now, but he knew it would be here soon. "He cut me. I was shot." Longer sentences seemed too difficult.

"Oh Lord bless us and save us, we need to go—" she said.

He was nodding.

She moved around him and started to work on the ropes at his wrists. He shut his eyes and the world swiveled again.

"Maude."

She was talking softly to herself about the ropes, and he could feel the pressure now where she was working at a knot, twisting and stretching.

"Maude."

"Yes? Are you alright?"

"How are you here?" He opened his eyes, listening. Things were coming into focus. The room. The light still above, harsh and pitiless. The pain of that blade in his skin.

Something gave—the rope. Suddenly tight and then his hands were free. Her soft fingers on his wrists, the rope falling away, the sound as she tossed it to the floor. His hands hanging, then he had them in front of him and she was standing looking down at him.

He looked down at himself. His torso was like a butcher's apron, soaked in crimson. He looked up at her and saw her make her face still, all her compassion and feelings hidden beneath a calm exterior.

"We have to go," she said. "Can you walk?"

He nodded. "How are you here?"

She offered her hand and he took it and tried to stand and the room swung away from him.

"Tommy!"

She kept him up, somehow, then wedged her shoulder into his armpit, and stretched an arm across the width of his back so that they could walk together.

His head hung. The pool of blood on the floor was so wide. It could not have all come out of his body, he thought. He wanted to sleep.

"We have to go, now. I don't know where the door is, but you'll just have to trust me."

"Maude. I trust you." He put his arm over her shoulders.

"Are you alright?"

He said, "No. But I'll be alright. I need water."

His mind was sharpening. He could feel it filling in, like lights being lit in a big house. She moved them forward, one difficult, wobbling step, and he went with her.

"How are you here, Maude?" he asked again.

"They left me in a room with a lock I could pick. And they gave me a bucket with a metal handle. So I got the handle off and bent it and I picked the lock. Then I brained the guard outside with my bucket. I'd been looking for a way out for ten minutes before I find you looking like death warmed up."

"I thought I was dreaming."

"You weren't dreaming. Sister Diana is here somewhere, too. And Gearoid, if they haven't killed him."

Another step across the room, then another, more solid.

"How long have you been here?" he asked. "How many nights?"

"Only one. They took us yesterday evening."

He nodded. "There's an attack coming. We have to get out."

They were at the door.

"What kind of attack?"

"A gang. With guns. They're going to hit these fellas as hard as they can. We can't be here."

He put a hand out and steadied them against the wall. He needed water. Once in Turkey he had been a few meters away when a shell landed snug in the middle of a forward observation trench and killed every man around him. The shockwave had blown him twenty feet against a sandbag wall and shrapnel had torn his right hip to shreds. He lay unconscious and bled profusely while a Turkish attack and an Australian counter-attack happened around him.

When he awoke hours later, his ragged crater still in the middle of contested no man's land, he felt as if he might die at any minute. He could barely move. He managed to crawl and fall across the crater and sucked down the dregs of water from a canteen pockmarked with a bullet hole. Almost at once he had felt the water affect him; strength suddenly flowing into his muscles. He had imagined it like the roots of a plant absorbing water from earth. Then he had stumbled back to the lines and ever since he had regarded water as a somehow magical liquid.

"I need water," he said again, almost to himself.

"I know you, I know you do," she replied.

She maneuvered him against the wall beside the door and he leant there, waiting, while she opened the door and craned her neck outside.

"Where are we?" he asked. "What is this place?"

"It looks like a hospital," she said. "But it's not finished, they're building it still. Right, so be quiet."

She managed to get them out into the corridor and as they limped tortuously along, he saw that she was right, this did look like a hospital, with yawning doorways to darkened rooms and wards beyond lined along the walls every few feet. But there were few actual doors, and the walls were unpainted. Fragments of scaffolding were visible through a window they passed. It smelled like a building site, the damp scent of plaster and wet cement, the nuttiness of sawn timber.

He could not suppress a groan and she stopped and looked at him.

"Are you alright?"

"I'm alright," he said. But every step was causing a wracking pain to fork down from his shoulder into his chest, and their shambling rhythm was also an issue. Each step she took sent his head wobbling away from her as she shuffled him along, and each time it happened he felt consciousness float sideways, a woozy feeling settling on him briefly and only shaken off by her next movement.

He needed to focus.

He groped for her hand but then he was on the floor and she was attempting to lever him up again. He had no strength in his arms or legs.

"You fainted," she said. She sounded so fierce, so determined.

"Come on. Tommy, come on."

He tried to push himself up but he could not. His fingers felt like they were bending under his weight.

She was groaning, but she managed to get him most of the way up.

He said, "Maude, no. No. Maude."

She stopped and looked him in the eye. They were virtually embracing. Her arms were around his back, hooked under his armpits, hers on her shoulders.

"We'll never make it this way," he said. "I can't do it. I

think I've lost too much blood."

Her face creased. He saw tears in her eyes now. But she persisted. "You can do it. You can."

"No. Get me into one of these rooms. A dark one. Put me in the corner. Hide me if you can. Then get out as quick as you can, get help and come back."

"Who can help us?"

"The police. Ask for a Detective Barry. He's a friend."

"I can't leave you."

"You have to."

"Tommy—"

"We haven't time, Maude. You need to go."

She nodded grimly and half dragged, half lifted him into the nearest doorway. Then she moved him along the wall, sliding his shoulder along until they reached a spot in deepest darkness. She lowered him and he lay propped against the wall, panting. She disappeared into the blackness then returned, laying a white painters sheet over his body.

She bent and held his hand. "I'll be as quick as I can."

He tried to nod.

She squeezed his fingers, adjusted the sheet so that it covered his face, and then she was gone.

Tiredness swept in over him again, something he could not withstand. He closed his eyes.

———————

IT WAS Mossy who woke him. A torchlight swooped and swung in the black.

"Jaysus, Tommy. You look like a butchered pig."

Conlon blinked at him. "Mossy."

"Saving your arse again, hah?"

Conlon became aware that he was still on his back, on the ground, and that he could barely see his friend, crouched above him and whispering. He had no way of telling how much time had passed, but it was still dark. The same night? A day later?

Mossy said, "I'm going to lift you. We haven't got long before this place is on fire. It'll hurt. Try not to scream."

He felt Mossy's big hands on him and then the world was tumbling and he was upside down. A lurch and he knew he was over Mossy's shoulder like a sack of potatoes.

The torchlight died.

"Good man," Mossy said. "Not a peep out of you. Right."

Conlon heard the cold clack of a pistol being cocked. "We're outside in less than a minute. If I have to run, you'll faint. You right?"

Conlon made a sound indicating assent. An actual word had been beyond him.

Pain came again—a hideous spasm of it in his chest and shoulder, then another. He felt like he was being swung by his ankles.

The ground was a blur, shadows in motion, the report of Mossy's feet heavy on the floor. He was running. Running, with Conlon on his shoulder. Conlon felt a burst of pure love for Mossy at that instant, for his madness and insane courage and his strength. And then the pain cracked him open again.

At some point he passed out once more.

———

HE AWOKE IN A BED. Daylight. Morning sounds outside large, light windows. Medicinal smells. A hospital. The pain was there but held back now. Instead there was a tightness in his chest, his shoulder. A nurse noticed that he was awake. She helped him drink some water but wouldn't answer any of his whispered questions.

"I'll call your friends for you," she said. "They've been very concerned."

While she was gone, when he looked around and allowed the world to seep in, he came back to himself. He was bandaged tightly across his chest and around his shoulder, accounting for the constricted sensation. But he had movement and feeling in his hand and fingers. He waggled them in front of him and the man in the bed across the ward chuckled and waved back at him.

"Alri', Sleepin' Beauty?" he called. Conlon laughed, and that hurt.

His legs and lower body were fine. His face hurt in various places, but he remembered he had taken a beating.

Maude. Maude and Mossy, Sister Diana, Gearoid. He had no idea what had happened to any of them. Finch's assault on the Americans. Now that it had come to mind, he could think of nothing else.

The twenty minutes or so before Mossy strolled in, his shirtsleeves rolled up and jacket over his shoulder, cap set back at a jaunty angle, were long and difficult for Conlon.

Mossy nodded and kept nodding as he pulled a chair over to the side of Conlon's bed, flicked off his cap, and slapped Conlon's leg through the bedsheets.

"Good to see you back with us, ye lazy fucker."

"What happened?"

Mossy laughed. "Ah, right, you don't have a clue, do ye? Well, we won."

"The sisters?"

"They're grand, they're grand. All safe and sound. And the wee girls, too. We did win, I'm not just shining your balls for ye."

"So, how did you find me? That wasn't a dream, was it?"

"I hope not! Right, bear with me, Tommy. So, off you go that morning—"

"What day is it? How many days ago was that?"

"Three days ago. You've been here for two days. So off you go, in your weird mood, like Robinson got that time after he saw Stewart get castrated by the shrapnel over breakfast outside that church, do ye remember?"

Conlon nodded.

"You were that queer, man, I swear to God. I didn't know what to say to ye."

"Sorry, Mossy." Conlon shook his head.

"No, no, fuck off. You've seen me in much darker places and you've helped me out, haven't ye? I just let you go off and hoped a walk'd do ye some good! Anyway. So I go and observe the Shelbourne for a while. And basically that wasn't the best plan, Tommy. You never would've survived it. I might've had a shot on one guard but you would've been blind for most of any incursion. Stupid boy. But I did some reconnaissance anyway. Went down to the bar and had a chat with a handsome young barman. He eventually told me that there were as many as ten guards on that floor, guarding Mr. Swaney. And that some of our British friends from the Castle had been regular visitors. So I set myself up in the lobby with a paper and I watched their comings and goings. I counted seven of them, and assuming there was one or two who never left the suite the whole time I was there, ten was a good number for them."

"Too many," Conlon said.

"Now I know you. If I put you in a forest with that lot and gave you a knife, they'd all be dead in an hour. Or in a room, hand to hand, no weapons. But in a corridor, or small rooms, with them all set up and armed; your only advantage is superior skill, and their firepower would win out every time. So I started getting a bit worried about it all."

"Mossy."

"Now if you'd been normal in the morning, I wouldn't have. I've followed enough of your plans over the years, I know they always work, more or less. But you weren't a bit normal. You were acting so peculiar. So I took matters into my own hands."

Conlon couldn't help laughing at the dramatic delivery. "What'd you do?"

"I took a prisoner."

"Where'd you take them?"

"I dragged him up to my rooftop. Nice sunny day. Nice and quiet."

Conlon laughed.

"So his name was Melvin. He was from Baltimore. The city in America, not the town here."

Conlon nodded.

"Big lad he was, said he'd been in the army but never made it to the War. He'd ruptured something in basic training, he says. He put up a bit of a fight and then again on the roof so I had to break his arm. And his nose. And those boys were very, very scared of Mr.

Swaney, hah? He wouldn't tell me a thing. Just went quiet, refused to answer."

"Really?"

"Until I tied a rope around his ankle, attached the other end to a chimney, and threw him off the roof. Then he fucking talked, I'll tell you."

Conlon laughed, despite the pain in his chest. Laughter rolled around the ward and looking around, they realized that all the other men in the room had gone silent and were listening to Mossy's story.

Mossy continued, oblivious. "So anyway, he told me how many guards there were, and that they had shotguns and rifles and enough ammunition to last 'til Christmas and that any fucker stupid enough to come out of that elevator without the right face would get his head blown off before he'd taken two steps. He also told me where they were holding your nuns and the wee girls they were planning to ship off to America. Very helpful, so he was."

"God almighty."

"I know. The ol' Mossy luck, I think we used to call it."

"I remember," Conlon said.

"So I went to the first place he told me about—"

"What did you do with him?"

"He tried to get away again when I was getting him back on the roof. Kicked me in the chest, so he did, the little fucker. Tried to go for my rifle as well."

"He's dead?"

"He is. Anyway, the place was a printers out the back of the Phoenix Park, took me about an hour to find it. I hate Dublin. They had a guard on the roof but he was asleep when I got to him."

"Really?"

"Snoring and all. Four of them inside."

"What did you do?"

"The Major's old trick."

"He had a few."

"Set a fire in the chimney and smoked them out. They all ran out like dopes. One of them was in his long johns. Then I put out the fire and went in and got the kids. Twelve of them, scared out of their wits. I called the peelers and left them in a pub."

Conlon laughed at that, too.

"What about the four guards?"

"I didn't kill any of them. They all will've had headaches when they woke up though. So then I went back to meet you and when you didn't show up I knew immediately."

Conlon raised an eyebrow.

"Alright," Mossy said. "I thought you were dead, to be fair. But I knew something was wrong. You've never been late in your life. So I thought I'd go and check out the second place your man gave me. And that was a big hospital out by the coast, in...ehhh...Sutton? Sutton. They hadn't finished building it yet. Big building site basically, but no builders to be seen, just a load of scaffolding and some suspicious looking chancers with guns on patrol. It was a nice spot. I understand why they chose it. It was back a ways from the road, lots of trees around—private, quiet. So I thought I'd have a closer look, and it was getting dark at this point, which'd help me get in without being spotted. I don't quite have your gift for concealment."

"You do alright, come on."

Mossy shrugged. "I was literally going in the door

when your little nun walks out and right into me. Not a word of a lie, honest to God. So she tells me where you are, where the rest of them are, and I get them first, then I go find you, and you remember the rest."

"I remember fainting."

"Ah, of course you did. Putting you over my shoulder must've hurt. You looked worse than you ever did in the War, Tommy. Like somebody had dripped all the blood out of you."

Conlon nodded. A memory of Gunnar's knife opening his chest made him shudder.

"So what happened? Gunnar?"

"Who?"

"I think he's like their Sergeant. Swaney is the Officer, Gunnar makes things happen. Lanky fella. Looks like he could be dangerous."

"Is he the one who cut you?"

Conlon nodded.

"I haven't seen anyone like that. Finch's lot did their part, though. Five attacks, more or less. A few more stragglers over the next day, in the streets. The papers think it's the Fenians, of course."

"Swaney?"

"He's still in the Shelbourne, holed up now. Half of his guards have left him and there's nobody left in the city to come to his rescue. If I was Finch I'd wait 'til he makes a break for it and tries to leave the country and take him then, when he's vulnerable. Otherwise you're just going to lose too many men."

Conlon said, "So that's it?"

Mossy shrugged. "It's over. We won."

Conlon thought about that. Here he was, damaged but alive. They had recovered all of the girls and dismantled the operation before anymore could be sent overseas. He had done his best, and certainly fulfilled his obligation to the sisters who had engaged him.

But...Swaney was alive. Gunnar was alive. That didn't sit right with him.

"When are you going home, then?"

"Well I have been waiting on your lazy arse."

"I know you have, and I appreciate it, but there's no need anymore."

"Perhaps Dublin is growing on me."

Conlon raised his eyebrows, smirking.

Mossy went on. "Some decent pubs, sure. Once you find a decent pub, sure you could be anywhere in the world. Didn't we only find that out in France, didn't we?"

"We did. Well I appreciate you being here. When are they saying I can leave?"

"Ah I don't know, ask them yourself. There was a peeler here, asking after you."

"Barry?"

"That's the one. Odd little man, isn't he? I felt like he was laughing at me every word he said. And ordinarily I'd want to burst him for that, but I just wanted to laugh, too."

"That's Barry alright. He's a good man. You two would get on well."

"I get on with everybody, Tommy. Or else I shoot them."

———

CONLON DECLARED himself fit enough to leave a day later. His shoulder had little movement but his chest was healing well and he felt strong again, strong enough to find lying in bed all day intolerable.

It was a lovely moment, walking down the steps of the hospital on a bright summer afternoon, thankful for his life and freedom, aware of his fortune, even if the pain in his shoulder caused him to walk with a slight drag on one stride and carry himself a little stiffly.

He returned to his flat for the first time in days, and although he had just fled hospital, tired of rest, he promptly lay on his own bed and fell asleep, waking almost twenty hours later, still dressed, his mouth dry as sand.

He washed and, discovering that there was absolutely nothing to eat or drink, he went out and over to Cooneys, where Gunnar's men had taken him.

Flann almost wept at the sight of him. "Jaysus we thought you were dead. We called the peelers and all."

"Ah, it takes a lot to kill me, Flann. But I'm close to starving to death, so if you could arrange some scrambled eggs and toast for me I'd be in your debt."

He read a paper as he ate, and drank two pots of tea sitting there, occasionally looking out through the window at the passing traffic and people in the street, an endless line of hats bobbing and jerking past. The shadows swept slowly across the buildings on the other side of the street like a sundial.

He paid, joked with Flann some more to reassure him that he wouldn't be attacked by gunmen every time he came in for a cup of tea, and was on his way.

———

JORDAN WAS OUT, but Mrs. Devereaux invited him in nonetheless. He saw her replace the pistol on a little shelf at waist height just beside their front door, as she ushered him in. She was in another expensive dress of black and red. She dressed like nobody he had ever seen; her hair was perfectly piled and gathered, her face made up to an extent he rarely saw in Dublin. There was something hypnotic about her, in the manner of a cobra.

She busied herself in the kitchen and returned with scones and tea. Stuffed as he was, still it felt impolite to refuse. And he sensed that this woman watched and measured every single thing he said or did.

She sat on the same settee as he did, and gave him a smile that felt genuine in his warmth. "It's good to see you, Mr. Conlon. We had thought you might be dead."

"I've almost died twice in the last few weeks. Once with the Black flu, and once when they got their hands on me. But here I am."

"Here you are." Her raised eyebrow was flirtatious, and he found himself smiling.

"You haven't come out of it too badly," he said.

"No, it seems to have worked out nicely. Of course, there are a few wrinkles we still have to iron out, but we fully intend to have that arranged within the next few days."

"Swaney."

Deadpan, she said, "Oh, haven't you heard? Mr. Swaney passed away."

"When was this?"

"Last night."

Conlon shook his head, half in bemusement, half in admiration. "How?"

"He was a man of immense appetites, Mr. Swaney. He could not contain those appetites despite the fact that he was surrounded by enemies in a foreign city. Still he insisted on having a young girl delivered to his suite for his pleasure each night. Once we determined from where these young girls were being sourced, Mr. Finch simply substituted one of the young girls with one of our young girls. And later that night something that Mr. Swaney ate...disagreed with him."

She shrugged. "A shame."

Conlon said, "He has men coming, doesn't he?"

"Apparently so. They will be met at the dock with his coffin and enough guns to ensure none of them want to leave the ship they arrive in."

"Nicely done, Mrs. Devereaux."

"Please, Mr. Conlon. Call me Molly."

"Molly. I'm Tommy."

"Tommy. We are aware that your role was significant. They seemed to be so obsessed with finding you they missed our preparations to attack them. Mr. Xavier is grateful."

Conlon nodded, uncomfortable with this, but seeing an opportunity.

"There is a way he could repay me."

She tilted her head.

"Gunnar."

"Ah. The big man. He's disappeared."

"He'll show up. He stands out."

"You want him."

"I'd like a crack at him, yeah."

She nodded. "We can arrange that, I'm sure. But you seem hurt, Tommy. He's a killer. Perhaps you need some time...?"

"I'll make it work."

"I'd hate for anything to happen to you. We're just getting to know one another."

He smiled. "It's not my time yet. He had me in his hands and I got out. He won't get another chance."

"I'll inform Finch. We will let you know if he turns up."

"Thank you."

"So. Your clients," she said.

"Yes?"

"Are they pleased with the outcome of your investigation?"

"You know who my clients are?"

"It's my business to know as much as I can, Tommy."

"I haven't seen them yet."

"You came to me first?"

"I knew you'd have the information I wanted. I'm heading over there next."

"Speaking of information, there is one thing I'm unclear about."

"Well, since we're friends now, Molly, of course I'll do my best to clear it up for you."

She nodded. "Was it the church that hired you? Or the nuns your friend rescued?"

"Why is that unclear?"

"Finch did some...chatting with a few of the Americans. Before they died."

Conlon nodded.

"There was somebody inside the church they were in touch with. They didn't know who, just that somebody had helped them find the children."

"Helped them."

"They said they were directed to your nuns, Tommy.

Told that they'd lead them straight to the kind of children they were looking for."

Conlon was silent, thinking. Somewhere cylinders were clicking into place, a door about to open. The break-in at the Convent. That they knew where to look for the keys. That they knew about the Choristers Hall at all.

She was watching him.

"It makes sense," he said.

"Why didn't you see it before, then? Is that what you're thinking?"

"A bit."

"A good Catholic boy like you wouldn't be expecting that of somebody working for our lord, now would you?"

He said, "That's not it."

She was silent a moment. Then she said, "You were distracted. That pretty young nun."

Conlon darted a look at her and she laughed, taking that as confirmation.

"Oh Tommy. I had heard that women were your weakness. Everybody knows how you and Xavier came to part ways."

"I'd stop now, Molly, if I was you."

"I knew her well, your Orla."

He felt the mention of her name raise the hairs on his flesh instantly.

"Did you know that?" she asked.

"I didn't know you existed until a week ago."

"She was lovely. I understood why you did it. And my, she loved you. I could see it in her. The change over those last months was remarkable. It's a pity the way it went."

Conlon was quiet. He could hear his own breathing, feel the bandages constricting his shoulder like iron bands. She went on, her confidence so blithe and relaxed. He suddenly saw how dangerous this woman was, how clever and careful she was. Everything she said painstakingly considered and planned and perfectly timed for maximum effect.

"But this nun is not for you, Tommy. She's a simple girl, from a nice family, and she has decided to devote her life to God. She can't be running off with the first handsome gurrier who comes along just because she's never had a ride."

He looked at her now, his face blank.

She said, "And you...you need a real woman. Somebody who can handle you."

He said nothing and watched her. She returned the gaze, and one finger slowly traced a line along her own neck.

"A real woman like you?" he finally said. "Could handle me?"

She smiled and said nothing, then a moment later, she said, "So what now, Tommy?"

"Gunnar."

"I won't forget. And then?"

"A rest, I think."

"Yes. You look like you need one."

––––––––

HE WENT to see Barry before he visited the Convent. They met in Stephens Green and walked for a few minutes before choosing a bench. Barry unwrapped what he said was a beef sandwich and ate it with precise little chews and bites and discrete maintenance of his chin and lips as they spoke.

Conlon was used to it now; this part of the city with its wealth and wealthy people strolling in their finery, even the way the grass here was cut so short, so exquisitely cropped back from the paths; the way the ducks seemed to raise their bills that bit higher here; the huge trees swaying in the breeze, the occasional man in a hat ride by on a horse like a roman general—all of it. Something about talking with Molly Devereux had set him on edge, and he found it infuriating today. All of it. Only Barry's gentle wit kept him even.

Barry's first words were, "Can you even bloody die?"

Conlon shrugged. "Someday. I think."

"Aye. Someday. Even the Black Flu couldn't kill you, for Jaysis' sake."

They shook hands. "Sure it's good to see you up and about."

"It's good to be up and about."

"How are the injuries? You looked a bloody mess in the hospital."

"I'm sore. But I'll be fine."

"Is it done? Are you finished? Are they gone?"

"Yeah they're gone. You heard about Swaney?"

"I did. The coroner will say natural causes, I presume. And it'll have been far from that, will it?"

Conlon nodded.

"Your pal Finch arrange that, did he?"

"Probably."

"Did you ever think of retirement, Tommy? Because whenever you take on a case, it seems to end up with a load of people dying."

"I can't afford it, Barry."

They sat together, looking out over the pond with its snooty ducks.

"Ah sure I suppose it's mainly bad people who die, isn't it?" Barry said, almost to himself.

"That is the intention," Conlon said.

Barry nodded, chewing. "I met your pal. Interesting fella."

"Mossy."

"That's the one. I wouldn't like to be fighting him for the last piece of sponge cake."

Conlon laughed. "No, you wouldn't."

"Ah, I'm sure you have him well trained."

"Have you looked into them at all?"

"The Americans?"

Conlon nodded.

"They were well organized, as you said. They basically left no footprints, no trail, nothing to follow. Because they were all part of the unit and they only used our goons for muscle, none of them were any use because they had no clue why they were doing what they were doing. So we know what you told me. They came in looking to take over and they wanted young girls to send back to America. Most of them were ex-military."

"Was there any hint of an inside man?"

Barry looked at him. "Apart from the small-timers they used for their donkey work?"

"Yeah. I heard something that made me curious."

"We haven't even learned enough to get to the point where we might speculate. But it would make sense. Somebody to act like a local guide."

"I heard somebody in the church."

Barry nodded, looked back at his sandwich, and very deliberately finished it.

Conlon said, "What are you not saying, Barry?"

"The church keeps things in-house. They don't bring us in if somebody accuses a priest, say, of doing something untoward with the child of a parishioner. Or several children of several parishioners. Or if a priest—maybe even the same priest with a liking for young girls—gets himself a gambling habit and owes quite a bit of money to some bookies."

Conlon watched him.

Barry said, "But a decent policeman—he hears things, and he remembers. When I heard the name of that priest who got himself killed in that gunfight..."

"Brailsford."

"That name rang several bells for me, Tommy."

"It wouldn't be hard for them to take on his debt and use it, would it?"

"Not an outfit so well-organized, no. And they could have let him have some access to some of those girls they were shipping out to America, too..."

"Jesus. That's how they found me. He told them."

"And he ended up shot, eh? God has some sense of humor on him."

"Yeah, hilarious. And now I have to go and tell the sisters."

———

SISTER MAUDE ANSWERED THE DOOR, and in that instant, the desire to move into one another's arms was fairly palpable. It had been that way between them for a while, but now, after the shared intimacy and trauma of her finding him bleeding and tied to that chair it was far worse, far more powerful, and he felt the sting of it as soon as he saw her.

But they did not move towards one another. Instead they were polite and reserved. Her smile was warm and fragile but a touch wary, too. They had been through too much and gone too far together for this to be easy, and he wondered if they would even acknowledge any of this.

She brought him inside and they made their way towards Sister Diana's office.

"I'm so relieved that you're alright," she said.

"Thanks to you. You saved me, Maude."

"Ah, I was only returning the favor. You saved us at the house."

He laughed derisively. "No I didn't. They took you."

"But they came to kill us all. They only took us because they didn't know what else to do. You should have heard them arguing."

"How are you? Are you sleeping?"

"I have nightmares. And on some days it's hard to think about anything else. I get images, and memories of how scared I was, but I pray to our Lord and that helps."

He nodded.

She looked at him. "I wish you could know that comfort, Tommy."

"I don't have nightmares."

"Don't you?"

They were quiet for a moment, and then she asked after his injuries. He shrugged and said he was fine, he'd be fine. They were at Sister Diana's office now,

Maude giving him a shy, somehow apologetic smile as she opened the door.

It had always been a light room, since Sister Diana sat with a huge window at her back, but the sunshine today made it dazzling to enter. Sister Diana had a pen between her fingers, a ledger open before her. She came around her desk as he squinted in the glare to take his hands and thank him and ask after his recovery, and then she returned to her chair, and Maude sat where she had on his first visit here, what now seemed like months before. For a moment he stood, and then, with Sister Diana gesturing, he, too, sat.

"How are you, Sister?" he asked. "You look very well, considering your ordeal."

"We pray for strength in our recovery, Tommy. And that prayer provides its own strength."

He looked at Maude, hearing some echo of her words there. She was looking at him, too, the expression on her face utterly enigmatic to him.

Sister Diana went on, "So is this the routine? Do you visit your clients to review the case? Or are you looking for payment? We've already made arrangements for your payment."

She said that with a little smile, but he caught the sting in her words.

"Most of my cases don't end the way this did. I just wanted to make sure you were alright. And to say goodbye."

"That's good of you, Tommy."

"I have a question, as well."

"Always the detective."

"Well, it turns out I'm not a very good one. When did you know about Father Brailsford, Sister Diana?"

He saw that register in her eyes, for all that she responded incredibly quickly and dismissed it.

"God rest his soul. I'm not sure what you mean, however. Know that he was dead?"

He looked at her silently and she stared back, unblinking. He glanced at Maude, who looked confused. She said, "What are you talking about, Tommy?"

"Father Brailsford had a bit of a history of complaints about him, didn't he?"

"Sister?" Maude said.

Sister Diana finally nodded, just once. "He liked young girls."

"He had his needs. He had his struggles. He was a human being."

"You should have told me."

"I couldn't, Tommy. I couldn't have you poking around in our closets and uncovering church affairs. Especially not once I'd seen how little you believed."

She looked at Maude and sharply commanded. "Sister, please give myself and Mr. Conlon some privacy. I'll call for you when we're ready."

Conlon and Maude shared a look and then she was moving out of the room, her head low. Sister Diana looked at him.

He said, "If I'd known, things would've been easier."

"Why? What difference would it have made?"

"He was working with them, Diana."

"No."

"You must have suspected it."

"I...considered it briefly. I—"

"He led them to the children. He knew just where to

go. He picked out the ones he could see wouldn't be missed. Until you started missing them."

"No, no, he was a good man. He—"

"Sister. How else did they find us? At his house?"

"But—but they killed him?"

"They were either sloppy, or more likely, that was the intention. He was a weak link. They snapped him off the chain."

She was silent, her eyes darting as she worked things out and tried to find a balance here, a way to feel at peace with this.

Conlon said, "I told you. You should have let me know. And, yes, he was flawed. But in this world, those kind of flaws can have serious consequences. He had large debts. Did you know that?"

She shook her head, her eyes wide with shock now.

"So either he worked with them to pay his debts, or he worked with them because they were blackmailing him or he worked with them because they made sure he met some of the young girls he liked. But he worked with them. And people have died because of that. We all almost died."

He watched her struggle with herself for a moment, and then he rose.

She said, "Tommy."

He looked at her. "Sister."

"I am sorry. I will pray for forgiveness."

He nodded.

She said, "Don't come back here. You mustn't ever see Sister Maude again. Your presence confuses her. I've seen it between you. It can't be, and you both know it. So say goodbye to her today and don't come back."

"I know. I will. Goodbye, Sister."

"Goodbye, Tommy."

He glanced back as he closed the heavy door behind him. She was on her knees behind the desk, eyes closed, hands clasped together, face creased with passion.

———

MAUDE WAS WAITING. At the sight of her he felt a sudden chip of emotion in his chest. She appeared uncertain, her eyebrows high, quizzical.

"What was that about?"

He shook his head. "It doesn't matter. How's Gearoid doing?"

She talked warmly about Gearoid most of the way to the front door, as he had hoped she would. The church was finding him work as a caretaker, it seemed, and he seemed happy and looking towards his future.

He stole glances at her as she talked, and they made their way through the high-ceilinged halls and corridors of the convent, the echoes of activity distant but constant. But then there they were, the door looming over them, holding back the sound of the street, but only just, and it was unavoidable now.

He turned to look at her.

She said, "What's next for you?"

"This isn't finished. Gunnar's out there."

"Be careful, Tommy."

"I'll try. No promises."

"The only good thing that came out of all this was meeting you," she said, suddenly. "I've never met anybody like you before."

"I'm not sure if that's a good thing."

"It is," she said. "It is."

He said, "In another world, or another life..."

She said, "I know. I'm sorry."

"Don't be sorry. That's part of why it's been so..."

"Nice?"

"Yeah. Thank you for saving my life."

She laughed. "I never thought a man like you'd be saying that to me."

"Well I just did, Sister."

"Well, I'm sure you're welcome. And I need you to remember something. Listen to me. I thought about it and prayed for you. For all the violence in you and all the terrible things you've done. Killing and beating and shooting people. All that pain. But then I realized, you're like an angel. You don't hurt people because you want to or need to or because you're told to. You're protecting people. Good people. You're protecting people who can't protect themselves. You're like an avenging angel doing God's work. And avenging angels do terrible, frightening things, but they have God's blessing. And that's what I think you are, Tommy Conlon. So remember that, the next time you catch yourself feeling bad about what you've done. And remember that I'll always say a prayer for you."

"Remember that I'm like an angel?"

She nodded, smiling slyly.

"I'll do my best."

There was an instant of awkwardness then. And he said, "Come here." And he stepped towards her and held her tightly, for about half a minute. She put her arms on his shoulders and let herself be held. She was small and fragile against him.

There was a charge between them when they broke apart and her eyes were wet.

She said, "Will I ever see you again, Tommy Conlon?"

"No, I don't think so, Maude."

She nodded. "I will. We'll be together in our lord's kingdom."

He smiled at the thought. "I hope you're right."

He opened the door and the sounds of Dublin rushed in, a garbled storm of people and traffic and movement.

"Goodbye, Maude," he said.

"Goodbye, Tommy."

And with one last look at her, he stepped out of the door and he walked away.

18

Two days later, at around six in the evening, a knock on the door brought Conlon downstairs. He had been reading—Conan Doyle, which now seemed hilariously far-fetched to him, if still boundlessly entertaining—and felt a flicker of irritation at the interruption. His shoulder was still tight, but his chest was much better, and he stretched as he descended to the front door.

There was a note there.

Chapelizod Gate, 0100. — Finch

He read it and knew that it meant they had a line on Gunnar.

That memory again – the knife cutting across his chest, peeling him like a grape. His rage and fear. The face of the man hurting him; a killer, a vicious animal who was enjoying himself. Was he ready for that?

Unconsciously he had put a hand on his shoulder

and realizing this, he smiled at himself. He had to be ready. An avenging angel, indeed.

————

FINCH WAS THERE ALONE in the morning. Conlon arrived early and waited across the road and a hundred feet away, partly obscured by the shadow cast by the canopy of a big, gently springing chestnut tree. The moon was hanging bright in the dark sky. The air felt cool and thin; and he knew this was him, that hyper-sensitivity that often came over him in a fight, opening his senses to the world so that they could keep him alive.

But yes the air felt cool and thin. Noises were amplified. An automobile somewhere off in the dark, its engine growling. Voices raised in drunkenness somewhere much closer. Music hidden behind walls and windows. It was a Wednesday night and Dublin was sleeping. But not all of Dublin.

He heard Finch before he saw him. The scuff and slap of his tread. And then there he was, approaching slowly, walking along beside the Park wall, his hat back on his head, eyes alert and busy. There was nothing interesting about this man, and yet Conlon knew him as a cunning, cruel and careful man, a man of terrible will and admirable loyalty; a man to be hated for all of the dreadful acts for which he was responsible, and a man to be feared for his power and ruthlessness.

Finch stopped at the gatehouse, leant against the wall and lit a cigarette. He didn't even look up as Conlon crossed the road.

"Finch."

"Good evening, Tommy."

"No bodyguards tonight?"

"Sure I don't need them anymore. Don't we only control the whole city now?"

"What's happened to Fitzy?"

"We're still deciding. I'd like to see him running a bordello, I think. Xavier will probably give him some influence to keep his men happy."

"And then in a few years when he tries to grab some more power, you'll have to deal with him?"

Finch nodded, smiling. "That's exactly what I said to him. See, you and me think the same way, Tommy."

"What did Xavier say?"

"He told me I'd get to enjoy teaching him a lesson if that was the case."

They were silent a moment, Finch dragging on his cigarette, Conlon listening to the sounds on the faint breeze. Bells? Something tinkling, metallic.

"Gunnar?" Conlon said.

Finch said, "He's trying to get out on a ship. He's arranged to meet a sailor at half past one at the Wellington Monument. This sailor has arranged him passage on a ship bound for Rotterdam. Now it goes without saying that the sailor won't be showing up, and he's all yours."

"Good. Thank you, Finch."

"If he kills you then don't worry. We'll have a few fellas in the trees. He won't get twenty feet. Is he going to kill you, Tommy?"

"Plenty have tried."

"But he's already made a start. You're not moving right."

"I'll make it work. Are you staying around to watch?"

"I'll be around. Wouldn't miss another chance to see the great Tommy Conlon come out of retirement."

"What's he been doing?"

"Hiding out somewhere. He approached our sailor in some pub in the docks. He's a big fella, isn't he? Looks like he can handle himself. The pot is grand and big for this one."

"The pot?"

"My boys have been betting on you and him. Most of the money's on you, because they've heard the stories, and a few of them are old enough to have seen you back in the old days, but now they've seen you walking like you've lost an arm, that'll certainly change."

Conlon said, "Goodbye Finch."

"Good luck, Tommy."

———

HE WALKED QUICKLY. It was roughly a half hour walk, following the wall and the Liffey along the southern edge of the park from east to west. He saw one man, hatless and in an untucked shirt, riding a horse at a canter along the road, and nobody else. The flu was making the city seem a ghost town at certain times in certain places. People hiding from each other, sick in bed, fearful of germs, drinking their bovril.

Instead the wildlife had reclaimed the space. He heard the rustling of small animals in the grass, the high, eerie hoot of an owl, and he even thought he heard the distant rumble of deer across the pasture, their feet beating a tattoo into the earth.

And then after a few minutes he could see the monument, a needle of reflected light against the night sky. He kept his eyes upon it and increased his pace. As he approached, he saw a figure on the steps at the base. The shape stirred and detached itself from the structure. Conlon could make out a tiny pinprick of red in the dark—the tip of a cigarette. A beacon to snipers in the trenches.

Gunnar flicked the cigarette away, onto the steps, and advanced. They met on the path perhaps a hundred meters from the monument itself. Gunnar stopped fifteen feet away from him. In the light of the full moon they could just make out one another's faces, their fleeting expressions. Conlon wondered how much Finch's gunman could really see.

Gunnar smiled at him. "Well, I had a feeling that was too easy."

He was dressed like a laborer, like a docker, in oily work clothes, a tattered cap and boots.

"You've done well to hide this long."

"I'll tell you the truth. I've hated it. Hiding ain't my style. And I hate this fucking town. I just wanna go back to Boston."

"That's not going to happen."

Gunnar nodded. "I know it. But at least I get to go out in style, huh? With your windpipe in my hand." He chuckled at this.

Conlon took off his hat and dropped it to the ground at his side. Then he carefully removed his jacket, too, and folding it, placed it on top of the cap. "I told you I was going to kill you."

Gunnar had shed his own cap and coat and was rolling up the sleeves on his shirt. "Yeah, you said you were gonna beat me to death."

Conlon nodded.

"That seemed pretty improbable at the time. I still think it's a fat chance, but we'll see."

"You ready?"

Gunnar said, "Is Swaney dead?"

"Of course."

"Goddamn. I knew we shouldn't have come to this country."

Conlon took a step towards him and Gunnar raised his fists and sprang on his feet, two steps to the side. Instantly it was a boxing match. Conlon raised his fists and was reminded of the injury, still healing, to his shoulder. Gunnar would surely target it. Conlon would have, if roles were reversed. They circled and shaped for a bit, adjusting to the dimness, the heaviness of the ground.

Gunnar began; he was aggressive. He jabbed his way forward—three rapid shots, his fist a piston, forcing Conlon to block, and then swept in a hook, aiming for Conlon's shoulder. Conlon rolled under it and pivoted away.

"That shoulder still smarts, huh, Tommy?"

Conlon turned the pivot into an attack and knifed an uppercut into Gunnar's solar plexus, then sprang away.

Gunnar spat and nodded. "Nice. You got moves. But you're hurting. And I'm hungry and ain't got shit to lose."

Conlon had known fighters like this; talkers, always trying to get under your skin—psychological combat as much as physical. Gunnar's voice was a whine in the dark to him, and he tried to tune it out and focus instead on the figure before him, weighing his style up, picking out his weaknesses.

Gunnar came forward again—two jabs, then a cross, which Conlon barely evaded, finally caught by the fifth punch of the combination, a raking left hook which clipped his temple.

"Damn! An inch lower and your jaw is broken, boy."

Conlon backed up, then came on, an undertow in motion. He threw a two-one-two; a straight right followed by a jab, then another straight, and both straights connected. He felt the force of the punches travel up his arm, his knuckles stinging. Gunnar went down.

And bounced straight back up.

He was still springing, bouncing from foot to foot, circling Conlon. "See, I'm not some little fucking middleweight you can bully."

And he came in as if to punctuate that, throwing a lance of a jab and then a hook. Conlon got his forearm in the way of the jab, but the hook found his cheek with unerring, devastating accuracy. His vision exploded in light and he stumbled.

Gunnar laughed. "You're in with a man now, Tommy."

Again he came in after the last word, a vicious left hook to the body and then a straight into Conlon's shoulder. Conlon cried out when that hit and reeled away. His shoulder felt like it had been ripped open.

Gunnar was laughing again. "You should have waited. That shoulder ain't ready for me."

Again he attacked. A flurry of jabs and straights, and finally two close hooks, the first doubling Conlon up as he protected his liver, the second rocking him back as it clipped his ear.

Gunnar said, "Maybe you could've lived with me if you were fit and in your prime."

He came in again; an almost contemptuous arcing hook and an uppercut. Conlon ducked the first and stepped away from the second, but Gunnar had thrown it to disguise the straight that followed, and it hit Conlon in the mouth and threw him onto his back.

Gunnar said, "Get up you little prick. I'm enjoying this."

Conlon, panting now, nodded, and picked himself up. "You talk too much."

"Because you're making this so easy, Tommy. I don't understand where your reputation came from, I really don't."

"Well, let's find out. Come on." Conlon beckoned him on. Gunnar laughed and came forward again.

Conlon feinted a straight and stepped around it and stamped down suddenly, thunderously on Gunnar's leg. The sound was awful—a crunch as bone tore itself free from ligament. Gunnar's head shot back and he let a silent scream turn into a groan.

"This isn't a fucking boxing match," Conlon said. "It's a street fight."

Gunnar bellowed at him and swung a wild punch, like something from a Saturday night pub brawl. Conlon blocked it with his forearm, and jerked his other arm up into the Gunnar's elbow. It snapped like a biscuit; clean and crisp. This time, Gunnar screamed into the dark. Conlon let him fall away and he hopped onto the ground, holding himself.

Conlon said, "While you were talking, I was seeing what you had. And you don't have much, do you?"

Gunnar groaned and pushed himself up, then stood there, swaying, the odd little hop keeping him straight.

"Finish it," he said, his voice strained and barely recognizable through the pain.

Conlon nodded. He moved in. Gunnar grabbed at him with his good arm. Conlon warded that off with one hand and adjusted his feet in an instant. Gunnar was making a sort of growling noise of rage mixed with pain.

Conlon hit him three times. First, a straight to the nose, the kind of punch that ends most fights, stunning him, his eyes already rolling up in his head before the second punch found him. The second was a left to his kidney; a precise punch that you only land with extraordinary luck or rare skill. And then an uppercut into his larynx, thrown from low down in the pelvis, his right fist battering upwards and smashing into Gunnar's throat, crushing his Adam's apple, severing his windpipe. He fell back, already gurgling and gasping, blood sputtering from his lips.

Conlon turned, peered around in the gloom, then retrieved his cap and jacket. He dressed quickly, not looking at the man dying in the grass nearby. He wiped his knuckles—already beginning to ache—on a handkerchief, then he waved to the unseen gunmen and Finch somewhere off in the dark, and he walked away.

Gunnar was silent, still; dead.

19

In the days after saying goodbye to Sister Maude, Conlon found himself in a funk unlike any he had experienced since the months after he had lost Orla.

Back then, he had drank and fought and wept his way across England until he woke up one day in a London slum and decided to join the army, hoping for the oblivion of the trenches. And instead found a calling of sorts, discovered that he was a warrior, and that he should embrace his gifts.

Now, in his Dublin flat, all danger extinguished and the evening sun stretching out over the city, he sat, drinking whisky, and thought of his last conversation with the nun and what they had said to one another and the expressions on her face throughout.

A feeling of bitterness and solitude swept over him then, but it was not Sister Maude that his thoughts circled. It was Orla. He could not flush her out, no matter how much he drank or where he went.

The fleeting connection he had felt with Maude had brought Orla back to him so vividly because it was a reminder of the way it had felt with her—not as exciting, not as charged, not as easy—and that just made him feel her loss all over again, and down he went, down, down into that black pit of his own pain.

He stayed in his flat, curtains drawn. He drank and slept and wept and said her name over and over again until his voice was a wasted rasp. When he had drunk all of the alcohol he had, he began to jab at a wall and only stopped when his knuckles were battered and bloody.

And then after a few days he awoke, and he felt better. Clearer. He drank a pint or two of water. Ate some scrambled eggs. He did some exercises, bandaged his bruised fist.

He knew what he had to do, what Orla would want him to do. He had to move on, he had to let her go, he had to stop being so afraid.

He had been afraid he would lose her even more; that loving anybody else would mean she would slip away from him. But he had to move on or this would kill him. He had to move on.

He knew what he had to do.

———

HE MET Barry at the bar in the station. There was a fog of cigarette smoke, the smell of hops hanging there in it, men in shirtsleeves jawing and gnashing on ham sandwiches in between drags on smokes, guffaws and drawls in the air, somebody playing the piano near the back of the room, a jolly reel Conlon didn't recognize. It was dark, underlit by small, flickering lamps behind the bar and in alcoves, but also so thick with smoke it felt like a November evening.

Barry was in the brightest spot, a table near the door, writing something in his notebook with a nub of a pencil, his hat on the table, a drink half-empty nearby. Conlon went to the bar and returned with another for him and a pint for himself.

Barry raised an eyebrow at him, tucked his notebook away and said, "Been a quiet few weeks, wha?"

Conlon laughed and took a drink.

"So is it over, Tommy?"

He nodded. "It is. They're gone."

"By that would you be meaning 'Gone away gone' or 'Dead gone'?"

"Dead gone. Finch didn't hold back."

"I've heard he's like that, alright."

"So now Xavier controls the crime all over the city."

"Well. Crime doesn't really work like that. There are always goin' to be little gangs, independent operators, chipping away at the sides, doing what they want, causing trouble. That's the nature of the industry. The Fenians, now. They're criminals, under one interpretation. And Xavier has no control over them. I'd even go so far as to say he's worried about what they're planning. And if it comes down to it, he won't win a war against them. They're willing to die for their cause, and his people just want money. So he'll keep his head down, and let them get on with their next revolution, and see where the pieces land, if he knows what's good for him. But even apart from them there are hundreds of little gobshites, stealing and stabbing and up to no good."

"You're feeling cynical today."

"Ah, I'm tired. It's good to see you up and about. Did you get the bowsie who cut you up?"

"I did."

"Finch?"

"He was helpful, yeah."

"And?"

"He won't be doing anymore cutting."

"I wish I got to say things like that."

Conlon laughed. "You asked...!"

"I know, I know, I set it up for you."

"Thanks for visiting me, anyway. I had no idea at the time, but I appreciate the thought."

"I was hoping to get a statement. But I did get to meet your big pal, as I said."

"Mossy."

"Jesus Christ almighty. From the army, is he? He must've made a fair few Germans spoil their trousers."

"He's a good soldier, I'd say. He liked you. I'm sure he didn't show it."

"No, I barely got two words out of him. And those two I could hardly understand."

Conlon laughed. They drank and chatted about football, the weather, Barry's children. Barry spun a long fantasy about introducing them to Conlon as their "Uncle Tommy, who'll teach them how to kill people with their bare hands."

"So why are we here? Where are you off to?"

"Well, the coast is clear."

"Ah. You're getting your ma. And Theresa? Bringing them back."

"Yeah. I might take a week or two. Just in the peace and quiet."

"I can't imagine you outside Dublin, Tommy."

"Believe it or not, I've lived in other places."

"The Somme isn't really what I meant."

"Don't you ever need a break from the city?"

"Of course I do. So I head out to Howth. Skerries. The sea."

"In Dublin. I think I need to get a bit further away."

"Fair enough. When are you going to make an honest woman of that Theresa, anyway?"

"What?"

"Oh, come on. The way she looks at you. The way you look at her..."

"You'll be the first to know, Barry."

"Well, you should probably tell her, first."

"I'll see how it goes."

"You old romantic."

Conlon finished his drink, and stood. "I have to catch my train. I just wanted to say thanks for your help, the last year or so. You're a good man and a good friend."

"That sounds like a goodbye, Tommy."

"No, it's not. I just...I don't say these things enough, to my friends. I know it's not always easy, with me. I appreciate it."

Barry stood, too, and they shook hands. "Don't mention it. We're on the same side. You do things I never could. And you laugh at my jokes. I appreciate that, too."

Conlon nodded, put on his cap, and made his way out of the bar and across the concourse for his train.

———

THEY WERE STAYING in a hotel in Salthill, so his train took him right across the spine of Ireland and to Galway, all of it golden beneath a full, blinding sun which hung in a cloudless blue sky. The train windows were open, and still his fellow passengers sweated and fanned themselves, the wind only serving to push the warm air around them in hot little flurries.

In Galway, he caught a tram out towards the coast. The town was busy, soldiers and shoppers bustling in its tight little center. He bought two bouquets of flowers then stood near the tram's door, feeling the breeze on his face and bare arms as they wound their way out of the town. It was cooler here, with the Atlantic's bared teeth on the wind.

He watched as the town ebbed away into a short quiet section of bumpy, pitted road, bordered by fields and only the occasional farmhouse, before they reached Salthill and again there were more houses, the odd automobile, the sense of activity and business.

He disembarked and didn't have to search too hard for their hotel—he had been here before, a few months earlier, searching for a young man who had run off with most of his parents' savings—and knew that there were only a few in town.

Back then it had been early spring, and quiet, but now he could see that the beach was much busier, and there were more people around in general. The porch of the first hotel he passed was lined with people squinting at the sun from the shade.

He found his mother instantly. She was in the large, comfortable common area of the lobby, which was all couches and low tables, with waiters circling. She was oblivious, playing cards with two other women around her age, laughing and drawling off one-liners as he approached.

"Don't let her con you, ladies, she's a real card-shark," he said, standing behind her. Laughing, she rose to greet him and he hugged her. The flowers were accepted with smug, theatrical gestures towards her friends, who laughed along.

She stepped away with him for a minute to quietly ask if he was alright, and then she took his hand in hers and said, "She's been awful worried about you. But she's too strong to say it."

"Where is she?"

"She went for a walk down along the front. She gets bored with us old ones."

"How could that be possible?" he said and kissed her cheek.

"Ah go on now you. Go and find her. Say what you need to say."

"I'm not sure what that is, though, Ma."

"Yes you are. You just need to be brave. You're such a brave boy in your life. And so scared with her." And she squeezed his arm and returned to her game, the flowers brandished like a torch before her, her friends roaring their laughter at the joke she bit off as she went.

He watched her for a minute, and then he turned and headed out and across the road for the front. There were couples strolling, arm in arm, and families, too. It was a Saturday, after all, and a nice day to visit the seaside. Stalls had been set up at little tables—men sold lemonade and sandwiches, apples and sweet cakes.

A mountain of white cloud lazily toppled, isolated out above the Atlantic, but aside from that the horizon was endless blue in two different shades, a huge, distorted mirror.

He scanned for her, trying to ignore the nerves that were circling in his stomach. And after a minute of walking he saw her, he thought, a hundred meters or so ahead, leaning against the railing, a yellow hat on and a blue dress, her small frame unmistakable to him.

The walk took what felt like an instant, because suddenly he wasn't ready, he would never be ready, and yet; here he was, standing behind her.

"Not a bad day," he said.

She turned quickly, startled, her eyes wide. And then he watched her take control of herself, and the startled look became careful and coolly perceptive.

"Well. You decided you needed a break, did you?"

He didn't want this; their usual dance around the edge of their feelings. He had to break the pattern and make her see that things would be different from now on.

"I think we need to talk, Theresa."

And that registered in her eyes; a jolt. "Are you alright? What happened?"

"It's been a difficult few weeks."

"It hasn't been easy for me either. Not knowing what was happening to you, or if you were even alive. I don't know how your mother does it. I've been a wreck."

"I'm sorry."

"I know you are. Is it done?"

"It's done."

"Was it bad?"

"Very bad. I—" He didn't have the words now. He had to find them. "I realized what I want. What I need."

She was quiet, watching him.

He said, "I want you. I want to be with you."

She shook her head. "No, no you don't. You've had a year...you haven't shown any interest...you're always after other women—"

"Theresa."

She stopped.

"I want you. If you think that'd be a mistake, or you don't want it, then tell me now. We'll go on the same way. I'll look after you as best I can. But I think you feel the same way I do. I think you always have. I don't want to lie to myself anymore. I want to try."

"Tommy, do you think you can just come and say these things and I'll just melt and come into your arms? It's not that simple."

"Yeah, I did think that."

He stepped towards her.

"Tommy," she said. "I have a gentleman. I'm—"

"If you don't want this, then just say no," he said.

She stared at him, her mouth just a little open, her eyes wide and startled again now. For once he had caught her off guard, and she was vulnerable. He reached for her, his hand stroking her jaw, and she took it in both of her hands. He smiled, and she smiled, too.

"It's going to be alright," he said.

"Oh, I don't think it is at all," she said, and then she did come into his arms, and they kissed for the first time.

A LOOK AT BOOK THREE:
RED BEAM OF DAY

Dublin, Ireland 1918

When WWI veteran—and part-time private detective—
Tommy Conlon is hired to find the troubled daughter of a
wealthy Irish businessman, he uncovers a mysterious cult
whose army of followers are willing to do anything to keep
their activities secret.

On a collision course to find the girl, Conlon faces several
armed men in a harsh pursuit of destroying him and his intel.
Conlon, though, is not deterred. In fact, he's hellbent on
destroying the intrepid cult funded by wealthy and powerful
men—even if they are determined to kill him.

But when Conlon turns the tables and brings his own style of
combat to their back doors, the results are bloody...and
explosive.

*A vivid and gripping historical crime thriller, Red Beam of Day
brings exhilarating action scenes, well-developed characters, and
riveting storylines to a revolutionary Dublin in intriguing noir
tradition.*

AVAILABLE MAY 2023

ABOUT THE AUTHOR

David Michael Nolan was born and brought up in Dublin, Ireland.

He studied English Literature and Film Studies at University College Dublin and is obsessed with movies, comics, books, rock music, soccer and boxing—many of which find their way into his writing.

Currently, he lives in Manchester with his family.

9 781685 492533